# LOST GALLEON

## A John Decker Thriller

# ALSO BY ANTHONY M. STRONG

## THE JOHN DECKER SUPERNATURAL THRILLER SERIES

Soul Catcher (prequel) • What Vengeance Comes • Cold Sanctuary
Crimson Deep • Grendel's Labyrinth • Whitechapel Rising
Black Tide • Ghost Canyon • Cryptic Quest • Last Resort
Dark Force • A Ghost of Christmas Past • Deadly Crossing
Final Destiny • Night Wraith • Wolf Haven • Lost Galleon

## THE CUSP FILES

Deadly Truth • Devil's Forest

## THE REMNANTS SERIES

The Remnants of Yesterday • The Silence of Tomorrow

## STANDALONE BOOKS

The Haunting of Willow House • Crow Song

## AS A.M. STRONG WITH SONYA SARGENT

**Patterson Blake FBI Mystery Series**

Never Lie To Me (Prequel) • Sister Where Are You
Is She Really Gone • All The Dead Girls
Never Let Her Go • Dark Road From Sunset
I Will Find Her

**Standalone Psychological Thrillers**

The Last Girl Left • Gravewater Lake • A Place to Die For

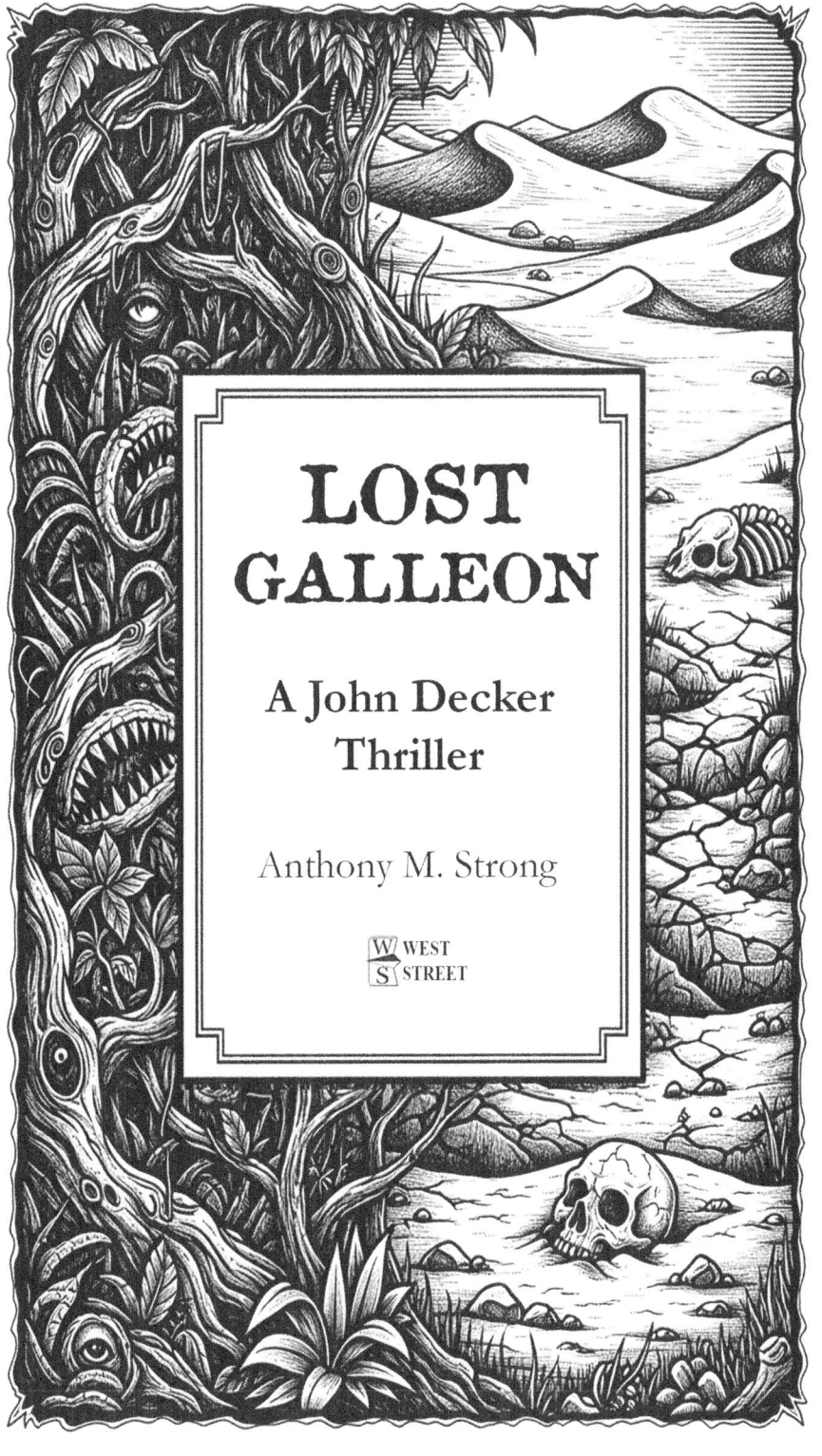

Lost Galleon
West Street Publishing

This is a work of fiction. Characters, names, places, and events are products of the author's imagination. Any similarity to events or places, or real persons, living or dead, is purely coincidental.

Copyright © 2025 by Anthony M. Strong
All rights reserved.

No part of this book may be reproduced in any form or by any electronic or mechanical means, including information storage and retrieval systems, without written permission from the author, except for the use of brief quotations in a book review.

No AI training or use without express written permission.

*Cover art and interior design by*
*Bad Dog Media, LLC.*

ISBN: 978-1-942207-58-0

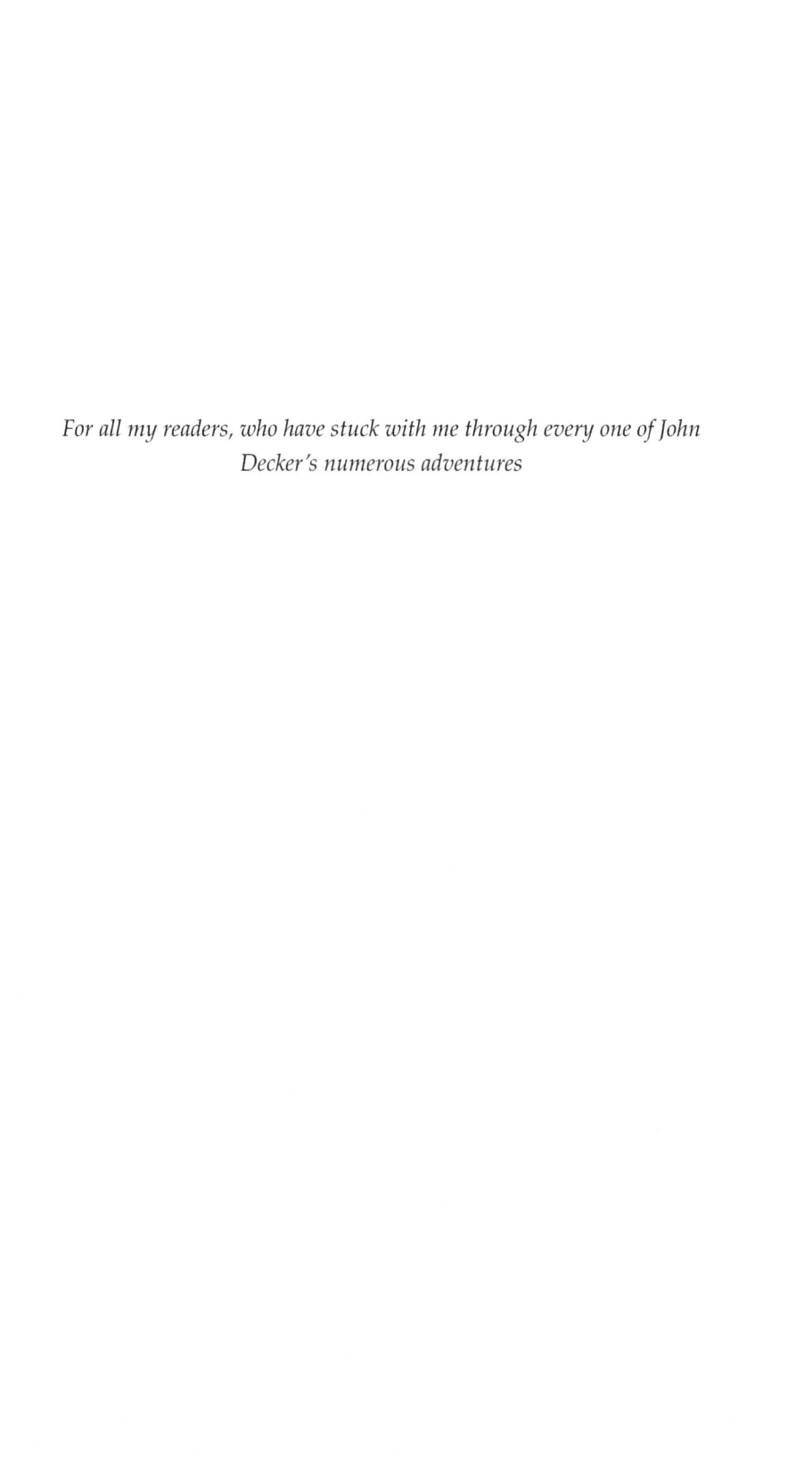

*For all my readers, who have stuck with me through every one of John Decker's numerous adventures*

# PROLOGUE

## SONORAN DESERT, SOUTHERN CALIFORNIA-PRESENT DAY

THE UNRELENTING SUN bleached the sands of the Anza-Borrego Desert State Park a dull white. Low lying scrub dotted the landscape at intervals, a testament to the hardy nature of life in this unforgiving corner of California.

In the distance, dry mud hills shimmered in the afternoon haze. To the east the land sloped steadily downward toward the Salton Sea, while to the west the hills gave way to the San Ysidro Mountains, their granite peaks born deep in the earth as the shifting North American and Pacific plates pushed against each other in an endless battle of creation and destruction.

In the distant past the semi-nomadic Kumeyaay and Cahuilla Indians roamed this land. Now it was a playground for a different kind of wanderer. Off road vehicles, camping enthusiasts, hikers, and the occasional archaeologist.

The quad bike was not an unusual sight as it barreled across the flat desert surface, it's 400HP engine producing a low rumble that carried on the breeze. It wasn't the most powerful all-terrain vehicle on the market, but it could certainly move. Several hundred feet behind it was another bike, this one with a slightly smaller engine, that struggled to keep up.

Sandra Miller kept one hand on the handlebars of the quad bike as she maneuvered a small two-way radio out of her pants pocket with the other hand. Although she didn't slow down—she had already fallen too far behind—she was careful not to allow the handlebars to turn while she retrieved the radio. One-handed, there would be no way to control the vehicle if it started to veer, and she didn't feel like having four hundred pounds of ATV flip and land on top of her.

"Hey, ease up a bit," she said into the radio before releasing the button. The two-way crackled momentarily. She waited for a reply.

Up ahead, Brett Sanders put his bike into a hard left turn. The vehicle kicked up a fresh screen of dust that swirled and spread on the breeze.

The radio sprang to life. Brett's voice sounded thin. "Aw come on, where's your sense of adventure."

"I can be adventurous without riding like a lunatic."

"What's the point of coming out here if you're not going to open her up." Brett was pulling further away. "Don't you want to see what she's got under the hood?"

Sandra considered throttling the ATV, punching the speed up a notch, but she was already pushing the machine past the point where she felt safe. Besides, she refused to be baited into riding faster just because Brett was in the grip of a self-destructive adrenaline rush. She shouldn't have been surprised. He always played it close to the edge, looking for the next big thrill. He craved extreme excitement the same way an alcoholic craved vodka.

Brett let out a whoop of joy and she briefly saw the quad bike through the dust as it left the ground with the aid of a small outcrop. The vehicle thudded back to earth and was instantly lost to sight once more.

"You're an idiot," she shouted into the radio.

"Come on, don't be such a killjoy."

She caught a glimpse of the bike again, barreling along through the scrub, weaving left to avoid a large rock.

Then it swerved just a bit too much.

At the speed the bike was moving it couldn't handle such sharp turns. The back wheels lifted as the front wheels slowed. She saw Brett rise from the saddle and glide over the handlebars like a bird in flight. The bike continued its upward arc and seemed to hang for a few seconds in an almost vertical position before crashing into the sand upside down, wheels still spinning.

"Brett!" Sandra throttled the ATV, pushing it to a speed that a few moments before she would never have considered. By the time she arrived at the crash site the other machine was quiet, although the wheels still turned in lazy rotations. The engine had stalled and when she cut her own engine the abrupt silence seemed unreal.

Brett was lying face down about eight feet from the crashed quad. At first, she thought he might be dead, but then he slowly raised his head, shaking sand from his hair.

He groaned. "Damn. That hurt like hell."

He pushed up onto his knees and examined himself for injuries.

Sandra slumped with relief. "Are you okay?"

"I think so, but the radio may have seen its last trip." Brett held up the smashed two-way. He grinned. "I think it broke my fall."

Even though her heart was still racing, Sandra couldn't help a nervous laugh. She hopped off her quad and hurried over to her boyfriend. "What happened?"

"There was a rock sticking up out of the sand." Brett stood and brushed his clothes off. He pulled a face. "I think I have sand in my boxers."

"Gross." Sandra rolled her eyes. "Could you focus for one second?"

"Sorry."

"Can you walk?"

"I'm fine." Brett studied the crashed quad bike. "Damn. Chuck's gonna to be mad as hell."

"He'll understand," Sandra said. Chuck was Brett's older brother. A Marine, he had been shipped out to Afghanistan six months ago. He was due back from his tour of duty the following week.

"Understand? He doesn't even know I took the bike."

Sandra groaned. "You're kidding me."

"I figured what he didn't know wouldn't hurt him."

"Well, I think when he gets back it's going to be a case of *what* he *does* know may hurt *you*."

Brett walked over to the bike and tugged on the handlebars. "Give me a hand?"

Sandra joined him and together they pulled the bike upright.

Brett groaned, his eyes alighting on the cracked and scuffed rear fender. "Great. Just freaking great."

But Sandra wasn't paying attention to the damaged fender. She was staring at the rock that had caused her boyfriend to lose control. Except it wasn't a rock. "Oh my God."

"What?" Brett glanced sideways at her.

"Look." Sandra's voice wavered. She pointed to the object.

A leathery face peered up at them from the desert floor. The empty eye sockets had been picked clean by scavengers. The mouth was pulled back in a rictus grin that revealed stained, yellow teeth. The desert sand mercifully covered most of the corpse. One arm had, however, escaped concealment and reached upward toward the sky, tatters of clothing clinging to the mummified skin. The hand was tightly clenched as if the corpse was shaking a fist at death. And in that hand, fingers curled around the strap, was a scuffed and weather-beaten leather satchel, still partly buried under the shifting sands.

"Whoa." Brett stared, wide eyed, at the corpse. "Is that a dead dude?"

"Yeah." Sandra turned away in disgust, fighting the bile that was rising in her throat. Then she bent over and lost the contents of her lunch onto the desert floor.

# ONE

**NORTHERN MEXICO CIRCA 1305**

CHIMALLI STOOD at the apex of the great pyramid and stared out over the vast rainforest beyond the city that had been his home since birth. Above him, the clear night sky shimmered in a glowing celestial river that traversed the heavens, within which burned Tianquiztli, the seven brighter points of light that the Greeks a millennium before had known as Pleiades. It was to this cluster of stars in the Taurus constellation that a human sacrifice had been made less than an hour ago. A prisoner of war who was held down, terrified, on the sacrificial altar as his chest was ripped open so that a priest could cut out his heart, which was then swiftly burned inside the very cavity from which it had been removed. Torches were lit from the sacrificial fire, and runners were dispatched across the city and beyond to let the people know that the world was safe for now and the demons who dwelled in the heavens would not swoop down to devour them.

Now, the priest and his attendants were gone, leaving only Chimalli to guard the body until morning, when it would be removed from the stone altar high atop the pyramid and placed on a pyre, which would then be set ablaze, incinerating the rest of the sacrificial offering in the same manner that his heart had been burned.

Chimalli surveyed the landscape with pride. He was lucky to be chosen for the task of watching over the prisoner's earthly remains until the New Fire Ceremony was completed. It brought honor not just to him, but also to his family. In many ways, he felt as if destiny had played a role in his selection, and if he desired any proof of this, he only had to look to his name, which meant *shield* in Nahuatl, the language of the Aztecs.

A warm and gentle breeze stirred the rainforest and rose across the top of the pyramid, almost as if the land below was breathing a sigh of relief that destruction would not rain down upon it tonight. In fact, the world was safe for another 52 years, a century in the Aztec calendar, at which point the priests would return and watch for Tianquiztli to reach its zenith, then perform the ceremony all over again.

Chimalli cast his gaze over the city, which he knew would not be sleeping. Right now, its citizens would be destroying all that they owned. Furniture, cooking utensils, jewelry, and even their clothes, so they could start the new century cleansed and unburdened by the possessions they had accumulated in the one that came before. He held this moment dear, because it would not come again, at least in his lifetime.

"Brother."

A voice cut through Chimalli's musings. He turned to see his younger sister, Quiauhxochitl, or Rain Flower, standing at the edge of the pyramid's flat top, near the ceremonial steps, with a wooden bowl in her hands.

"What are you doing here?" he asked, annoyed. Rain Flower was barely in her teens, and as such should be at home. And even if she were not so young, the sacrificial altar on the night of the New Fire Ceremony was no place for a woman. "If you get caught, it will be bad for both of us."

"There is no one to catch me, brother. Everyone is busy purifying themselves for the new century."

"As should you be," Chimalli told her. "Now go."

"I brought you some soup," Rain Flower said, holding the bowl out toward her older brother. "You must be hungry, and it's many hours until dawn."

Chimalli smiled, ignoring his rumbling stomach. "I appreciate that, but this is not a suitable place to eat. It is disrespectful to the Gods."

"The Gods would not want you to starve." Rain Flower looked down at the bowl, before her gaze shifted to the mutilated corpse laying on the blood-soaked altar. "Do you think he knew that he was saving the world?"

"I think that he understood his place and purpose." Chimalli would rather have spared his sister the grisly sight upon the altar stone, not because he feared that she was squeamish, but rather because he did not want her to witness the high price demanded by the Gods who watched over them. She was young enough to retain a measure of innocence, and he wished to preserve that for a little longer. "Now, stop asking questions. I have a duty to perform."

"Then take the bowl, and I will leave."

Chimalli shook his head in wonder. "So young and yet so stubborn."

"I had an excellent teacher." Rain Flower grinned mischievously, looking up at her brother.

"Very well." Chimalli sighed and reached for the bowl.

But Rain Flower was not paying attention to him anymore. Her gaze had wandered skyward. And as it did so, the bowl slipped from her hands and clattered to the ground, spilling its contents across the cold, hard stones. Her mouth fell open, and her eyes grew wide. When she spoke, her voice was barely more than a whisper. "Look."

Chimalli followed her gaze to the source of his sister's

wonder—a bright orange ball of fire streaking across the night sky, even as a sharp boom shook the earth.

The fireball arched toward the horizon and vanished behind the trees. A second later, another rumbling boom more powerful than the first rolled across the landscape, and a blinding white light burst toward the heavens, then quickly faded. The ground heaved and the stones beneath Chimalli's feet shifted. For one terrifying moment, he feared that the great pyramid would collapse upon itself, swallowing up the altar and the sacrificial offering that lay upon it, and crushing both himself and Rain Flower amid a tumbling cascade of falling blocks. But then, as quickly as it had begun, the ground stopped shaking, and calmness fell once again across the landscape. Except for the shocked cries of his brethren in the city below, and his sister's gasping, terrified breaths.

# TWO

THEY MOVED through the rainforest with the stealth of a big cat, which was fitting, considering that the small group of six men who had left the city hours before were all members of an elite group known as the Jaguar Warriors. Some of the most ferocious fighters in the Aztec army, the small contingent of warriors wore jaguar skins that covered them from head to toe, with only their faces showing. They carried clubs inlaid with obsidian glass blades capable of slicing a foe open with one swoop. But these elite warriors were not hunting an enemy to drag back to their sacrificial altar or chasing some fugitive who had broken the rules of Aztec society. Not today. Instead, they were following the path of the fireball that had streaked across the night sky hours before, in order to find the place where it had fallen to earth.

Chimalli led the way, because his location atop the pyramid had afforded him the best view of the fireball as it passed overhead and slammed into the forest with a fiery explosion that rattled the very foundations of the city. At first, the priests and nobles had worried that they had angered Xiuhtecuhtli, the god of fire, also known as the Turquoise Lord, for whom the previous night's ceremony had been performed. If the ritual failed and a new century did not come to pass, then the earth would be destroyed. The flaming ball that passed above the city and slammed into the ground not long after the sacrificial offering had been made must surely have been a sign of the Turquoise Lord's displeasure.

But the world had not ended, and soon those same priests began to wonder what exactly they had witnessed. Which was why they had dispatched Chimalli and five other warriors to fight their way through the rainforest toward the point of impact. But it was not an easy journey. They were forced to walk many miles through the gloomy humid forest, where little sunlight penetrated, because the fireball had fallen in a remote spot far from the city. It was also a dangerous place where they often encountered warriors from neighboring tribes like the Tepehuan. In fact, the man they had sacrificed, and whose body Chimalli had guarded the previous night, was captured in this region. Which was why the warriors were on high alert. It also underscored the urgency of their mission. Rather than being a sign of Xiuhtecuhtli's anger, the fireball in the night sky might have been a gift sent in gratitude for the successful completion of the ritual, and they did not want it falling into the hands of their enemies.

"Look. There is smoke," said one of the warriors, pointing.

They had reached a spot where the land rose and were now standing atop a ridge that afforded them a sweeping view of the rainforest beyond. And there, rising above the trees a couple of miles distant, was a curl of black, acrid smoke that drifted upward before being snatched away on the breeze.

"If we move fast, we can reach that spot and still make it back before nightfall," Chimalli said. They were prepared to make camp if necessary, but he would rather not spend the night so far from home. There were dangers here beyond enemy warriors. Like the jaguars for whom they were named, and also pumas, poisonous spiders, and snakes. Of the latter, there were a myriad of deadly species, such as the jumping pit viper, the neotropical rattlesnake, known to cause blindness in anyone who was bitten, the cantil, with its long deadly fangs, and the boa constrictor. The rainforest was not a friendly place, despite the Aztec warriors' familiarity with their environment, and Chimalli preferred to spend as little time here as possible. He watched the column of smoke for a few seconds longer to get his bearings, and then started down into the valley below, taking the lead with the rest of his group following behind as they were once again swallowed by the densely packed rainforest.

They trekked for another two hours, fighting their surroundings all the way. Then, finally, they reached their destination and Chimalli could hardly believe what he saw.

They stood on the rim of a huge crater amid a circle of trees that had been toppled, as if they were twigs. Of the trees that had stood in the epicenter of this massive explosion, there was no sign. They had been destroyed so completely that naught but scorched earth remained where they had been growing only hours before. And even the ground itself was changed. Instead of the soft, loamy forest floor, there were fragments of glasslike material scattered all around, both within the crater and elsewhere, that reminded Chimalli of the obsidian blades in the clubs they carried.

But what took his breath away was the object at the center of the impact zone. A small metallic orb that shimmered and pulsed with an almost ethereal light as it hovered, suspended miraculously in the air, a few feet above the devastation that it had caused.

Chimalli felt a tug from somewhere inside him, as if the unknown object was calling out. He took a step forward, reached the rim and scrambled down the sloping side of the crater, ignoring the cries of alarm from his companions, and approached the strange object. It was about the size of his fist, with a smokey metallic surface covered by strange symbols that he could not read and deep grooves that throbbed with an almost hypnotic light from within. And as he stared at the orb,

Chimalli was overcome by an overwhelming compulsion. A longing to become one with this weird object. To embrace it. He reached out and touched it, his fingers lightly brushing its surface. The orb was warm, and he felt a strange vibration from somewhere deep within.

Chimalli closed his eyes, overcome by a sense of calmness the likes of which he had never experienced. Upon opening them again, he was somewhere else, just for a moment, before the real world snapped back into place. But in that brief interval, he glimpsed craggy mountains rising from a verdant forest, a cerulean sky, and a pair of bloated moons hanging near the horizon. Above the forest, swooping in wide graceful circles, was a winged serpent with a long, slender neck and whiplike forked tail. And even as the vision faded, and he found himself back in familiar surroundings. Chimalli knew where he had gone, if only briefly. Because he recognized the creature frolicking in that cloudless blue sky. He knew it from the carvings in the temple atop the pyramid that bore the creator god's name, and from the stories he had been told since childhood. It was the winged serpent deity, Quetzalcoatl. And as he pondered this, a realization dawned upon him. That they had been sent a greater gift than anyone could ever have imagined . . . a doorway into the realm of the gods.

# THREE

**NORTHERN MEXICO CIRCA 1524**

JUAN CAVALLERO STOOD atop a rise at the edge of the rainforest and watched the activity in the city below them. It was late—almost midnight—but the streets were a hive of activity and ablaze with fiery torches.

"What should we do?" asked Captain Francisco de Alvarado, Cavallero's second in command, who stood next to his leader. Behind them, camped in the forest, was a contingent of a hundred men who had made the days-long trek inland from their galleon moored off the coast.

"We wait and we watch." Cavallero had figured the citizens of the Aztec city below would be asleep at this time of night, making it easy to take them by surprise. He hadn't expected this. His training was telling him to withdraw, because he did not want to linger here lest they be discovered and end up in a confrontation with the feared Aztec Jaguar and Eagle Warriors, known for their prowess in warfare. In a location like this, the Spaniards would be at a distinct disadvantage. The warriors were familiar with this terrain, while his own men were not. They would be easy pickings, especially in the darkness. But his instincts told him the opposite. Something big was happening, and it might be beneficial to know what. After all, they had come a long way to steal the riches of this city, and he had no intention of returning to his ship empty-handed.

"The men are restless, and attacking the city right now would be foolish." De Alvarado did not share his leader's convictions. Of the two, he was the more cautious, which worked as a foil to Cavallero's more impulsive urges. But tonight, he was overridden.

"We stay," Cavallero replied with a shake of his head. "Instruct the men to keep alert. I want to move quickly when the opportunity presents itself."

De Alvarado observed his companion with narrowed eyes, perhaps gauging if further protest would be wise, but then he nodded silently and retreated into the forest toward the encampment.

Alone, at least for the moment, Cavallero turned his attention back to the city. It was a fluke that they had discovered the remote settlement after encountering a lone jaguar warrior—the only survivor of a clash with an unfriendly neighboring tribe—while the Spaniards were exploring a coastal area looking for fresh water. They had been sailing up the Pacific coast for months, far from the Aztec's old empire further south, now renamed New Spain, and did not expect to find a settlement so far north.

He wondered what this lonely outpost was doing here, and why its people were willing to live in such a harsh environment so far from their former homeland. Did they even know that Tenochtitlan had fallen? The jaguar warrior, whom they had swiftly captured, had provided no answers to these questions. It had taken three days of creative persuasion before the warrior had even given them the location of his home. Beyond that, they had learned nothing before the man expired from his injuries.

Cavallero yawned and closed his eyes, overcome by deep weariness. The march to the city had been grueling, and it was almost impossible to get any rest in this harsh and deadly place. Apart from the snakes and spiders, and ants that could drive a man insane with their excruciating bites, there were more mosquitoes than he had ever seen. A good night's sleep was a luxury that would have to wait until they returned to the ship. When he opened them again, something had changed in the city below.

The activity, which was unusual for such a late hour, had reached a frenetic crescendo. A snaking line of torches weaved their way along the wide central plaza leading to a huge four-sided step pyramid that dominated the smaller dwellings around it. Atop this imposing monument, upon a flat platform, was a temple with a wide stone altar at its center. It was to this pyramid that the torch carrying Aztecs now processed. They approached in pairs, and started up the western slope, climbing a steep and wide staircase that went all the way to the top. Then, at the apex, the lead pair came to a halt and waited, motionless. Behind them, a line of men standing two abreast stretched all the way down the side of the pyramid, through the plaza below, and into the city beyond. By Cavallero's estimate, they numbered in the hundreds.

"What's happening?" De Alvarado asked, returning from the encampment in the forest.

"I don't know." Cavallero stepped closer to the edge and squinted to see past the blaze of the distant torches.

At first, he saw nothing unusual, but then the air atop the pyramid undulated, much like the heat shimmer that sometimes stirred the air above a roaring campfire. It twisted upon itself and burst into a point of blinding white light that expanded from the top of the pyramid. It reminded Cavallero of the beacon atop the Farum Brigantium, a lighthouse built by the Romans in the first century that still stood on Spain's northwestern coast near the city of A Coruña. He had sailed past the lighthouse on many occasions and watched its beam sweep across the dark water.

But this was no navigational beacon.

The light grew in intensity, forcing Cavallero to turn his head momentarily. When he looked back, the light was already fading, and in its place stood a solitary Aztec soldier dressed in the feathered uniform of an Eagle Warrior, and brandishing a long spear. Next to him was a sight that took Cavallero's breath away.

Gold.

More gold than he had ever seen in one place. Rough ingots stacked in a pile at least six feet high. Ingots that had not been there before.

Now, the line of Aztecs that weaved through the plaza and up the pyramid steps started to move. They marched forward in pairs, each one collecting an ingot, then heading back down the steps on the opposite side, where they vanished from view.

"We are rich," De Alvarado said in a voice barely above a whisper. "Richer than those who sacked Tenochtitlan."

"We're not rich yet," Cavallero replied. "Those natives down there won't relinquish their wealth without a fight."

"Then what are we waiting for?" De Alvarado's voice was bloated with greed. "The gold is right there for the taking, and we have the element of surprise."

"We'll take their gold. But that's not the real prize."

"I don't understand." De Alvarado glanced toward his superior, confused.

"Look. In the temple, atop the altar." Cavallero's gaze was fixed upon an object sitting on the wide stone plinth. An object that, just like the gold, had not been there a few minutes before. A glowing orb that seemed to pulse with an inner fire. "I don't know how, but the gold came from that."

De Alvarado squinted through the darkness at the strange object. "We should take the gold and be content. The savages are using some kind of witchcraft, and I want nothing to do with it."

"Nonsense." Cavallaro shook his head, his gaze never straying from the orb. "We take it all. Ready the men. We strike at dawn."

# FOUR

## PRESENT DAY

SANDRA MILLER STOOD with her arms folded and watched a peace officer, Anza-Borrego State Park's equivalent of a park ranger, and a couple of deputies from the San Diego County Sheriff's Office study the remains unearthed from the desert sands. Brett's quad bike, or at least the one he had *borrowed* from his brother, still lay on its side near the now mostly uncovered, mummified corpse he had almost crashed into.

She was bored and restless.

After finding the body, they had raced back to the parking lot where Brett's truck was parked and called 911, because there was no cell service at the site of their discovery. Twenty minutes later, after loading the still operational quad bike into the bed of Brett's truck, the pair were riding back into the desert in the rear of a state park quad-cab truck with the peace officer at the wheel and the deputies following behind in their own vehicle.

Now, over an hour later, they were still there, because the sheriff's deputies had originally thought they might have discovered the corpse of either a lost hiker or a murder victim.

Also, Brett did not want to abandon his brother's quad bike, since he would already be in enough trouble for wrecking it. Not that it mattered. They couldn't go anywhere until the deputies and the park ranger had finished with the corpse, which they had now determined was too old to be either a missing hiker or a murder victim. They had found coins in the man's pocket that dated the corpse to the late 19th century, and the remains of a mule, still weighed down with pickaxes and other old mining equipment, which the deputies had uncovered nearby, only reinforced that assessment.

Whether the man and his animal had met their end through foul play, or whether they had died of exposure after getting lost in the desert, was something that would have to be determined later, but since the corpses were basically antiques, the deputies and the park ranger appeared to have lost interest. At least, until they examined the leather satchel the man had been carrying.

"There's something in here," one of the deputies said, reaching into the satchel without releasing it from the dead man's grip. He pulled out a large, leather-bound volume at least three inches thick, which he quickly opened to reveal pages covered with looping cursive.

"What is that?" the park ranger asked.

The deputy shrugged. "Looks like a diary of some sort, or maybe a journal."

"What does it say?"

"Not a clue." He glanced around the group. "Anyone here read Spanish?"

None of the group stepped forward.

"Guess it will have to wait, then." He bent to slip the book back into the satchel, then stopped. "Well, what do we have here." Putting the book aside, he reached into the satchel and pulled out a roll of paper loosely held together by a knotted piece of string. The sheets were frayed at the edges, the paper mottled and discolored.

The other deputy perked up. "Would you look at that. Maybe it's a treasure map or something."

The first deputy shook his head with a bemused grunt. "It might be a map, but I wouldn't get your hopes up. I doubt it leads to much treasure out here in the middle of the desert."

"And if it *is* a map, it didn't do this guy much good," said the park ranger with a chuckle. "I wonder how long the poor guy was walking around lost out here before he died, and for that matter, why."

"Only one way to find out." The deputy who held the roll of papers started toward the park ranger's truck and lowered the tailgate. He laid the rolled paper in the bed and tugged the string, pulling carefully until it came free. Then he carefully unrolled it, holding the edges down to keep it flat, even as the other men crowded around to see what they had found.

Sandra yawned, wondering when they would be able to retrieve the damaged quad bike and get back to civilization. She hadn't wanted to come out here in the first place. Her friend Jessica was having a party tonight, and she had intended to go. Now, it didn't look like that would happen. It was already late in the afternoon, and the drive back would take at least ninety minutes, and probably longer since they would hit rush-hour in San Diego. After that, they would still need to drop off the bikes, then shower and change into fresh clothes. She was tired and hungry, and her will to do anything other than pick up Chinese food and veg on the couch was waning fast.

But apparently, Brett didn't feel the same way. In fact, his interest was piqued.

He nudged her, leaning close and whispering. "If that's a treasure map, then the treasure belongs to us because we found it."

Sandra rolled her eyes. "We didn't find anything. You almost drove over a dead guy and crashed your bike. And anyway, there is no treasure. The man was obviously a prospector or something. It's probably just a map to his mine."

"Right. And what were people like that looking for back then?" Brett sounded excited now. "I'll tell you what. Gold!"

"Don't you think that if there was an old gold mine out here, someone would have found it already?"

"Not necessarily. We're surrounded by over half a million square miles of desert, and that's just the land inside the state park. There could be a whole city out here and you wouldn't find it if you didn't know where to look."

"That's a bit of an exaggeration." Sandra glanced back toward the ruined quad bike and wished, not for the first time, that they had driven in any other direction and never come across that corpse. "And anyway, even if there is treasure, it won't belong to us. We're in a state park, so anything we find would belong to California."

"I don't think that's right." Brett shook his head. "And even if it *is* true, there might be a finder's fee."

Sandra snorted. "I doubt it."

"We'll see." Brett took a step closer to the truck and peered over the shoulders of the huddled men.

Sandra stood there for a moment longer. She turned and looked at the newly unearthed corpse, leathery skin pulled tight against its bones. The man's dead face stared back at her, jaws locked in an eternal scream, and she shuddered. She didn't care about the party anymore. All she wanted to do was put as much distance between herself and their grizzly find as possible.

But instead of packing up and heading back to civilization—instead of leaving the dead prospector and his mule to be collected by the state medical examiner, or fawned over by a bunch of archaeologists, or whatever else happened when someone found a body from a couple of centuries ago—the men were chatting excitedly among themselves as they stared down into the bed of the truck.

And now it was Sandra's turn to be curious, because she wondered what was causing all the commotion. She stepped forward and joined Brett, then stood on to tiptoe to see over the shoulders of the deputies and the park ranger. And there it was. A real-life treasure map. Just like her boyfriend had hoped. But instead of X *marks the spot*, there was a crude drawing of a three-masted sailing ship. And beneath it, written in faded brown ink, were three words.

*The lost galleon.*

# FIVE

## THREE DAYS LATER

JOHN DECKER RAN through the dimly lit tunnel, past walls of human skulls stacked from floor to ceiling. The bones had been there for centuries, the earthly remains of more than six million Parisians who had been removed from cemeteries around the city and reburied in the limestone quarries that eventually became known as the Paris Catacombs. Earlier in the day, there would have been tourists traipsing through these passages, gawking in wonder at the grizzly and seemingly never-ending tableau presented by the bones.

But in the early hours of the morning, the catacombs should have been quiet and empty. Except that they weren't. Because behind him in the darkness, Decker could hear the creature giving chase and sending the bones of the long-dead residents of the city above clattering to the ground as it tore along the narrow passageway.

He weaved left into another narrow passageway, leading his pursuer deeper into the warren of tunnels and into a section where no tourist ever set foot. Thankfully, Decker knew where he was going. Or at least he had a good idea, because he had studied the layout of these catacombs before he had entered them a couple of hours earlier through a little-known entrance near the former Barrière d'Enfer, or Gate of Hell, a pair of tollhouses that once stood at the entrance to the city but were now long gone and buried under the modern Place Denfert-Rochereau in the 14th Arrondissement. The Gate of Hell was, he thought as he fled the beast he had come here to find, also a fitting name for his current location.

"Decker." A voice echoed in the darkness. "Where are you?"

*In the last place I want to be right now*, Decker thought to himself. But he didn't answer, because it would waste valuable oxygen, and he was already winded enough. Instead, he ducked into another tunnel, following the sound of the voice.

More clattering bones. The creature was still giving chase, even if its pursuit was clumsy.

Decker risked a glance over his shoulder, caught a glimpse of the beast, broad shouldered and almost too wide to fit in the passageway.

It was gaining on him.

He turned his attention forward once again, but not in time. His foot landed on something lying in his path. A bone. It shifted under his weight, sent him tumbling forward. He reached out looking for a handhold, but all he found were skulls that popped from their resting place under his flailing grasp.

The ground rushed up. He landed hard. The breath exploded from his lungs, then he rolled onto his back and reached instinctively for his hip and the gun that he knew was not there anymore. He had lost it earlier in the chase and was now defenseless against the living nightmare he had come here to find.

Instead, it was going to find him.

He pushed himself up in a vain attempt to regain his feet, but it was too little, too late.

The beast was upon him. Five hundred pounds of sinew and muscle that only a few hours ago had been cold, hard stone crouched upon the roof of the famous Notre Dame Cathedral.

A gargoyle.

To the millions of tourists who visited the church each year, the gargoyles were nothing more than an interesting Gothic adornment meant to funnel rainwater off the roof and keep the corruptions of the outside world at bay, at least symbolically. And most of them did just that. But a few of these carved statues, the ones that crouched upon the parapets and looked down on the city, were anything but. They were nothing short of demons turned to stone and placed there by the builders of the church in an attempt to contain their evil. But it hadn't worked. At least, not completely. Because when the conditions were right, these ancient creatures would reanimate and take to the skies above the city looking for victims. They would swoop down and snatch unsuspecting Parisians in the darkness, and drag them off, never to be seen again.

Which was where CUSP came in.

They had dealt with gargoyles before—at least, according to the archives—but never one with the power and ferocity of this creature. And now, deep beneath the city of lights, Decker was about to fail his mission.

He raised his arms, swatted away a claw bristling with razor-sharp talons.

The creature's rancid breath was hot on his face. Its mouth was filled with rows of pointed teeth that had surely ripped the flesh from countless victims over the centuries. It pressed down on his chest, making it hard to breathe. The creature's eyes burned yellow, as if fueled by an unholy fire.

"Decker." The voice came again, closer this time. "Close your eyes."

He did as he was told, even though he was afraid the creature would take advantage of the moment to tear out his throat.

It didn't.

Instead, the surrounding air exploded in a crackling frenzy that made his hair stand on end. A pulse of brilliant blue light illuminated the darkness behind his eyelids, a momentary flash that he was sure would have burned his retinas if he hadn't done as he was told.

The weight on his chest lifted, even as the creature let out an angry squeal.

He could breathe again. Even better, he was still alive.

Decker opened his eyes and waited until they adjusted to the gloom, then sat up.

Everything ached.

"That didn't quite go as planned," said his rescuer, holding out her hand and helping him to his feet.

"Tell me about it." Decker glanced toward Daisy, who was still holding the gun and looking past him down the tunnel. It could have been a prop from a sci-fi movie—A chunky black pistol with pulsing bars of blue luminescence running down each side of the barrel. But this was anything but a harmless fake. It was a localized EMP weapon, just like the one he had lost during the chase. The result of a highly classified project straight out of Area 51, the electromagnetic pulse released by the weapon, when properly aimed, could disable a ballistic missile, stop a speeding car, or cut power to an entire city block. Or in this case, Daisy had theorized, short-circuit the central nervous system of a gargoyle and render it inanimate long enough for them to contain it. Except that when Decker turned to look behind him, the tunnel was empty.

"Crap." He rubbed his neck and looked down at the gun. "Guess that toy of yours didn't work."

"It worked well enough," Daisy said. "You're alive, aren't you?"

"Yeah. But so is the gargoyle. I thought you said the EMP would turn it back into stone."

Daisy shrugged. "A girl can't always be right."

Decker pulled a face. "That creature could've killed me."

"But it didn't." Daisy holstered the weapon, her gaze drifting to the wall of skulls that stared back at them with dark, empty sockets. "Let's find your gun, then get out of here. This place gives me the creeps."

# SIX

THEY EMERGED from the catacombs and onto the dark streets above. A full moon hung low above the city, bathing them in a faint silvery light. It was this full moon that had roused the gargoyle from its granite sleep to wreak havoc, just as it caused the werewolf to turn, and tugged at the oceans, swelling the waves. Tomorrow, the moon would wane, and the lunar cycle would begin anew, once again trapping the gargoyle in stone. It would, Decker mused, be easy to deal with the creature in this inanimate state, except that Notre Dame was off-limits, and any attempt to convince the relevant authorities that one of their statues had a habit of coming alive would not go well. They would have to wait until the next full moon if they wanted to capture the beast and render it harmless.

They walked in silence for a distance along the Rue Froidevaux before Daisy spoke. "I'm sorry for what happened down there in the catacombs. I should have been more prepared."

"Your theory was sound," Decker said. "You couldn't have known the gun wouldn't work as expected."

"That's kind of you to say, but it's my job to know. Especially under the circumstances. You only returned from your honeymoon last week. I'd rather not get you killed on your first assignment as a married man."

"I can take care of myself. Besides, it's not your job to keep me safe."

"I'm not sure Nancy would agree with that. I have a feeling she would have preferred that you find a less dangerous occupation, even if she won't admit that outright." Daisy pulled her coat closed against the biting wind that swept down Rue Froidevaux. "Either way, it's good to have you back."

"Thank you." Decker had been in two minds about returning to CUSP, but given the spectacular failure of his law enforcement career it wasn't like he had many other options, short of becoming a private investigator, which felt like a step down, or a mall security guard, which was rock-bottom. And of course, he would also have to find a mall that was still in business, which was probably a harder proposition than catching the gargoyle.

He yawned, then reached into his pocket and took out his phone. "Much as I would love to walk all the way back to the hotel and soak up the Paris air, it's late, and I'm tired. Mind if I find us a ride?"

Daisy looked at him with narrowed eyes. "Really? It's not every day that you get a chance to stroll the streets of Paris."

"And it's not every day that you get chased through the catacombs by a gargoyle. I ache all over, and it must be a good forty-five minutes on foot. If you want to walk, be my guest, but I'm calling a cab."

Daisy grinned. "Bet you wouldn't be so grumpy if Nancy was here with you."

"But she's not." Decker was already dialing the number for the taxi company. "And no offense, Daisy, but this trip has been far from romantic."

# SEVEN

WHEN DECKER ARRIVED BACK at the hotel, he went straight to his room after bidding good night to Daisy, who had decided that a cab ride sounded better than a brisk walk after all. Now he stood in his room which overlooked the Champ De Mars, the wide, grassy public park in front of the Eiffel Tower, and stared out of the window toward the legendary wrought-iron lattice structure. It twinkled against the night sky, standing over a thousand feet tall, and it made Decker sad to be alone, because he really would have loved to share this view with Nancy.

He took out his phone again and snapped a quick photograph, then sent it to his wife halfway around the world in Portland, Maine, with a short caption. *Thinking of you.* After that, he closed the blinds and stepped away from the window, then undressed for bed.

In the bathroom, he stood in front of the mirror and studied his chest, where bruises were already forming thanks to the gargoyle's assault back in the catacombs. He would come face-to-face with this creature again, he was sure, and the next time it would go differently. They would capture the gargoyle before it could kill anyone else. But to do that, they would need to wait until the next full moon, when it turned from stone, back into flesh and blood. His employers would not keep him in Paris until then. He was sure of that, too. There was no way that Hunt and Mina would let him enjoy a month in one of the most expensive cities in Europe on their dime. Besides, there were other matters that would need the attention of a monster hunter. The question was, how long would they wait to reassign him?

He got his answer sooner than expected.

He had barely stepped back into the bedroom and was about to climb into bed when his phone rang.

It was Mina.

"John," she said when he answered. "I hear things didn't go as planned with the gargoyle."

"Not quite," Decker replied. Apparently, Daisy had been talking to her mother already. "You *do* realize that it's almost three o'clock in the morning here. Can't whatever you're calling about wait until I've gotten some sleep?"

"You're not in bed yet, right?"

"I was about ten seconds away from it."

"Good! Then I'm not waking you up." Mina sounded way too chirpy for the late hour. But of course, it was only 9 PM in Maine. "Since our window of opportunity to apprehend the gargoyle has closed for now, I have a new mission for you back stateside."

"What will I be chasing this time?" Decker asked. "Please tell me it's not a werewolf. I've had enough of those guys for a lifetime. Vampires, too."

"Actually, it's neither of those. It isn't even a monster. I figured you might like a more sedate assignment to ease you back into it."

"You just eased me back into it with the gargoyle," Decker said grimly. "And I have to say, it was no walk in the park."

"Okay. Fine. We're a bit shorthanded right now, and everyone else is busy with other jobs."

"You could try recruiting some more operatives."

"If only it were that easy." There was a note of exasperation and Mina's voice. "This is an easy assignment, but if you'd prefer, I can find a nice banshee for you to chase, or perhaps an ogre or two—"

Decker glanced wistfully toward the bed. "Just tell me where I'm going and why."

"California. The Sonoran Desert, to be precise."

"And Daisy?"

"She's going to stay in Paris for now."

*Of course she is*, thought Decker.

"She has valid business in the city," Mina continued, as if reading his mind. "But don't worry. You'll be working with a familiar face. We've booked you on a flight to Phoenix out of Charles de Gaulle tomorrow afternoon. From there, you'll be taking a helicopter to Canyon de Chelly. It's a national monument situated on Navajo land a couple of hours—"

"I know where it is," Decker replied. "But I'm confused. Why are you sending me to Canyon de Chelly if the assignment is in California?"

"To rendezvous with your partner for this mission," Mina said. "He's working out in the desert right now on a side project that has nothing to do with CUSP."

That raised more questions than he was willing to ask at three in the morning, so Decker decided to skip the question-and-answer session and get right to the point. "Who would that be?"

"An old friend who I'm sure will be delighted to see you," Mina said. "Rory McCormick."

"Rory, huh? I'm assuming this mission has something to do with archaeology?"

"You could say that." Mina paused, perhaps for dramatic effect. "A map has come into our possession that shows the location of a Spanish Galleon loaded with treasure, and we would like to reach it before anyone else does."

"Since when did we become treasure hunters?" Decker

asked. "And more to the point, how did a Spanish Galleon and up in the middle of the Sonoran Desert?"

Mina sighed. "Rory will fill you in. He's better at this stuff than me. Like you said, he's an archaeologist."

"Great. That still doesn't answer my question. Why are we going in search of treasure?"

"Because the Spanish Galleon wasn't just carrying gold and jewels. We believe there was something else on that ship. An object you've encountered before. And we need to make sure that it doesn't fall into the wrong hands."

# EIGHT

CALIFORNIA'S STATEWIDE Museum Collections Center was a nondescript warehouse building on the west side of a sprawling business park near downtown Sacramento. Originally built to house supplies for the Air Force base that had once occupied the land, it was now the permanent home of over a million historically significant objects and almost as many photographs, which were frequently lent to museums and other institutions throughout the state.

Inside this building was a research facility where all the artifacts found within California's state parks were sent for evaluation and study. It was to this unassuming and little-known facility that the mummified corpse unearthed in Canyon de Chelly, along with the satchel and its contents, had been sent for preservation and study.

The map and leather-bound book discovered in the dead man's satchel by the San Diego Sheriff's deputies were lying on a table in a small laboratory deep in the bowels of the building. They had arrived the previous day and would stay there until they were studied, catalogued, and any necessary preservation work had been performed. That process had already begun. Earlier in the day, scans of the objects had been performed to provide a digital record of them prior to any further work commencing. Tomorrow, a team of archaeologists and preservationists would examine them. Now, at midnight, they sat alone in the darkness within the empty building.

Except that the building wasn't truly empty.

There was a security guard patrolling the corridors and storage vaults, wandering slowly through the hallways with the lethargic gait of someone who had done the same thing so many times without trouble, that they didn't expect any now. Tonight, though, would be different. Because two more figures were currently working on the building's rear door, next to the bays where trucks pulled up to collect and drop off the many artifacts that frequently left the facility for touring exhibitions, loans to museums, or temporary transfer to other research establishments.

The door had an alarm, but they made quick work of gaining access to the building and bypassing the security system with the consummate skill of professional burglars. Except that these two intruders were not simple burglars. They were highly trained operatives who didn't care about the wealth of treasures locked away in the vast repository they were currently entering. Except for two specific objects, that was.

Dressed from head to toe in black, wearing ski masks and gloves, they all but merged with the shadows in the dimly lit corridors as they proceeded forward. Neither one of them had ever been inside the building before—it was not open to the public except by appointment and even then, access was limited to certain areas while accompanied by a tour guide—but they knew exactly where to go.

They also knew about the guard.

Which was why, when they heard footsteps approaching and saw the swing of a flashlight carving through the gloom, they ducked quickly sideways through an open doorway and into what appeared to be a break room with tables and chairs, a TV fixed to the wall, and a beverage center with coffee urns, a water cooler, and a soda dispenser.

A couple of minutes later, once the guard had passed safely by, the intruders were on the move again. They slipped from their hiding place and stepped back into the corridor, intending to continue along their way. But before they could move, a voice rang out.

"Hey. You two. Stop right there."

The intruders turned to see the security guard, not as unobservant as they had hoped, standing in the corridor behind them with a pistol grasped in his hands.

The pair exchanged glances. The taller of the two nodded almost imperceptibly. A silent communication to confirm their next move.

He took a step forward, lifting his arms in the air as if surrendering.

"I said don't move." The guard's hands trembled as he clutched the pistol hard enough that his knuckles turned white. Because even in the dimly lit corridor, he surely must have seen the holstered weapons at the intruders' hips. Weapons bigger than his own.

The man came to a halt.

"Just . . . just stay where you are . . . okay? Try anything, and I'll shoot." The guard let go of the gun with one hand and reached down, pulling a cell phone from his pocket.

He fumbled with the phone's lock screen, made a clumsy one-handed attempt to dial 911, never taking his eyes off the intruders. In the process, the handset slipped from his grasp.

That was all it took.

The guard let his gaze drop, a look of horror flashing across his face.

A split-second later, a pair of bullets slammed into his chest. Two center mass shots that lifted him from his feet even as his finger twitched on the trigger of his weapon, sending a third bullet slamming harmlessly into the ceiling. He landed on his back; the weapon bouncing from his grip and clattering out of reach.

Not that it mattered, because he wasn't in any condition to fight back, and was, quite possibly, already dead.

But that didn't stop the taller of the intruders from walking up to him, aiming his weapon downward, and putting one last bullet through the guard's forehead.

Satisfied, he holstered his weapon, a silenced Makarov PV semi-automatic pistol identical to the one carried by his partner, then turned away from the newly minted corpse. "Come on. Let's find what we came for and get out of here. I doubt anyone heard the guard's gun go off, given the time of night and our location, but I'd rather not stick around to find out."

"Idiot." The other man cast a quick glance at the dead guard. "He should have just let it be and kept on walking."

The taller man chuckled and stepped past his comrade, then started back down the corridor. "They never do, my friend. They never do."

# NINE

AT NOON THE NEXT DAY, Rory McCormick stood on a rocky outcrop overlooking the dig site in Canyon De Chelly, Arizona, and blew a fine covering of dust from the object in his hand. From his exterior demeanor, only those who knew him best would have an idea of how excited he was right now. He was a model of calm professionalism.

He turned the object over in his palm and let his finger run along its edge. The arrowhead was still sharp after thousands of years in the ground. In the valley below, a team made up of research assistants and students from the Archeological Sciences Program of the university where he was a part-time professor—his cover and the place he occasionally worked when he wasn't on assignment for CUSP—were slowly removing layers of earth to reveal the buried village beneath.

"Isn't it beautiful?" Abigail Thorpe—Abby to practically everyone who knew her—bounded up the hill to join him, then looked back over the dig site.

"It certainly is."

"I've been looking over the data. This just might be the most complete early Anasazi settlement ever found. It's incredible."

Abby spoke quickly, the words tripping over themselves as they tumbled from her mouth. "We're making history here."

"Let's not get ahead of ourselves," Rory cautioned.

"Come on, enjoy the moment. It's not as if discoveries like this come along every day."

"Even so . . ."

Abby rolled her eyes. "It wouldn't kill you to show some emotion once in a while, you know."

"There's a time and a place. This isn't it," he admonished her.

Abby had been Rory's assistant for five years. He had offered her the job the day she graduated from college. She was the brightest student he had ever come across and he found her company stimulating—at least in an academic sense. She had also proved invaluable as his eyes and ears on campus when he was not around, which was most of the time. She did not, however, know what he did during the long sabbaticals when he was off saving the world—sometimes literally—for his primary employers.

"Come on, prof, you can't tell me you're not the tiniest bit excited right now."

"I'll be excited when we've confirmed what we have here," Rory said, glancing sideways at Abby. He found her bubbly over exuberance refreshing. It made a change from the introverted, academic tendencies of the usual suspects who were drawn to a life of digging in the dirt. Not that he didn't occasionally try to rein her in, however, if only to keep his assistant on her toes. "Haste has been the downfall of many a researcher."

"It speaks for itself. The pieces we're pulling out suggest that this settlement is at least 3500 years old. It may be even older."

"And we'll confirm all that, but for now let's just document what we have and see where the evidence leads us."

"You can be a real killjoy, prof. You know that?" she replied, then drew in a quick breath. "Oh, I almost forgot, there's a call for you on the satellite phone."

Rory almost asked why she hadn't led with that piece of information, but let it go. "Do we know who?"

"Nope. She wouldn't give me her name. She said she'd only speak to you."

"A mysterious woman. How intriguing!" Rory raised an eyebrow. "Well, I guess we'd better not keep our unknown caller waiting, had we."

---

The air in the tent was no more than a few degrees cooler than the air outside, but it was still a relief to be out of the sun.

Rory picked up the satellite phone. The chunky handset was an anachronism compared to his smaller, lighter cell phone, but out in the middle of the desert there were no towers to pick up a signal, so the satellite phone was the best choice for communicating with the outside world. "Hello?"

"Rory, is that you?" The voice on the other end of the line was barely audible behind an infuriating crackle of static. Sometimes, even the satphone had its issues.

"Mina?" Rory had hoped it would be someone else. He sat down, his gaze wandering to a framed photograph of Cassie Locke, his girlfriend who was out of the country filming episodes for the second season of her reality TV show, *Hunting Cryptids*. The show had been a huge success, and Rory was pleased for her. The only drawback was that their combined work schedules meant that they barely spent any time together. The last time he'd seen her in person was at Decker's wedding, and that was almost two months ago.

"I know you're in the field on a side project, but we need you."

"Yeah. I figured this wouldn't be a social call." Rory couldn't help noticing how his boss dismissed the excavation as a *side project*. Then he reminded himself that CUSP was the priority, and the university gig was only for show.

Mina must have picked up on his tone of voice. "I'm sorry. I didn't mean to belittle your field work."

"It's fine." Rory looked up from the desk toward a wall of topographical maps pined to boards hung around the periphery of the tent. Each one showed a small area of desert where they had been digging. Some were marked with red pen outlining where they had found the remains of dwellings. Numbered dots related to artifacts removed from the ground. GPS co-ordinates were scrawled next to each discovery. It was vital to know where each piece had been found, in order to draw a complete picture of the site. "This place has been buried for centuries. It's not going anywhere anytime soon."

"Good, because something has come up, and you're going to love it."

# TEN

THE SHROUDED figure moved along the narrow dirt street with the ease of one accustomed to life in this hard and unforgiving place. On both sides, he passed dwellings constructed from whatever cheap or free materials their builders could scavenge. These huts housed some of the country's poorest people. One building was assembled from battered sheets of corrugated steel held together by rough wooden posts, another seemed to be almost entirely composed of dismantled shipping pallets. Sheets of dirty plastic and tatters of ripped fabric served as barriers to keep unwanted eyes from prying into the gaping holes that served as entranceways to the dark, cramped living spaces.

Although he seemed to be a perfect fit for this environment, in truth the man had been born nowhere near the slums of Mexico City. Not that the squalid, disease filled streets repulsed him. Quite the opposite in fact. He liked the gritty texture of his surroundings. Places such as this were more real, more visceral, than any upscale urban landscape in a city like New York, Paris, or London. Even so, he took no joy in seeing these wretched people struggle to survive on the brink of starvation. The poverty surrounding him wasn't his fight though. He had a higher purpose.

At the end of the street the man took a left turn, avoiding the rotting carcass of an animal that had been partially covered by dirt. Although the body had almost completely collapsed into decay there was still enough shape left to make out that it had once been a goat.

Up ahead stood a structure that appeared to be a little more solid than the buildings clustered around it, which wasn't saying much. Constructed of assorted red brick and concrete blocks, with a tin roof sagging under its own weight, the building would have been condemned years ago in most modern cities. Here it was the best house on the block. It even possessed a stout wooden door to keep unwanted guests out, it's paint peeling and chapped.

The man drew close to the building and paused for a second in the shadows, glancing around to make sure he had not been followed. Satisfied that he was alone, he rapped twice on the door.

A narrow streak of lightning pierced the darkness, ripping the night in two and illuminating the street for a split second. The man huddled close to the door and waited.

After a few seconds the sound of bolts being drawn back broke the silence. The door opened a crack.

"Hola?"

"It's me." The man's voice was hard and coarse, weathered by years of hard living.

"You are late."

"Let me in."

The door swung a few inches wider. Not much, but enough. The man slipped through the opening and was instantly engulfed by the gloom within.

The interior of the building was about as rotten as the exterior. The smell of urine and stale sweat hung in the air like a toxic cloud.

"He is waiting for you, señor." The man who occupied the building was of obvious Mexican heritage. Small in stature, he observed his visitor with almond-colored eyes. His dark tanned skin gleamed in the pale glow from a single bare bulb that fought in vain to adequately illuminate the shadowy interior.

"Gracias. You should go now. What we have to discuss is not for your ears."

The Mexican nodded and picked up his coat. He pulled open the door and hurried out into the night. For a brief second the breeze whipped into the small building, kicking up a whirlwind of dust from the floor, before the door slammed shut with a thud.

"Señor Chava. I have looked forward to meeting you for some time." A voice floated from the shadows.

"As I, you." Chava said. It felt odd to hear someone speak his name, almost like it didn't belong to him anymore. He had spent too long in solitude.

"I assume you are here because of the vision."

"Yes." Chava stepped closer, and the old man came into view. He was wizened, with stringy white hair that fell to his shoulders, and dark skin ravaged by the passing of time. Only his dark brown eyes still carried a glint of youthful energy. "Tell me what you saw."

"Very well." The old man motioned to a wooden chair sitting against the wall. One of the only pieces of furniture in the room besides the chair the old man occupied. "But first, sit."

Chava sat down.

The old man cleared his throat, the sound phlegmy and brittle, then he started to speak.

Chava listened, his unease growing by the moment. When the old man finished, he sat quietly, absorbing what he had just heard, and what must to be done.

The old man gave him a moment, then filled the silence. "You will have to move swiftly. I had hoped the orb, stolen by the Spanish so long ago, would restore to us the lands taken in blood and violence when it reemerged, but that is not what will come to pass. Others are searching for the orb, and if they find it, a great darkness will be unleashed. A scourge that will feast on the flesh of mankind."

"Not if I find the orb first." Chava said, his voice projecting a resolve he wasn't sure he had.

"I sincerely hope you do, for all our sakes," said the old man, then he leaned forward, taking Chava's hand in his. "But be warned. Nothing in this world is free. There will be a price to pay for your success. This too, I have seen."

Chava met the old man's gaze, read the sadness in his eyes. He sat in silence for a moment, then released the old man's hand, stood and turned toward the door.

"You aren't curious?" The old man asked softly.

Chava shook his head. No man should know his fate ahead of time. "I'll find out soon enough."

"Yes." The old man's voice trailed him back out onto the street. "Yes, you will."

# ELEVEN

THE LOW RUMBLE of the rotor blades could be heard almost a full minute before the helicopter itself came into sight, flying low over the canyon walls.

Rory stood in the entrance to the tent and watched the Bell 525 come to rest on the ground a few hundred feet away, bumping the surface a couple of times as it settled as though the machine was testing the sand first to make sure it was safe. At least the pilot had the good sense to put the helicopter down away from the dig area. It wasn't, however, far enough away to prevent the wash from the rotors kicking up a miniature sandstorm that threatened to engulf the contents of the closest trenches.

Several of the students bolted into action and began pulling a large blue tarp over the excavation. The tarp was on constant standby to protect the remains from the occasional inclement weather the region could produce such as rain or high winds.

The helicopter had barely stopped moving when the cabin door flew open, and a tall figure dressed in a pair of faded denim jeans and a white polo shirt stepped out, a pair of dark sunglasses shielding his eyes.

Rory watched as the man bounded toward him, lowering his

head to avoid the still spinning rotors, even though he was in no danger of coming into contact with them.

When the man drew closer and he recognized John Decker, he smiled. "Would you like to try that again? I don't think your entrance was quite dramatic enough."

"Funny." Decker came to a halt and brushed a fine layer of sand kicked up by the rotor blades off his shirt. "I guess you're a comedian now, in addition to being an archaeologist."

Rory shrugged. "I like to keep my career options open." He stepped aside to let Decker into the tent. "How was the honeymoon?"

"Better than the trip I ended up taking the first time I tried to marry Nancy."

"Aw, come on. You got to sail on the Titanic. That's kind of hard to beat."

Decker chuckled. "It had its moments, I'll admit." He looked around, taking in the tables filled with artifacts, the maps, desk, and the narrow cot standing against the far wall. "So, this is where you hide out when you're not working."

"You're as bad as everyone else." Rory rolled his eyes. "This *is* work. Just because I'm not in any danger of being killed by a gargoyle..."

"You heard about that, huh?"

"News travels fast on the CUSP grapevine, even when you're off *not working*."

Decker folded his arms. "Mina?"

"Yup. I can't believe you just walked away and let that creature get the better of you. That's not the John Decker I've come to know and love."

"I didn't walk away. We lost it. There won't be another chance to capture the beast until the next full moon."

Rory nodded thoughtfully. "Hey, at least it's one more all-expenses-paid trip to Paris. Can't beat that."

"Who's going to Paris?" said a voice from behind the two men.

They turned to see a slim young woman in her mid-twenties standing between the tent flaps. She wore dusty khaki pants, and a dark gray T-shirt that had probably once been black, with the slogan *I Dig It* stenciled on the front in faded white lettering. Her dark shoulder-length hair was tipped with red highlights. A small Ouroboros tattoo graced her wrist—a circular motif of a snake eating its own tail.

Rory wished he had pulled the tent flaps closed, but it was too late now. "Decker, meet my assistant, Abigail Thorpe."

"You can call me Abby. Everyone does." She looked from Decker to Rory. "Are you going to Paris, prof? I'd like to go to Paris. That sounds like fun."

"You have an assistant?" Decker asked, raising an eyebrow.

"Yes." Rory turned his attention back to Abigail. "I'm not going to Paris, and neither are you. Now, how about you get back to the dig so that we can continue our conversation."

Abby smiled. "Sure thing, prof." She went to leave, then turned back. "What's the deal with the gargoyle?"

"Never you mind." Now Rory really wished he had closed the flaps. Abby was a smart girl and a fantastic assistant, but she was a little too inquisitive for her own good. "And stop listening in on my conversations."

"I was walking past the tent," Abby protested. "It's not exactly soundproofed."

"Point taken."

"Which leads to my next question." Abby shuffled from one foot to the other. "What's the deal with the Spanish Galleon full of gold in the middle of the desert?"

"Dammit, Abigail." Rory realized that he sounded like a chastising parent, using her full name like that. "How many times did you walk past the tent?"

"Enough." Abby looked sheepish. "And yes, I know what you're going to say. The satphone call from that woman, Mina, was private. But honestly, it's almost impossible *not* to hear. You need to talk so loud just to use it, and have the volume turned up so much to hear a response, that privacy kind of goes out the window."

"Is there *anything* I've said today that you haven't overheard?"

Abby stared at him. "I'm not sure how to answer that. If I didn't hear it, then I wouldn't know you'd said it, so..."

Decker coughed politely. "This is getting a little off track and we're on a tight schedule. We need to go."

"Where are you going?" Abby asked.

"Again... none of your business." Rory glared at her. He had never seen Abby react with such audacity before. It was almost like she was *trying* to irritate him... or maybe something else altogether was going on. He had a sudden inkling that he knew what, and he didn't have to wait long for her to confirm his suspicions.

Abby grinned. "You're going to look for that galleon, aren't you?" She clapped her hands together, then continued without waiting for either of them to answer. "I knew it. I'm going with you."

"That is absolutely not happening," Rory said.

"Okay." Abby pushed her hands deep into the pockets of her khaki pants. "I guess I'll just stay here and tell everyone about your other job. You know, the one with that weird pseudo-black ops outfit." She glanced at Decker. "Which I'm assuming that your friend here also works for."

Rory stiffened. "What do you know about that? And more to the point, *how* do you know?"

"I know enough. And as for the how... let's just say that you're not as good as you think you are at this clandestine stuff." Abby shuffled her feet. "So, am I in?"

Decker nodded toward the satphone sitting on Rory's desk. "I think it's time for you to make a call."

"Don't suppose you want to do it?"

Decker shook his head. "Nope. This one's all yours."

"Fantastic." Rory snatched up the handset. He fixed Abby

with a withering stare. "I'm stepping out to find somewhere private to have a conversation. You're going to stay here with Mr. Decker. If you move a muscle, he *will* kill you. That's how us weird pseudo-black ops outfits work."

Abby went pale. "Really?"

"No. Not really. We don't go around killing people . . . mostly. Just stay put." With that, Rory stomped out of the tent, finally tugging the flap closed behind him.

# TWELVE

DECKER STOOD WATCHING Rory's assistant with a wary eye.

For a short while, neither of them spoke, then Abby shuffled further into the tent. "How about you fill me in on the Spanish Galleon and why you need to find it so bad while we wait?"

"How about you stand there and keep quiet?" Decker could feel the minutes slipping away. They had a schedule to keep and there wasn't time for this kind of unnecessary drama. If only Rory had been more careful, they would be on the helicopter and out of here by now.

"What's wrong? Don't you know?"

"I'm not telling you anything," Decker said, not bothering to hide his irritation, "so stop asking."

"Boy, you're grumpy."

"You have no idea." Decker had been traveling for almost twenty-four hours. He had flown from Paris to London, then boarded another flight across the Atlantic to Phoenix, where the helicopter was waiting for him. And he was still not at the end of his journey. From here, the helicopter would take them to a municipal airport in New Mexico, where a charter jet was waiting. Although in the wrong direction, it was the closest airport to Canyon de Chelly. From there, they would fly to Palm Springs. Once they arrived, Decker could finally get a good nights' sleep before they met up with the rest of the team and ventured out to find the long-lost Spanish Galleon and its unusual cargo, which legend told was located somewhere in the Sonoran Desert near a large lake known as the Salton Sea. If the ship even existed, that was. And it was a big if.

Abby sauntered over to Rory's chair next to the desk and sat down. "Okay. Fine. You don't want to talk about the galleon. How about you tell me about the gargoyle in Paris, instead, then?"

Decker said nothing, because there was no point.

Abby leaned back in the chair. "You might as well be nice to me since we're going to be working together."

"We're not going to be working together."

"We'll see."

Decker shook his head in bewilderment and wandered over to the wall of maps.

At that moment, Rory came back. He stormed into the tent and glared at his assistant. "Looks like you're coming with us."

"Yay." Abby jumped to her feet and turned to Decker. "See? I told you we would be working together."

Decker stared at Rory. "You can't be serious."

"Do I look like I'm joking?" Rory crossed the tent toward the cot. He reached underneath it and dragged out a backpack into which he started to throw clothes. "Mina said she'd rather have Abby with us than risk what she might say while we're gone. She said that we'll deal with the consequences later."

"What does that mean?" Decker asked. He wondered why Mina was so agreeable to an outsider tagging along on their assignment. It didn't make sense. Unless she knew something they didn't.

"Beats me." Rory zipped up the backpack. "Just doing what I'm told. I think it's ridiculous, but until someone tells us otherwise, Abby is part of the team."

"Whatever." Decker checked his watch. Under different circumstances he might have called Mina himself to clarify the situation, but it would just waste valuable time and whether he agreed with her decision or not, it was Mina's call to make. "We're running late. We need to go. Right now."

"Great. Give me ten minutes to pack a bag, and I'll be with you." Abby turned and bolted from the tent, shouting back over her shoulder as she went. "And you'd better not leave without me, or else."

There was a moment of heavy silence before Decker sighed. "Is she always so annoying?"

"Pretty much. Although not usually this level of super villain."

Decker sighed again. "Fantastic!"

# THIRTEEN

ONCE DECKER, Rory, and their unexpected passenger were aboard the helicopter, it took off for the short flight to Gallup, New Mexico, a small city on the old historic Route 66, and its municipal airport. Thirty minutes after the helicopter landed, they were in the air once again, this time in a sleek Cessna Citation X executive jet, which would have them on the ground at their destination an hour later.

Abby looked around the cabin in wide-eyed awe. "This might be the fanciest plane I've ever been on. Does it belong to you guys?"

"It's owned by the organization we work for," Decker replied.

"Wow. Now I see why you work for them. Pretty sweet. Can you use it whenever you want? Like, say, to fly out to Vegas and arrive in style. Make an impression."

"No. It's for official business only." Decker settled into the plush leather seat and closed his eyes, hoping to catch a quick nap, but Abby had other ideas.

"That's a shame." She leaned across the aisle and nudged Decker. "Okay. Now that I'm on the team, how about you tell me what the deal is with that Spanish Galleon, and why we're looking for it."

He didn't open his eyes. "You work for Rory. Ask him."

"How about I fill you both in on the details," said Rory. "It will save time when we arrive, since the rest of the expedition team has already been briefed." He took a deep breath. "First, some background. I'm sure you're both aware of the Aztec empire and how it fell to Hernán Cortés in 1521. He all but wiped them off the map in his quest for riches, namely the vast quantities of gold they possessed. But prior to their conquest, the Aztecs had ruled over a large empire for centuries. Originally a nomadic tribe of hunter gatherers, they eventually settled and built their capital city, Tenochtitlan, on a small island in Lake Texcoco in 1325. But legend says that it was not the first place the Aztecs settled. There was another, older city called Aztlan, which has never been discovered, and many scholars believe is nothing but a myth."

"I already know all this stuff," Abby grumbled. "Archaeologist, remember?"

"I don't," said Decker. Then, knowing how Rory tended to get off track lecturing them with irrelevant information, he said, "But I'm also not interested in a history lesson unless it relates to our current assignment."

"This does have relevance," replied Rory. "Because Atzlan was anything but a myth, at least according to the logbook recently found on a mummified corpse in the Anza-Borrego Desert State Park."

"What kind of logbook?" asked Abby.

"The logbook from a previously unknown 16th-century Spanish Galleon named the *San Isidore*. According to the logbook, they were sailing up the Pacific coast in 1524 searching for treasure and stopped somewhere along the way in northern Mexico because they were getting low on fresh water. They sent a party ashore to find a natural spring or some other source from which to replenish their reserves and instead came across an

Aztec Jaguar Warrior, which was the last thing that they expected to find so far north. Regardless, they captured the man and brought him back to the ship, then tortured him into telling them the location of his city. The Spaniards knew that where there was an Aztec city, there would also be gold, so they sent a hundred men, mostly soldiers, to find the settlement and plunder its wealth."

"Atzlan," Abby said.

"Exactly."

"They had that many soldiers on a Spanish Galleon?" Decker asked, finally opening his eyes.

"Absolutely." Rory nodded. "Depending on the size of the ship, a galleon could accommodate between fifty and a hundred and fifty soldiers and officers, in addition to a crew numbering up to eighty men."

"Did they find the city?" Abby was leaning forward in her seat.

"Yes. But here is where it gets weird. They trekked for hours through the rainforest and eventually found the city and the gold that they were looking for. But they also found the source of the Aztecs wealth, which the person who wrote the entries in the logbook claimed was a glowing orb sitting on a ceremonial altar atop a huge step pyramid. An orb that opened a doorway to another world, through which the Aztecs brought their gold."

Decker said nothing, because he already knew about the orb and Mina's suspicions regarding its origin.

Abby, however, was not so restrained. "A doorway to another world?"

"U-huh. The Aztecs believed it was a realm of the Gods."

Abby snorted. "That's ridiculous. Nothing but superstitious nonsense."

"I wouldn't be too quick to dismiss the story," said Rory. "After the Spaniards captured the city, they interrogated one of the surviving warriors because they wanted to know about the orb. The man claimed that it was a gift from the Gods that had fallen to earth a couple of hundred years before in a huge fireball. But here's the thing, they supposedly found it in a smoldering crater with what sounds very much like a strewn field of tektites."

Abby looked at Decker. "Tektites are formed from molten ejecta created by a hypervelocity meteorite impact."

"I know what tektites are," Decker said.

"Just trying to be helpful." Abby turned her attention back to Rory. "The Aztecs found the meteorite and figured it was sent there by the Gods. They probably worshipped it, got high, or went into a trance or something, and thought the orb was some kind of conduit. Plenty of indigenous peoples have mistaken drug induced visions for real experiences. It's well known that many pre-Columbian Mesoamerican cultures, including the Olmec, Maya, and Aztecs, used hallucinogenic mushrooms, peyote cactus, and other psychoactive substances in their rituals. No big deal. What I don't understand is why the Aztecs told the Spaniards that it was where their gold came from. Were they trying to stop the conquistadors from finding the real source of the gold?"

Rory shook his head. "I don't think so. From the description of the object in the logbook, it doesn't sound like a meteorite. It was a perfectly spherical orb covered with symbols."

"That's easy enough to explain. The Aztecs carved the meteorite into something else. It wouldn't be the first time an ancient civilization used meteoric material like that. A sword found in Tutankhamen's tomb was forged from meteoric iron, and the Japanese used the same material to make katanas, the curved swords wielded by the samurai. Bronze Age hunters fashioned arrowheads from meteorites. There's even a Buddha statue from around the eighth century that was carved from a meteorite. And then there are the beads discovered in—"

"Enough with the history lesson. We get the point." Rory said, interrupting his assistant. "It wasn't a meteorite. The logbook's author described the object in great detail. He even claimed to have seen the Aztecs bringing gold through a doorway from another world with his own eyes. After the Spaniards attacked the city and killed its inhabitants, they took all the gold they could find and anything else they deemed valuable, including the orb, which they intended to bring back to Europe and present to Carlos I, the king of Spain, so that he could benefit from the orb's wealth-making properties."

"I'm surprised they didn't keep it all for themselves," Decker said.

"That's not how it worked back then," Rory replied. "At least, not if you wanted to stay alive long enough to enjoy the spoils of your endeavors. In return for their loyalty, the king would take a cut and share the rest with the expedition leader and his crew. Everyone got rich."

"Since I've never read in the history books about this ship or the city they found, I'm going to assume they never made it back to Spain?" Abby said.

"They did not." Rory shifted in his seat. "After sacking the city, the Spaniards continued their journey, following the coastline north in search of more loot. They navigated all the way up through the Gulf of California, and if the logbook is to be believed, they kept going all the way into Lake Cahuilla—which is now known as the Salton Sea—thanks to a tidal bore that had temporarily connected the two bodies of water, just like it had done on numerous other occasions. When they reached the lake's northern shore and realized they could go no further, they turned around and sailed back, but the title bore had retreated, leaving the galleon trapped in the lake. With no other choice, the men abandoned their ship and set out on foot through the desert, hoping to find a friendly tribe who would help them make it back to Central Mexico and their Spanish brethren in what the conquistadors had renamed New Spain after conquering Tenochtitlan a few years before."

"But they didn't," Decker said.

"No. Or at least, if they did, there's no record of it. The most likely scenario is that they died of thirst somewhere in the desert and their bones are long buried."

"Okay. There's a lost Spanish Galleon full of gold somewhere out in the Sonoran Desert," Abby said. "Lake Cahuilla covered a much larger area than the modern lake. We'll have to search thousands of square miles to find that ship, and that's assuming that it isn't under the waters of the modern Salton Sea."

"Actually, we won't need to search anywhere near that large an area," Rory said. "The logbook wasn't the only thing found on that corpse. The dead man, probably a prospector who stumbled across the wreck, made a map showing the approximate location where he found it."

Abby's eyes grew wide. "Which will give us the location of the *San Isidore*."

"Correct. He even labeled the spot on the map as *The Lost galleon*." Rory nodded. "And it's absolutely not under the waters of the Salton Sea."

"Good enough for me." Abby settled back into her seat. "But I have one more question. The ship has been buried for five hundred years, so why did we have to race here in such a hurry? What's the big rush?"

"We're not the only ones who know about the map and the logbook," Rory said. "The San Diego Sheriff's Office, who handled the investigation into the mummified corpse, wasn't exactly quiet about what they'd found. Stories ran in several local newspapers and on the web. They even let reporters photograph the logbook before they turned it over to the State Archaeological Collections Research Facility for further study."

"Which means that other people will be looking for the ship, too."

"Yes. But at least they were smart enough not to release images of the map."

"Which would have sent droves of ill-equipped amateur treasure hunters out into the desert," Decker said. "But it won't stop the more sophisticated actors who think they stand a chance of finding it."

"Okay, I get it, but that still doesn't explain why the super shady black-ops outfit that the pair of you work for needs to find that ship so bad," Abby said with a frown. "Unless, of course, you guys are nothing more than treasure hunters who want to get your hands on that gold and keep it for yourselves just like everyone else."

"We're not treasure hunters," Decker said. "And it's not the gold that we're interested in. It's the orb."

"Why?"

"Because, like Rory has already said, we don't believe that the orb is a meteorite."

"Then what *do* you believe it is?"

"An artificially made object of extraterrestrial origin."

Abby stared at him for a moment, processing this information. When she spoke again, her voice was low. "You mean like a crashed UFO?"

"Yes." Decker sat up straight in his chair. "That's exactly what I mean. Or at least, a small part of one."

# FOURTEEN

FORTY-FIVE MINUTES after they took off, the pilot began his descent into Palm Springs. Decker was looking forward to escaping the cramped cabin and stretching his legs after spending almost an entire day cooped up inside various aircraft. He looked out the window and watched as they dropped below the clouds to reveal a barren mountainous landscape scarred here and there by meandering roads that snaked through the valleys and off into the vast plain of the desert beyond.

Across the aisle, Abby was also watching the dusty ground below them slip ever closer. After a few minutes, she tore her gaze away from the window and looked at Rory. "There's so much empty land out there. Even with the map to give us an approximate location, how are we ever going to find a five-hundred-year-old ship under all that sand?"

"I've been wondering that myself," said Decker. "I hope you have a plan beyond simply driving into the desert and digging randomly."

Rory looked bemused. "Actually, I do. Or rather, Mina does." He shot Abby a stern look. "This is highly classified information, so it can't be repeated, but she was able to convince the Pentagon to send one of their satellites equipped with a space-based ground penetrating radar over the area."

Abby shook her head. "That's impossible. There's no such thing as space-based ground penetrating radar."

"That's correct, at least officially. But the Pentagon has been working on a system for many years, and they finally deployed an experimental satellite several months ago as a classified payload atop an Atlas V rocket launched from Kennedy Space Center in Florida. While we don't know exactly what the satellite is capable of—the Department of Defense aren't exactly bragging about the abilities of their new toy—we do know that it's more than capable of looking down through the sands of the Sonoran Desert to find something as large as a buried Spanish Galleon."

"How exactly do CUSP know about the satellite?" asked Decker. "And why would the Department of Defense be willing to let us go on a treasure hunt with it?"

Rory shrugged. "How does CUSP know about anything? We have a lot of friends in high places, and that includes the Pentagon. Honestly, I think they were itching to take the satellite for a spin, and our search was a good excuse to do so."

"Okay." Abby folded her arms. "But why couldn't we—or for that matter, anyone else—just use conventional aircraft-mounted ground penetrating radar to find any ship sized anomalies beneath the desert floor?"

"Because the location on the map puts the ship somewhere within an active naval bombing range north of the city of El Centro, which means that it's restricted airspace. We can't just fly over it, and getting permission from the Department of the navy will take too long and require more explanation than we are willing to give."

"But venturing into an active bombing range without permission, and with no one knowing that we're there, is all good?" A flash of concern passed across Abby's face. "Seems like a good way to get blown to pieces."

"Relax. It will be fine," Rory said, although he didn't sound convinced. "Like I said, we have contacts at the Department of Defense, and there are no exercises planned for the next few days. That should give us plenty of time to get in and get back out safely."

"If you say so." Now it was Abby's turn to sound skeptical. "When is this supersecret satellite going to make its supersecret flyover, anyway?"

"That's a good question. According to Mina, the DoD wasn't forthcoming with that information. I guess they don't want anyone knowing exactly where their satellite will be at any given time."

"Makes sense," Decker said.

Rory nodded. "But they've already had almost twenty-four hours to make a pass over the area, so hopefully there will be some images waiting for us when we land."

"Speaking of which, what's the plan when we land?" Abby asked. "I'm hoping that we're not just driving straight out into the desert. I've been sleeping in a tent for weeks and I'd love one night in a comfortable bed before I jump right back in."

"You're the one who strong-armed your way onto this expedition," Rory said. "You're hardly in any position to complain about the sleeping arrangements."

Abby pulled a face. "All I said was that I'd like to sleep in a real bed for a change. Sue me!"

"I wouldn't mind a decent night's sleep either," said Decker.

"There will be a vehicle waiting for us when we land, packed with everything that we'll need to find that ship—including tents and sleeping bags, which I'm sure will be more than adequate," Rory said. "But have no fear. Mina was good enough to arrange hotel rooms for us tonight in Palm Springs. We'll head out into the desert first thing in the morning."

Decker nodded thoughtfully. "That will give us time to go over the GPR images and pick the best targets to explore."

"Hopefully, there will only be a few," Rory said. "There can't be many anomalies the size of a ship out there."

Before anyone could answer, a high-pitched whine filled the cabin. Somewhere beneath them came a thud. The plane's landing gear dropped into place. The lone flight attendant who had been looking after them made a quick tour through the cabin to make sure that everything was in order and they were wearing their seatbelts, then strapped herself into a jump seat at the front of the aircraft near the door.

Decker gripped his armrest, fingernails pushed into the leather, and settled stiffly back into the seat, eyeing the rapidly approaching runway through a window to his left. When the plane's wheels made contact with the tarmac and another bump shook the cabin, he grimaced.

"After all the flying that you've done for CUSP, you should be used to it by now," Rory said, observing Decker's unease with a bemused smile.

"Just happy to be on the ground." Decker met Rory's gaze briefly, then turned his attention back to the window. And when he did, he saw them. Three squat black SUVs with heavily tinted windows racing across the tarmac to meet the plane. He watched them approach with a growing sense of alarm. "Rory, many vehicles was Mina providing for us?"

"Just the one," Rory said, unclipping his seatbelt and sliding across the aisle to look out of a window on Decker's side of the plane. "And I can't imagine that she arranged for it to meet us on the runway."

"That's what I figured," Decker said, studying the speeding SUVs as they caught up with the taxiing plane and took up positions one at the front and two at the rear of the aircraft. An obvious escort. "Which means we're in a bunch of trouble."

# FIFTEEN

WHO ARE THESE GUYS?" Rory said, watching wide-eyed as the three black SUVs kept pace with the plane, which was moving slowly forward. But not toward the terminal buildings. Instead, the aircraft appeared to be heading to a remote area of the airport with buildings that looked like hangers.

As if to answer his question, the aircraft's PA system crackled, and the pilot's voice filled the cabin. "Just a heads up, ladies and gentlemen. I'm sure that you've noticed the rather ominous-looking vehicles that are accompanying us. The tower has diverted us to a hangar at the far end of the airport on their orders. And before anyone asks, I have no idea who *they* are."

"This isn't good," Decker said, unclipping his seatbelt and standing up. He turned to Rory. "You should probably get Mina on the phone."

Rory nodded and made the call, then stared at his phone screen in disbelief. "It won't go through. I don't have any service."

Decker took out his phone. "Me either."

"Same here," Abby said. "We are in Palm Springs. There is no way they don't have cell towers."

Decker pushed his phone back into his pocket. "Whoever these guys are, they must be jamming us."

"Is that even possible?" Abby asked.

Rory nodded. "Actually, it's pretty easy, especially for the kind of people who drive black SUVs with tinted windows and have the power to intercept a private aircraft on the runway of a civilian airport in plain sight."

"You think this has anything to do with that secret spy satellite you borrowed?" Abby asked.

"I don't see how. I'm sure that Mina did everything aboveboard," Rory said. "Spoke to all the right people. It's not like she hijacked it."

Decker leaned down and looked back out of the window. "Yeah, well, someone's feathers have been ruffled."

"It won't be long until we find out who," Rory said, because they were approaching the hangar now. A huge metal building with wide doors that were sliding back to reveal a darkened cavernous interior. The plane rolled forward, following the lead SUV into the hangar, cutting off the sunlight and leaving the aircraft's interior illuminated only by the warm white overhead up-wash LED lights mounted on the ceiling.

No sooner had the aircraft cleared the doors than they began sliding closed, cutting off what little sunlight remained. The two SUVs that had been following them now peeled off to each side of the plane and came to a halt.

The flight attendant wasted no time in opening the cabin door and deploying the airstairs, then she stepped aside and waited for her passengers to disembark.

"Here goes." Decker started down the aisle. "This should be interesting."

"That's one way of putting it," Rory said, following along behind. "I really don't want to disappear."

"I'm sure they just want to have a friendly chat," Decker said dryly, ducking his head as he stepped out of the jet and started down the stairs toward the six men, all wearing white shirts under black suits, who stood waiting for them in a tight line. Behind them, occupying the hanger's second bay, was another small jet aircraft, painted deep black, just like the vehicles that had intercepted them. Decker noted with alarm that it bore no tail number.

When they reached the bottom of the airstairs, one of the men stepped forward and spoke in a deep, gravelly voice. "John Decker and Rory McCormick. We've been keeping an eye on the two of you for a long time, and now here you are. It's a pleasure to make your acquaintance."

"Just us?" Rory asked. "What makes us so special?"

"Not just you. We like to keep tabs on everyone who works for your organization."

Abby stepped forward. "What about me? Have you been keeping tabs on me?"

The man fixed her with an unblinking stare. "No."

"Huh. That doesn't seem fair." Abby feigned a pout. "Guess you're not an equal opportunity spook."

The man looked at Decker with narrowed eyes. "Who is this person?"

Decker opened his mouth to answer, but he never got that far.

Rory got there first, positioning himself between the stranger and Abby. "She's nobody."

"Hey!" Abby pushed past Rory. "I am *not* nobody. I'm his assistant, and I'm a damn good one."

"I'm sure that you are." The man motioned for them to step away from the plane. "Now that the pleasantries are over with, you need to come with us."

"There were pleasantries?" Decker asked.

The group of unknown men stared at him, expressionless.

"Okay. No sense of humor."

"Along with their lack of fashion sense," Abby said. "You get a bulk discount for those suits?"

"Just come with us." There was a note of weariness in the man's voice.

"Yeah. I don't think so." Decker shook his head. "Not until you tell us who you are and where we are going."

"You'll find out soon enough." The man motioned toward the other aircraft. "If you wouldn't mind accompanying us aboard?"

"Again, I don't think so." Decker glanced toward the CUSP jet. He could see the pilot through the cockpit window, staring down and watching the action in the hangar below him. Decker wondered if the pilot had decided that the safest option was to remain in the cockpit, or if he had been instructed to do so by the tower. "How about we take our own transportation, and we'll follow you?"

"Your aircraft has been impounded until further notice."

"And our pilot?"

"He's free to go just as soon as we depart."

*That's something, at least,* Decker thought . . . assuming that it wasn't a lie. "Once we step on that plane, we're at your mercy. You could fly us to some secret facility and hold us against our will or even shoot us."

"If we wanted to detain you, we would have done so already." The man glanced around the hangar, perhaps to highlight the secluded nature of their location. "Likewise, if we wished to kill you."

Rory looked at Decker. "He has a point."

"I suppose he does, but I can't imagine they'll let us walk out of this hangar and go on our way."

The man gave a small nod. "That is correct."

Decker's gaze drifted to the waiting jet. "Then I suppose we have no choice but to do as they say."

# SIXTEEN

AFTER BOARDING THE JET, they were escorted to seats near the rear of the cabin, where they were told to sit down and buckle up. Decker couldn't help noticing that the blinds were pulled over the windows, blocking their view. When Abby reached to lift one up, the man who had previously done all the talking barked an order for her not to touch it. She withdrew her hand as if the blind was scorching hot and sat staring sullenly ahead.

The rest of the men who had intercepted them filed onto the plane and took seats up front. Unlike the CUSP jet, there was no flight attendant to offer them drinks.

Soon after they boarded, the plane started up, reversing from the hanger and out into the late afternoon sunshine. From his position, Decker could make out airport buildings, distant mountains, and a patch of blue sky through the still open windows near the front of the cabin. At least, until those blinds were pulled closed, cutting off his view. Within minutes, they were barreling down the runway and lifting into the air.

Once they reached cruising altitude, the man who had done all the talking made his way down the aisle. He took a seat opposite Decker, Rory, and Abby, then observed the trio in silence for a moment before speaking. "Now that the bluster and indignation are out of the way, I think it's time to have a little chat."

"I couldn't agree more," Decker said, studying his adversary. He was a large man, possibly 6 foot five, with broad shoulders and piercing blue eyes. He appeared to be in his early fifties, but his dark brown hair showed no signs of turning gray. "Why don't we start with who you are and the organization that you work for?"

"Who do *you* think we are?" the man asked.

Decker had been wondering about that ever since they first noticed the SUVs racing toward them across the tarmac. "Well, I'm fairly certain you're not FBI. You would have identified yourselves as such immediately if that were the case. And you're not CIA either, because we're on American soil and that particular agency is prohibited from conducting operations in the United States."

"Doesn't mean they don't do it anyway," Rory chipped in.

Decker glanced sideways toward him. "Agreed. But regardless, I don't think our friends here are with the Central Intelligence Agency." He turned his attention back to the man sitting opposite them. "You could be Secret Service, but again, I don't think so. I'm not getting that vibe. Then there's the National Security Agency, which, considering that we're on an aircraft with no tail number, is a viable assumption. But my instincts are telling me no."

"Okay. You've rattled off a list of organizations that you don't think we're associated with, so how about you tell me who you think we are?"

"I think that you're a government black ops outfit similar to the CIA's Special Operations Group, except that I'm betting you run independently and with very little external oversight, if any. Not that I could begin to guess the name of your group, obviously." Decker realized he was clutching the armrests of the seat in a tight grip that made his fingers ache. He forced himself to relax. "I assume that our request to use the top-secret GPR satellite rang an alarm bell somewhere within your organization and that's why we are currently your unwilling passengers aboard this mystery flight."

The man smiled, showing a glimmer of emotion for the first time. "How very perceptive of you. And yes, your little excursion with that satellite raised a few eyebrows, not only because you knew of its existence, but also because of the location you requested for the flyover."

Rory snorted. "This is about the lost galleon."

"In a roundabout way." The man rested his hands in his lap. "I think some introductions are in order. I'm Commander James Cade."

"With?"

"That's need to know, and *you* don't."

"And the rest of those men at the front of the cabin—do they have names, too?"

"Of course they do. But there is no reason for you to know them, either."

"Huh. Not much of an introduction." Decker wondered if Cade had told them his real name and decided that it was unlikely. Not that it mattered under the circumstances. They were along for the ride, regardless of what this man called himself. But Decker did want to know one thing. "I don't suppose you want to elaborate on where we're going?"

"You'll find out soon enough."

"Okay, then how about you tell us why that Spanish Galleon is of so much interest that you're willing to abduct civilians to stop us looking for it?"

Cade shook his head. "You're hardly civilians. The organization that you work for has a long and storied history, as I'm sure you already know. Founded as the Order of St. George in the 19th Century by Queen Victoria and tasked with eliminating threats that regular police and military forces were ill-equipped to deal with, like the vampiric Jack the Ripper. In the 1940s it morphed into an international organization operating outside of traditional governmental oversight on either side of the Atlantic. Grendel and his mother. Werewolves. The Bermuda Triangle. The secrets you guys are keeping make the rest of us look like amateurs." He looked at Decker. "For example, there's a photograph of passengers strolling the promenade deck of the Titanic, and there's a man who might as well be your twin, with an attractive young woman on his arm. And here's where it gets really weird. According to the historical record, both of them survived the sinking. They arrived in New York aboard the Carpathia and disappeared into the city. The man is never heard from again. He literally vanishes as if he never existed. But the woman . . . well, let's just say that she pops up many times in the decades that follow. She appears in dozens, if not hundreds, of photographs. She shows up at galas and parties, posing as a socialite. She's been photographed with the likes of Winston Churchill, Franklin Roosevelt, JFK, and a host of other historical figures who had a hand in shaping the twentieth century. There's even an image of a woman who looks just like her at the Cavern Club during an early Beatles concert. And not a single person can identify her. But here's the thing, she doesn't age in any of them. Now, how would you explain that?"

"I'd say that you have an active imagination, and that you're seeing what you want to see," Decker replied, trying not to let his alarm show. "My organization is nothing more than a group of like-minded people trying to preserve relics of the past before they are lost or destroyed. And as for that couple on the Titanic, well . . . you do know how preposterous that sounds, right?"

"Ah. The classic *nothing-to-see-here* misdirect." Cade nodded. "But we both know that's not true. I don't know how or why, but you were on the Titanic and now you're here. Maybe it's time travel, or maybe you don't age for some reason. I won't bother to ask how any of that is possible, because I'm sure that you won't tell me. But please, let's dispense with the useless protestations. You know very well what we're interested in on that Spanish Galleon because it's the same thing that *you* want, which is why we felt the need to intervene."

"What's he talking about?" Abby asked, looking at Decker and Rory with a startled expression on her face. "Time travel? The Titanic? Has everyone lost their mind?"

"Oh, that's right." Cade smiled. "You're new to this." His gaze shifted to Rory. "You might want to use the remaining flight time to bring your new recruit up to speed, because she has no idea what she's gotten herself into, even if she thinks that she does."

Cade stood and started back through the cabin, retaking his seat at the front.

Abby looked at Rory and Decker. "Well? Want to do as he said and fill me in?"

Decker shook his head. "We're not authorized to do that, and even if we were, it would take way too long."

"Okay, then at least answer this. Were you somehow on the Titanic when it sank?"

Decker said nothing.

Abby's eyes grew wide. "Oh my God. You were. Otherwise, you just would have denied it."

"No comment," said Decker. He glanced down the cabin toward Cade and his men, none of whom were paying their reluctant passengers any attention. Then he reached out and lifted the blind covering one of the windows. He looked down toward the ground far below them, then quickly closed the blind again. "I have an idea where we are going."

"Really?" Rory looked skeptical. "How?"

"Easy. At this moment, we're flying over Las Vegas, and given the position of the sun and the time of day, I'd say that we're heading roughly north to northwest. We're clearly not landing in Vegas, and unless we change heading, there isn't much else, except the Tonopah Test Range, and possibly Reno. But I don't think we're going to either of those places."

"So, where do you think we're going?" Rory asked.

"To the only place that makes sense under the circumstances." Decker glanced down the aisle, then spoke in a low voice. "I think they're taking us to Area 51."

# SEVENTEEN

DECKER WAS RIGHT. Less than an hour after they flew over Las Vegas, the aircraft landed on a dusty runway in the middle of the desert, surrounded by tall mountains that provided natural cover for the remote facility. He studied their surroundings with interest, noting the length of the two visible runways, which were much longer than their counterparts at any commercial airport, and a control tower. Several nondescript one and two-story buildings and a row of large hangers stood nearby. Further away was a water tower, and more structures that looked to be in a state of disrepair. There was also a large, fenced boneyard, with piles of scrap metal, old jet engines, and other assorted junk. The skeletal remains of several military aircraft were also parked there, including a couple of partially dismantled F-16s and a wide-body transport plane with a set of airstairs pushed up to its sunbaked fuselage.

To the untrained eye, the place didn't look like much, but Decker suspected that the underwhelming facility visible to any spy satellite that wandered above was merely window-dressing. Whoever was operating this base would not be doing their work in plain sight.

And he was right.

They were quickly herded into a waiting SUV, much like the ones that had intercepted them earlier and were driven across the airfield to one of the buildings. Once inside, a pair of uniformed men carrying large guns ushered down a long corridor with doors on both sides that looked like they had probably once been offices and maybe even laboratories. Now, they appeared to be empty and abandoned. Except for one smooth metal door at the end of the corridor, which Commander Cade accessed with a retina scan.

Beyond the door was an elevator.

Cade motioned for them to enter, then followed, leaving their armed escort behind as the doors slid closed. But he didn't press any buttons, because there weren't any. Instead, the elevator car started moving of its own volition, shooting them straight down with a speed that made Decker's stomach lurch. He glanced at Rory and Abby, who were both grimacing and obviously affected in much the same way.

When the elevator reached its destination, Decker stepped out with a grunt of relief.

They were in another long corridor. But unlike the one above, this was pristine and bathed in a cool white light that appeared to emanate from within the walls themselves. At the end of this corridor was another metal door, which Cade quickly opened. The space beyond reminded Decker of a big city downtown hotel lobby. A large circular atrium ringed with walkways rose eight floors above them. The central plaza contained seating areas, a coffee bar, and what appeared to be a self-service cafeteria. There were dozens of people strolling or sitting. Some wore military uniforms. Others were in street clothes. A few wore white lab coats. They paid the newcomers scant attention.

Cade whisked them through the lobby to a bank of elevators on the far side, talking as he went. "This is what we lovingly call the Beehive. It's the living quarters and social hub for the base and can house up to a thousand people. The rest of the facility is built into the surrounding mountains."

"The bit where the good stuff goes on," Abby said.

"Exactly."

"Like the hangers for all those extraterrestrial craft you've recovered."

Cade let a stony silence do the talking for him, which, Decker mused, could either mean Abby's statement was true, or the commander deemed it not worth answering.

"Nothing?" Abby said, pressing the issue. "Not even a half-hearted denial?"

"What we keep here is none of your business, young woman." Cade glanced sideways at her. "Unless you have a top-level security clearance that I'm not privy to."

"Hey. You brought us here, remember?" Abby returned his gaze.

"Cool it." Decker cautioned her under his breath. "We don't want to antagonize these people."

"What, you mean the people who kidnapped us?" Abby hissed back.

"Yes." Decker glared at her. An uneasy feeling had settled into the pit of his stomach. This didn't feel like any military base he had ever visited. And worse, nobody knew they were here.

"The buildings on the surface," Rory asked, echoing Decker's suspicion that the visible base was a decoy. "Are they just for show?"

"Not entirely, but a remote location and secrecy are not enough to hide a facility such as ours in the modern world, so we moved everything that we didn't want to be seen underground. We still use the infrastructure above, including the runways, for training flights and testing what we call smokescreen projects."

"Smokescreen projects?" Decker asked.

"The best way to hide advanced developmental technology is to misdirect attention to something less advanced that you don't care so much about."

"Decoys."

"Yes. Sometimes we even invent unrealistic projects just to deceive our adversaries and tie them up working on technologies that are impossible to implement, thereby putting them even further behind."

"How devious," Decker said.

"It's what we do." There was a note of pride in Cade's voice.

"Now who's asking questions." Abby said. "You should probably stop, or they'll have to kill us."

Cade chucked. "I'm sure that won't be necessary."

The elevator arrived, and he motioned for them to step inside. Three floors above, he led them around the walkway to a door where another pair of armed men were waiting. He opened the door to reveal an oblong room with a small living area that included a sofa and a coffee table, wall-mounted TV, and a compact kitchenette with a microwave and refrigerator. There were two closed doors on the wall to the left. Surprisingly, there was also a window on the back wall, beyond which a herd of wildebeest grazed lazily on a wide-open grassy plain beneath a darkening sky tinged by the fiery glow of a perfect sunset on the western horizon.

Once they were all in the room, Cade turned to them. "These will be your quarters while you're our guests. Please don't try to leave. There will be armed guards stationed outside the door for your own protection. Dinner and breakfast will be brought to you, and there are a selection of snacks and drinks in the kitchenette. Any questions so far?"

"None that I think you would answer." Decker wondered who or what exactly the guards were protecting them from. He glanced around, taking in every detail of their new digs, including the false window.

Noticing the look on his face, Cade said, "We've found that people react better living underground when they have the illusion of space. There's an app on the TV that controls the view outside the window. You can choose vistas ranging from cityscapes to rolling hills. Whichever view you select will change based on the time of day to ensure that your circadian rhythms are not interrupted. If it's midnight on the surface, it will also be dark outside of your window."

"How thoughtful." Decker glanced toward the two closed doors. "I assume that's where we will be sleeping?"

"Yes." Cade walked over to the doors and opened the first one to reveal a cramped bathroom. The second door opened onto a sparsely furnished bedroom, containing two sets of bunk beds standing against opposite walls, with a pair of nightstands between them. The space was illuminated by a single sconce light on the wall above the nightstands.

"We're all sharing the same room?" Abby asked. "You can't be serious."

"This isn't a five-star hotel, Miss Thorpe, it's a top-secret government facility. Space is limited, and we aren't accustomed to having guests. These are the same quarters that we assign to our own personnel."

"That's ridiculous." Abby's face was full of indignation. "We don't even have our bags. What are we supposed to do, sleep in the buff and walk around in dirty clothes?"

"Absolutely not." Cade motioned toward three bags sitting on one of the bottom bunks. "We took the liberty of procuring the luggage from your jet and bringing it with us. I trust you have no further objections?"

"Would it make any difference if I did?" Abby asked sullenly.

Cade shook his head, his lips pressed together tightly. "No. It would not."

Rory went to his pack and unzipped it, then turned on Cade. "Where are they?"

"Where's what?"

"You know very well. The copies of the map and diary pages. They were here and now they're missing. You had no right to take them."

"We had every right." Cade's voice carried a hint of menace.

"That material is classified, and you weren't authorized to have it."

"Says who?" Rory's face had turned a bright crimson.

"Me, that's who," Cade replied, the edge fading from his voice. "And if you keep arguing about it, I'll have you thrown in the brig."

"Now, wait a minute—" Rory took a step forward.

Decker grabbed his arm. "Let it go. We won't win this."

"You should listen to him," Cade said. "Or would you like me to call a guard in here and have you taken to less salubrious accommodation?"

"That won't be necessary." Rory took a step back.

"Good." A half smile cracked Cade's lips. "I trust no one else has anything to say?"

Decker shook his head. So did Abby.

"Good." Cade turned toward the door. "I suggest that you make yourselves comfortable." Then he strode from the room, closing the door behind him.

# EIGHTEEN

"I SURE FEEL LIKE A PRISONER, considering that we're not supposed to be under arrest," Rory said, pacing the small living area inside their quarters. The remains of three meals that had been brought to them not long after Commander Cade departed sat atop metal trays on the coffee table, waiting to be collected by their hosts. And considering that it was now past 10PM local time, they weren't in any hurry.

"Better than the brig," Decker said.

"I guess." Rory didn't look convinced. "You think Mina knows where we are, or did we just drop off the radar?"

"No idea." Decker went to the door and tried the handle, noting that it was locked. Not that it mattered, because Cade had made it clear there would be armed guards posted outside. Apparently, he didn't want anyone wandering around the classified facility unaccompanied. "She should have been more careful requesting that flyover. I'm sure they already knew about the galleon, but we might have been able to beat them to it."

"Or they might have shown up while we were there and decided to just shoot us," Rory said.

Decker shook his head. "I don't think so. They've had plenty of opportunity to hurt us, and they haven't, which means they know who we work for and don't want to draw unwanted attention to themselves."

"Or they want something from us," said Abby, who was sitting on the couch with her arms folded. "Otherwise, why would they bring us to Area 51 and risk exposing their secrets? They could have just taken us to an abandoned warehouse, strapped us to chairs with duct tape, and held us there until they got what they wanted."

Decker nodded. "She's right. These guys probably have safe houses all around the country where they hold and interrogate people. They could have taken us anywhere. They could even have instructed the local authorities to arrest us on bogus charges until they were done. For whatever reason, they need us."

"Well, they're not giving me much incentive to cooperate with them," Rory said. "Whatever happened to asking nicely?"

"I think *this is* their version of asking nicely," Decker replied. "And I'm not sure why you're complaining. We're inside Area 51. I don't know about you, but I'm kind of curious."

"Oh, I'm plenty curious, but I also don't like being kept locked up."

"You think they'll give us the grand tour in the morning?" Abby asked.

"I doubt it." Decker shook his head.

"Yeah, that's what I figured."

"Whatever happens in the morning, it has to be more exciting than this," Rory grumbled, crossing the room and studying the fake window. "Although I have to say, this is impressive. It's obviously a screen, but the illusion of space is incredible. It's actually three dimensional, with no need for glasses or a visor, and there's no hint of pixels or anything. If I didn't know that we're heaven-only-knows how deep beneath Groom Lake, I'd swear that I was looking out over the Serengeti." He looked up.

"Even the moon phase is correct, which means they must be using some sort of AI to generate the image. Of course, it wouldn't really be night there now since Africa is eleven hours ahead of us."

"You're overthinking this," Abby said with a snort.

"But he's not wrong," said a voice from behind them. "The screen uses the latest in holographic technology. Not that you'll see it in stores anytime soon. At least, nothing anywhere near this advanced."

They turned to see Commander Cade standing in the doorway. He had arrived so silently that they hadn't heard him enter. Even the lock had made no noise when it disengaged. Behind him, waiting in the hallway, stood the pair of armed guards he had warned them about.

"You're back sooner than I expected," Abby said. "Change your mind about keeping us prisoner?"

Cade observed her silently for a moment, then diverted his attention to Decker. "If you and your team would like to follow me, I have something to show you."

"Right now?" Decker asked, surprised.

"I don't know how CUSP operates, but around here, we like to get things done pronto, and time is of the essence." Cade turned and stepped back out into the hallway. "Now, if you don't mind, please follow me."

"Guess it's a good job we haven't gone to bed already," mumbled Rory, following Decker and Abby out of the door.

Cade led them out of the central housing area and through the facility, which was even more massive than Decker had imagined. After leaving the towering central lobby they climbed into a vehicle that looked a bit like a large golf cart and were whisked along what felt like miles of wide corridors, each identical to the last, until they came to a square room hewn out of bedrock, with towering steel doors built into a wall of pure granite.

Cade brought the vehicle to a halt, and they climbed out.

With Cade in the lead, they approached the doors, which slid open at his approach, almost as if they recognized him.

As he stepped through the doors, Decker found himself inside an enormous hangar. His footsteps reverberated off the polished floor, which was as dark as obsidian. The air was heavy with a faint hum that Decker felt more than he heard. It was almost like a low-level vibration that seemed to penetrate his entire body and worm its way into his mind. But it wasn't the room and its strange atmosphere that caught his attention. It was the three craft that could only be described as UFOs, each more astonishing than the last.

The first hovered silently in the center of the hangar. A sleek, silver disc with pulsing blue lights running along its circumference. Its surface was smooth and seamless, lacking any visible openings, as if it had been sculpted from a single piece of otherworldly material.

To the left of the disc was a second craft shaped more like a large pill that sat on a bed of scaffolding complete with gantries and metal stairs that must have been built specifically to hold it. The vehicle's fuselage was elongated and tapered at the ends, and just like the disc shaped UFO, there were no windows or portholes of any kind. The craft's surface was covered with swirling patterns and symbols that looked almost like writing but were clearly not of this earth. It reminded Decker of the vehicle in the famous Tic-tac video taken by a U.S. Navy pilot, which made him wonder if there was a connection.

The third UFO was unlike anything Decker had ever seen. It was a huge triangular craft with sharp angles and a menacing presence. Its surface was a deep, matte black that absorbed the light so that it looked almost invisible. In fact, when he wasn't staring directly at it, the vessel seemed to merge with its surroundings, becoming nothing more than a vague shadow. Compared to this, stealth aircraft like the F-22 Raptor and B-21 Raider might as well give up and go home.

He stood in awe. The sheer scale of the hangar, the advanced technology on display, and the realization that he was standing in a place so secretive that few people would ever truly know it existed outside of conspiracy theories and myth, let alone see it, left him speechless.

Abby broke the silence, her voice barely above a whisper. "Holy freaking crap."

# NINETEEN

CLOUDS RACED across the night sky, blocking the moon and plunging the landscape into swampy darkness. Chava kept his head low and watched the Border Patrol jeep rumble past less than ten feet away on the border road. He had been lucky to find a natural dip in the landscape, or he might have been spotted, but then, he had always had more than his fair share of luck.

Not that he believed in luck. People made their own destiny by their beliefs and view of the world around them. Powerful men and women became that way because they aspired to be so, and saw no obstacles to their success. Those for whom fortune never smiled were so afflicted because they did not believe, in the deepest corners of their psyche, that they warranted any other life. This was subconscious for the majority of people. They went about their lives never knowing how much their beliefs shaped their future. But for those who had learned to master the power of true, unwavering conviction, and bend it to their will, destiny could be crafted into whatever outcome they desired. Chava had escaped the attention of the Border Patrol not by the blind luck of finding a fortuitously located gully to hide within, but because he truly believed that he would not get caught.

The sound of the jeep's engine faded away. A few seconds

later, the blackness of the night swallowed the dim red glow of the vehicle's taillights.

Chava was alone once more.

He slipped from his hiding place and approached the border. Moving stealthily, keeping low and taking long, measured steps, he watched for trip wires, infrared cameras, and motion sensors. It was unlikely there were any such devices in such a remote area, but it always paid to be cautious. His footfalls were so light that they barely disturbed the loose shale of the desert floor. Only the most ardent of observers would ever know he had been here.

As he crossed the border, the moon found a gash in the cloud layer and bathed the barren landscape in cold white light. Chava, confident that the border patrol was far away, didn't even break stride. He kept walking, picking his way across the terrain with a sense of purpose. After a while, more points of light appeared, twinkling from across the desert landscape, but Chava did not bother to hide this time. Because it was not the Border Patrol returning, but rather the distant lights of a small town somewhere beyond the nearby Ajo Sonoita Highway. The highway was nothing more than a remote atrip of asphalt cutting through the barren desert. It was also his destination. Or at least, as far as he was going to travel on foot.

He took out his phone and opened the *maps* app, then followed its directions to the GPS coordinates he had entered before leaving the shabby Mexican hotel room where he had slept for a few hours before traveling to make the midnight crossing.

A battered older model white pickup truck was waiting there, parked at the side of the road with the engine running and its lights off. When Chava opened the passenger door and climbed in, the dome light did not come on either, leaving the man behind the wheel cloaked in shadow.

"You're late. Problem?" The man's accent was hard to pin

down, but carried the barest hint of Mexican Spanish, much less pronounced than Chava's own accent.

Chava pulled his seatbelt on. His mind drifted back to the Border Patrol jeep. It was still out there somewhere. "Just drive."

The driver—Chava knew him only as Raul and that might not be his real name—grunted and slipped the truck into gear, then pulled onto the road. "I know it's kind of your thing, but you don't *have* to be so mysterious."

"I like mysterious."

"Fair enough." Raul glanced toward him. "Destination?"

Chava didn't reply. Instead, he once again opened his phone and the *maps* app and selected the second destination he had programmed into it back in his hotel room.

The phone chirped and started to issue directions.

Raul looked down toward the screen, then quickly back up at the dark and empty road that stretched ahead of them. "Might as well get comfortable. We have a long drive ahead of us. That's assuming the Border Patrol don't stop us first."

"They won't. It's not our destiny." Chava fell silent. He settled into his seat and watched the dark landscape flit past. They were heading five hours west toward El Centro, a small city in Imperial County, California south of the Salton Sea. After that would be a grueling trek to a spot in the desert given to Chava by the old man back in Mexico City. A location revealed to him in turn through a vision while in a deep meditative state. The old man was a seer. One of a few such mystics still left who had a connection to the many spiritual realms of the Aztecs, and in particular, Omeycan, the highest realm, which was known as The Place of Duality. The vision, he believed, had been granted to him by the most important of all the Aztec deities, Ometeotl, the creator. At the end of their journey, he hoped, was the orb crafted from an unknown metal that had become known as the Extlahualtin Teotl, or Gift of the Gods. This mysterious orb, lost for centuries after it was stolen by the conquistadors, would, so the legends said, release a vast army of Aztec warriors who waited in a realm beyond the physical plain to destroy the invaders who had settled their lands, and it would restore the Aztec empire to its rightful place in the world. Except that wasn't what the old man had seen when he was in his trance. He had witnessed something else come through from the other side. Something much darker and far more destructive. A terrible creature that would overrun the world and take it for its own. At least, if Chava didn't find the orb and stop it first . . .

# TWENTY

DECKER STARED at the trio of alien spacecraft, the enormity of what he was seeing slowly sinking in. CUSP had plenty of secrets, but nothing to rival this. Beside him, Rory gasped in disbelief.

Cade cleared his throat. "Welcome to the real Hangar 18."

"Hangar 18?" Abby looked at Rory.

"A conspiracy theory about a hanger on Wright-Patterson Air Force Base where they supposedly store alien spacecraft and bodies."

"Huh." Abby turned her attention back to the contents of the hangar. "I guess the conspiracy theorists were right. They just got the location wrong. Of course, there are plenty of rumors about alien spaceships at Area 51, too, so maybe not. Which one of these bad boys came from Roswell?"

"None of them," said Cade. "The Roswell disc suffered significant damage when it crashed, so we reverse engineered it. What's left is sitting in laboratories here and around the country. The disc-shaped craft in this hangar is of the same design, though."

"And the other two?" asked Decker.

"We call the one on the right that looks like a big triangle of black metal the Monolith," said Cade. "It flew over Phoenix in 1997, then drifted for many miles before *landing itself* in a remote canyon and shutting down. The occupants were all dead, and the craft was flying under some sort of automatic pilot we still don't understand."

"Huh." Abby cocked her head. "I guess the Phoenix Lights *weren't* military flares after all."

"Your sarcasm gets tiring rather quickly." Cade said with a deep sigh. "Regardless, that was not our most creative cover story."

"Even worse than the weather balloon story used at Roswell," Abby muttered.

"Do you want to hear what I have to say or not?" There was a note of exasperation in Cade's voice.

"Sorry. Continue."

"Thank you." Cade motioned toward the remaining vehicle. The one that looked like a Tik-tac. "This is what we call a USO, or unidentified submerged object. We retrieved it off the ocean floor in the Bermuda Triangle."

"Cool." Abby's voice rose a note. "Maybe that's what caused all those disappearances and the other weird stuff that's happened there."

Rory shook his head. "Not even close."

"Trust us, we know," Decker said.

Cade observed Decker for a moment, perhaps hoping that he would elaborate, then he nodded. "We believe that rather than causing the phenomena in that particular part of the ocean, this vessel was caught up in it, although we have no idea how long it was down there."

Decker's gaze drifted from the alien spacecraft to the hanger within which they sat. "We're thousands of feet underground, and this hangar doesn't appear to have any obvious doors. At least, none large enough to accommodate these vessels. How did you get them down here?"

Cade chuckled. "There are doors. You're just not looking in the right place." He pointed upward.

Decker raised his head and found himself looking up into a vast emptiness that towered at least ten stories above them. The space was illuminated by a bluish light that seemed to emanate from within the walls themselves, and at the top was a round metal hatch at least five hundred feet wide, and maybe larger. It reminded him of a missile silo, except on a scale far more massive.

"How do you hide a set of doors that large?" asked Abby, craning her neck to peer up.

"It really isn't that hard," said Cade. "The doors are camouflaged on the outside to blend in with their surroundings, and we make sure that there are no satellites passing overhead or planes within sight line of Groom Lake when we open them."

"Wait. If you're opening those doors, that must mean you're flying something in or out." He looked at the trio of spacecraft. "Can you actually operate these things?"

"That's not a question I'm at liberty to answer."

"I think you just did," said Decker.

"You may infer whatever you want from my reply," Cade said. "Because regardless of the operational status of these vehicles, you don't have the security clearances to receive an answer either way. In fact, from this moment on, I will only provide information that has direct relevance to your reason for being here."

"In other words, stop asking questions," Decker said.

"Not at all. You may ask whatever you want." Cade folded his arms. "I merely reserve the right not to respond."

"Right." Decker shifted his gaze back to the alien vessels. He couldn't help wondering if one or more of them was still not only operational but actually being flown in the skies above Nevada. It would certainly explain why the lonely stretch of road running through the Nevada desert parallel to Area 51 was known as the Extraterrestrial Highway. He had always thought it was a stretch that witnesses were mistaking military aircraft, even if they were prototypes undergoing testing, as alien spaceships. But even as he pondered this, a bigger question nagged at the back of his mind. He turned to Cade. "If we don't have the security clearance to know what you're doing here, why did you bring us here in the first place?"

"I'd like an answer to that question, too," Rory said, nodding. "Because there's no way that the tech in this hangar isn't beyond top secret. I bet most of the top brass at the Pentagon don't even know about this. Hell, I wouldn't be surprised if you've kept it from the President himself. Which begs the question of why you're willing to reveal it to a bunch of civilians you hadn't met until this afternoon."

"You're hardly civilians, as we've already established," Cade replied at length. "But you're correct that the existence of this hangar is known only to a select few outside of those tasked with its operation and maintenance. Obviously, I can't tell you who those people are."

"That still doesn't answer our question," Decker said.

"You're a smart bunch. Why do you think I brought you here?" Cade asked.

"I have a suspicion," Decker said. "We already know what you want on the galleon, because it's the same thing that we're going after. An orb-shaped object of extraterrestrial origin that fell to earth hundreds of years ago and ended up revered by the Aztecs until the conquistadors stole it. Given our current location, I suspect that your interest in the orb has something to do with the vehicles in this hanger. The most obvious reason is that you need it to repair one of your little alien toys here."

"Very good." Cade smiled.

"Wait," Abby said. "How will the orb help them repair a UFO?"

"Because it's what makes interstellar travel possible." Rory replied. "And they don't have one."

Cade nodded. "An excellent piece of deduction, Mr.

McCormick." He turned to Decker. "Which brings us back to the pertinent question of why I brought you here."

Decker's mind drifting to another time and place. "The orb. You brought us here because I've seen one before and you figure I'll be useful to you."

"Come now, Mr. Decker, don't be so humble." Cade said, his eyes narrowing. "You haven't just seen one. You've operated it."

# TWENTY-ONE

WHAT DOES HE MEAN?" Abby asked, her eyes flying wide. "You've operated a UFO?"

"No. Not quite." Decker shook his head and glanced at Rory.

Rory shrugged. "You might as well tell her. We've already told her everything else, and Mina cleared us to read her in."

"It's not her I'm worried about." Decker said, jerking a finger toward Cade. "It's him."

Rory sighed. "I'm pretty sure he knows more than we do, although I have no idea how."

"We have our ways," Cade said.

"Fine." Decker wondered what Mina's plan was for Abby once this was over. They could hardly let her go back to her old job as if nothing had happened. "A couple of years ago, I was sent on an assignment to an undersea research facility called Habitat One to investigate strange events that had no rational explanation. The facility was studying an impossibly intact sunken World War Two German U-Boat that had been fitted with an experimental drive by the Kriegsmarine that allowed it to attack Allied ships and then vanish, only to reappear hundreds of miles away in the blink of an eye. It was the perfect hunter-killer."

"The drive. It was an orb. Am I right?" Abby asked.

"Yes." Decker nodded. "An orb extracted from a Foo Fighter, or what we now call a UFO, that was involved in a collision with an Allied bomber. The Germans realized what it was and tried to harness its abilities, but they didn't fully understand it, and it eventually malfunctioned, stranding the crew on another dimensional plain and sinking the U-Boat."

"Huh?" Abby looked confused. "How did it do that?"

"Because it's an inter-dimensional star drive," Rory said. "We aren't really sure how it works, but the orb shifts whatever it's powering into a void between realities, then punches back into our dimension at the destination coordinates, effectively traveling massive distances in no time at all."

"It blinks out of existence and reappears somewhere else."

"In a way, yes." Rory nodded.

"Like a warp drive."

"No, nothing like that." Rory shook his head. "A warp drive would fold the fabric of time and space to negate a vast distance between locations, at least in theory. The inter-dimensional drive literally removes you from existence in a particular reality, then pops you back into it somewhere else. You could have it take you a mile down the street, or to the other side of the universe. It would make no difference if you knew where you wanted to go and take about the same amount of time, which would be a second or two from your point of view."

"Wait." Abby was silent for a few moments. "If this drive can punch out of our reality, could it open a doorway into a different one?"

Rory was silent for a moment. "I don't see why not."

"Which means that the aliens who created it might be from another dimension instead of another place in our universe." Abby sounded excited. "They could visit hundreds of Earths, each one a bit different to the next."

"It's possible." Now Rory's voice lifted with excitement. "Of course, everything we're discussing is purely hypothetical since we don't really understand the orb."

*It's not hypothetical,* Decker thought, remembering the strange landscape he'd seen with planets hanging in the sky like baubles on a Christmas tree when he'd rescued the trapped submariners from wherever the orb installed on the U-Boat had stranded them. He didn't say anything, though, because the only people who had access to his report on that part of his assignment were Mina, Daisy, and Adam Hunt. And maybe Cade, he mused, because the man appeared to have an unnerving knowledge of CUSP's mission and operations.

Now it was Abby's turn to frown. "Okay, so there's some kind of star drive on the galleon that the Aztec's mistook for a gift from their Gods." She looked at Cade. "But it still doesn't explain why you need it. I mean, you have all these spaceships already. Whichever one the orb fits into must have had one already, otherwise how did it get here . . . to Earth I mean, not this hangar."

"That's a good question," said Cade. "And one we didn't have an answer for until the galleon showed up. As best we can deduce, the alien craft in question has some kind of failsafe mechanism. The one we have is missing its *star drive*, as you called it. It will fly through the air like a regular vehicle with a speed and maneuverability that significantly outpaces even our most nimble fighter jets but has no way to move vast distances or between dimensions. We think that the craft ejects the orb in an emergency situation, although we don't know if this is to stop it being completely operational if it falls into the wrong hands after a crash, or to protect it from some sort of explosion or other catastrophic event."

"You have a craft without an orb to power it," Rory said.

"Yes." Cade glanced toward the saucer shaped vehicle. "That one, to be precise."

Abby furrowed her brow. "Then how did the Germans get their hands on an orb to install in their U-Boat?" She looked at

Decker. "You said that it was taken from a crashed Foo Fighter. I've read about those. They dogged both Allied and Luftwaffe planes during the Second World War. Both sides thought they were advanced tech being deployed by the other. But they weren't described as saucers. They were balls of light."

Rory answered quickly. "It's entirely possible that more than one race of aliens has developed similar technology, and they might not all have the same protocols for crashed spacecraft."

"Okay. Then how did an orb fall into the hands of the Aztecs?"

Cade rubbed his chin. "Best guess, a saucer encountered issues somewhere near our solar system and ejected its drive. Somehow, the drive made it through Earth's atmosphere intact and crashed near one of their cities."

"And the saucer?"

"That's a question I can't answer."

"You mean it could be floating up there somewhere with a dead crew, stranded billions of miles from home in a dimension not their own?"

"It's possible."

"I wonder if they were still alive when the drive was ejected."

"Again, I can't answer that," Cade said.

"Can you imagine?" Abby shivered visibly, a look of horror passing across her face.

"We're getting off track, and I'm exhausted," Decker said. "Can we cut to the chase?"

"Very well," Cade said. "Tomorrow, we're going after that orb. We'd very much like for you and your companions to work alongside us to retrieve it before our adversaries do. Your knowledge and experience will be beyond valuable."

"And what if we don't agree?" Decker asked.

"Then we'll keep you locked up here until we're done, instead." Cade's eyes were black under the soft light of the hangar. "Your choice."

"That really isn't much of a choice," Rory said.

"No," Decker agreed. "It isn't."

"I assume that's a yes?" Cade asked.

Decker nodded.

"Excellent. I look forward to working with you." Cade turned toward the doors. "Now get some rest. We leave at 7AM on the dot."

# TWENTY-TWO

CADE ORDERED a pair of guards to escort them back to their quarters. Decker was happy to leave the hangar behind, and also the odd hum that had permeated his body the whole time they were in there. But Rory hesitated at the doors, casting a wistful glance back toward the cluster of alien spacecraft, no doubt wishing he'd had the opportunity to examine them up close.

Abby fidgeted in her seat as they rode the golf cart back to the central housing area. "I can't believe it. Aliens are real. And not in an abstract *of course there must be other life in the universe* real, but completely, factually, seen it for myself, real!"

"Not really news to us," Rory said, but despite his attempt at nonchalance, a wide grin spread across his face. "Pretty awesome to see those spacecraft, though. Damn, I wish Cade had let us go inside one of them."

"Or all of them," Abby agreed.

"I'm content to stay on the outside looking in," Decker said. There was enough excitement in his life without tempting fate by climbing inside an alien spacecraft. He looked at his watch. "And anyway, it's past midnight. Cade wants to leave in less than seven hours. We don't have the time unless you want to skip sleeping."

"For that?" Rory raised an eyebrow. "I'd skip sleep for a week to get a peek inside those ships."

"Yeah, well you might not think that way once we're back out in the field. I have a feeling we're going to need all the rest we can get. The commander said something back there that's been bothering me."

"What?"

"He said we have to beat our adversaries to the orb," Abby said.

"Exactly." Decker lowered his voice. "I have a feeling that he knows something we don't."

"It's hardly surprising that other people would want that tech," Rory said. "Hostile powers, warlords, arms dealers who think they can make a quick buck selling it. But none of them have seen the map. It's safely tucked up in the State Archaeological Collections Research Facility and I was told that they are restricting access to both the map and the logbook."

"Which means that we're the only ones who know the location of the lost galleon," said Abby.

"Not the only ones," Decker said. "I'm pretty sure that Cade has a copy of that map."

"And even if he didn't before, he does now," Rory agreed ruefully.

"And I bet they have the satellite data from the flyover, too," Decker said. "But I'm more concerned with who else he thinks might have somehow gotten their hands of it."

"Maybe he's talking about amateur treasure hunters," Abby said. "You said people might go looking for the gold the ship was supposed to be carrying."

"I don't think he meant treasure hunters. The galleon is located on a military bombing range. It would be pretty easy for Cade to keep civilians away."

"Well, whatever he meant, there's not much point in worrying about it. We'll find out soon enough," Rory said as the cart entered the vast atrium of the central housing area and came to a halt.

They climbed out and let the guards lead them to the elevators, then up to their quarters. As before, they were ushered inside and locked in, only this time there was no pretense of civility. The pair of guards were stony faced and spoke only when necessary.

"You'd think we were a security threat," Abby grumbled once they were alone. "They could at least give us our phones back."

"And what would you do with it?" Decker asked. "We're thousands of feet underground in the middle of the desert. Not much chance of a signal."

"And even if cell phones did work, they wouldn't allow them," Rory said. "That *really would* be a security threat in a place like this. One photo of that hangar and its contents and there goes any hope of plausible deniability."

"I bet it wouldn't make any difference," Abby countered. "I could come up with a convincing photo of UFOs in a hangar in about ten seconds flat using generative AI. With today's technology, you could snap a selfie with the Loch Ness Monster, and nobody would believe it was real."

"She's got you there," Decker said with a smirk.

"Yeah, well, all that aside, it would be nice to check in with Mina. See what she thinks about all of this."

"My guess is that Cade has already spoken to her," Decker said. "It would be foolish of us to think that he's leaving our superiors out of the loop."

"I'm not so sure about that," Rory answered. "Cade doesn't strike me as an *ask permission* kind of guy."

"I never said he would ask permission. But he also won't want CUSP frantically searching for operatives who have been detained and spirited away by persons unknown. Because I guarantee that news of our abduction has already reached her. If he's smart, he'll seek Mina's cooperation."

"And she'll agree because it will give her future leverage with whatever shady government department he works for."

"Exactly." Decker nodded. "And we're not talking about some smalltime operation buried deep within the Pentagon. This is Area 51. The people who operate this base could be invaluable to her as friends, and a real headache as enemies."

"Which means were stuck going along with Cade," Rory said.

"Yup. At least for the moment." Decker stifled a yawn and glanced toward the bedroom. "Now, I suggest we get some sleep. Tomorrow will be here before you know it, and I have a feeling it's going to be interesting."

# TWENTY-THREE

THEY LEFT the base at 7AM the next morning, but not on the jet that had brought them to Area 51. Instead, Decker, Rory, and Abby were bundled onto an unmarked Black Hawk helicopter. They had been woken over an hour earlier when a breakfast of eggs, bacon, and pancakes with maple syrup was delivered to their room along with a steaming carafe of coffee and three glasses of freshly squeezed orange juice. It was a welcome early morning call even if it did mean that they were facing the day with less than six hours of sleep. It was also a surprise. Decker didn't know if everyone at the *nonexistent* base in the desert ate this well, or if they were getting special treatment, but he wasn't complaining.

Now, with his stomach full, he watched Groom Lake's runways and buildings fall away below them as the helicopter took to the air. Then he turned his attention to Cade, raising his voice to be heard over the roar of the engines. "I think it's time that you fill us in, because I'm sure there's a lot you aren't telling us."

"Like why you're so worried about someone else reaching the galleon before we do," Rory said. "Considering it's in a restricted area on a military bombing range and should be easy to secure."

Cade observed them with an expressionless face. "You were intending to trespass onto the range and plunder the ship. What makes you think others don't have the same idea?"

"We weren't going to plunder the ship. You make us sound like a bunch of pirates."

"Fair point, but my question still stands."

"Our boss appraised her contacts in the Pentagon of our impending presence," Decker said. "I doubt anyone else enjoys that level of cooperation with the military."

"Probably not," Cade agreed. "But that doesn't preclude sophisticated actors with a malicious agenda from making a play for the orb."

"Which brings me back to the question of what you know that we don't," Decker said. "Because I don't like walking into situations without full knowledge of the risks."

"Very well." Cade was silent for a moment, as if gathering his thoughts. "A couple of nights ago, there as a break in at the State Archaeological Collections Research Facility in McClellan Park outside Sacramento. Two men wearing ski masks and gloves to hide their identities breached the facility through a back door, killed the building's security guard execution style, and stole the artifacts recovered from the corpse found in the Anza Borrego Desert."

"The *San Isidore's* logbook and the map showing its location."

"Yes."

"How come we didn't hear about this?" Decker asked. If the theft had occurred two nights ago, Mina should have been aware of it.

"Because we didn't want you to," Cade said. "We knew that your organization had obtained copies of the logbook and map —in fact, you were the only entity able to do so despite the access to them being restricted—and we figured you would be easier to intercept if you weren't expecting trouble."

"So you buried the news of the murder and theft," said Abby.

"Yes. Although we would have done so anyway. In situations like this, where possible foreign hostiles are in play, it's standard protocol."

"Foreign hostiles?"

"Russians. Chinese. Maybe even the North Koreans. There are all sorts of people who would love to get their hands on that orb."

"Or maybe just garden variety thieves?" Abby asked.

"No. After reviewing the surveillance footage, we deduced that these men were not amateurs, but highly trained clandestine operatives."

"Spooks," Rory said.

"If you like."

"How do you know they haven't found the ship already and taken the orb?" Abby asked.

"Because we have one thing no one else does," Rory told her. "The satellite GPR images showing possible targets that might be the ship." He glanced at Cade. "Or at least, we *would have* had them if we hadn't been waylaid."

"Relax." Cade waved a dismissive hand. "We have the images and you'll be free to look at them just as soon as we land. And in the meantime, I've had our analysts go over them and identify the anomaly most likely to be the *San Isidore*. As soon as we land, we'll meet up with the rest of our team, and head straight there."

"Where exactly are we landing?" Decker asked.

"Naval Air Facility El Centro."

"Right back to the Salton Sea," Rory said. "Our original destination."

"You could have just taken us straight to the air base instead of that sightseeing detour to Area 51," Decker said. "It would have saved time."

"We needed you to understand exactly what is at stake," Cade replied. "The United States isn't the only country with an extraterrestrial saucer craft. That orb cannot fall into the hands of a hostile nation. Who knows what they would do with a fully operational spacecraft like that."

"Hang on," Abby piped up. "I thought there was an orb recovered from the U-Boat. Couldn't that one be used to power your saucer?"

"Yes, in theory," Cade said ruefully. "But it's malfunctioning. The last thing we want is a crew to end up stranded on some distant planet for the rest of their lives, or in another dimension. Which is why we've allowed Classified Universal Special Projects to remain its stewards. Not that it matters, because we would still be going after this orb for the reasons already stated."

Decker thought about this for a moment. "What makes you think that we won't want to take the orb? Our organization is better suited to this sort of thing."

"Do you have a saucer to install it in?"

"No," Decker admitted. "But I'm not certain that anyone on this planet should have a working spacecraft with the capabilities you have outlined. Humanity isn't ready to head out into the universe yet."

"Yeah. We can't even get along together here on Earth. Imagine what we'd do to civilizations on other planets," Rory said.

Decker nodded. "We're not equipped to co-exist with alien races."

Cade chuckled. "How do you know we aren't, already?"

Abby's eyes flew wide. "Are you saying there are actual aliens living among us . . . like right now?"

"I'm not saying anything. Just giving you something to think about," Cade replied. "And as for the orb . . . we're taking it. The matter has been discussed at levels higher than yourselves, and it's already settled."

"We only have your word for that," Decker said.

Cade nodded slowly, then he reached down into a backpack sitting at his feet. He pulled out their cell phones and handed them back. "Call your superiors. Confirm that what I've said is true. Then perhaps, we can start acting like we're all on the same side. Because I promise you, there are bad people out there who will do whatever it takes to get hold of that orb—people who won't hesitate to kill us if we stand in their way—and when the time comes to face them, I'll feel a whole lot better knowing that we have each other's backs."

# TWENTY-FOUR

CHAVA HAD STARTED his solitary journey into the desert at dawn, after swapping Raul's truck for a Suzuki DR650 motorcycle that could handle the rugged terrain. The bike had been waiting for him when he arrived in El Centro, along with a Sig Sauer pistol and ammunition, courtesy of a man who was paid well not to ask questions. As for Raul, he had taken his leave and the two would probably never see each other again. Such was the way within the Watchers, which was more of a loose collective than an organization with a rigid structure.

He wasn't sure exactly where he was going. The vision experienced by the old man in his trance had provided only an approximate location for the Spanish Galleon that contained the orb as lying in the dunes somewhere along the easternmost edge of Superstition Mountain several miles from Pinto Canyon. Chava had brought a backpack containing a small tent and enough dehydrated meals for several days, although his water would run out way before that because he hadn't brought as much as he would have liked. It was heavy to carry, so if his search lasted more than twenty-four hours, he would be forced to find a natural source of fresh water to replenish it. Not an easy feat given his location. But he was confident it wouldn't take him that long to find the ship. He believed that he would find the galleon quickly, maybe within the first hours of searching, and that force of conviction would shape the outcome of this task just like it had with so many others in the past. People called Chava lucky. But he knew better. It wasn't chance that favored him, but rather the universe, which he could bend to his will.

But there was one small obstacle. If the old man was to be believed, the ship rested smack in the middle of a navy test range—a dangerous place to be. There was a road that cut through the range, which he would be able to freely traverse, but the surrounding desert was strictly out of bounds. If he was caught there, his mission would be over. But a worse scenario would be to end up in the middle of a training exercise with live munitions. Then he might not come back at all. He needed to get in and out quickly. The nimble trail bike would help with that. He had picked this mode of transportation for its speed and ability to go where four wheeled vehicles could not. It also cut a low profile and kicked up less sand, making it harder to spot from a distance, which was a bonus.

Chava pushed the bike faster, his tires biting into the soft desert floor. It was still early and would be many hours until the sun reached its zenith, but the temperature was already rising. By noon, it would probably be in the low triple digits. Not exactly ideal, but there was nothing he could do about it, and anyway, he was used to the scorching heat. He had been born and raised in the small town of Porcicola Santa Bruna in Northwestern Mexico, where it could reach over a hundred and twenty degrees during the hottest parts of summer.

Up ahead, he could see the low hump of Superstition Mountain as a dark gray outline on the horizon. The sky was crystal clear with no hint of aircraft, military or otherwise. Not even an old contrail to scar the cloudless pale blue expanse. With any luck, it would stay that way until he had completed what he came here to do. He throttled the engine, squeezing a little more speed out of the bike and taking it to the edge of his comfort zone. All it would take was for the front wheel to glance off a hidden rock or some other half-buried obstruction, and he would be done for, but as usual, he had confidence in his abilities. And also, his propensity for avoiding trouble.

Even at the increased speed, it took another forty minutes to reach the foot of the mountain. At one point, he crossed over the desolate road that cut through the bombing range. If he followed this, he would soon find himself in a vast recreation area surrounded by dirt bike trails and primitive campsites. But that wasn't his destination.

Chava looked left and right, scanning the empty landscape. There wasn't another vehicle anywhere to be seen, but there was a large sign posted next to the road warning that he was in a restricted area and that it was expressly forbidden to venture beyond the paved roadway without permission from the commander of the nearby naval air station. The reminder of his peril did little to quell his resolve, and soon he brought the bike to a halt in the mountain's shadow. He slipped the pack from his back with a grunt of relief and flexed his shoulders, then opened the bag and pulled out a bottle of water, which he drank while stretching his legs.

Ten minutes later, he was back on the bike and following the base of the mountain, looking for the identifying feature that the old man had seen in his vision. A narrow sand filled canyon flanked by a pair of huge rocks, one of which bore the vague outline of an eagle's head. If he found that, the galleon would not be far away.

But after two hours of searching, he had seen nothing that resembled the landmark. What he did come across was the sandblasted remains of what had once been a military helicopter, half buried in a dune. The rotor blades had sagged until they touched the ground. The cockpit glass was gone, long ago blasted from its frame, and the fuselage was peppered with lines of ragged holes. Telltale signs that the aircraft had been strafed multiple times during target practice, probably from the guns of a more modern combat helicopter.

Chava navigated around the wreckage, barely giving it a second look. There were plenty of other pieces of old military hardware peppered throughout this part of the desert as targets, he was sure, and maybe even the remains of a few aircraft that had crashed during training exercises. None of it was of any interest to him beyond a cursory glance.

He turned the bike back toward the mountain, intending to double back and continue the zigzag search pattern that he had instigated at the start of his search.

And that's when he saw it.

A jeep sitting a couple of hundred yards away near the base of the mountain and tucked in behind the skeletal remains of the helicopter.

Startled, Chava came to a stop, his back wheel kicking up sand as he did so. At first glance, he assumed the vehicle must be a relic placed there for the same reason as the helicopter, but its condition told him otherwise. There were no bullet holes or signs of damage, and the tires were fully inflated. There was also a set of tracks across the desert that obviously belonged to the jeep.

Chava cursed under his breath. He should have been more observant, even if the vehicle itself was obscured by the wrecked helicopter. But that didn't stop him from noticing something now. Even though it was painted a light tan to match the surrounding landscape, the jeep bore no markings to indicate that it belonged to the navy. And now that he looked closer, Chava realized it didn't bear much resemblance to a military vehicle. In fact, it looked more like something you might find on a used car lot. The wheels were completely wrong. The tires weren't sturdy enough, and the rims were shiny black. Even the paint job looked off. It was sloppy with over-spray on the vehicle's windows. Alarm bells rang in Chava's head. Someone had tried to make this vehicle look like it belonged on the bombing range, but in reality, it was almost certainly a civilian model.

A prickle ran up his spine.

Chava glanced around but saw no one. His hand fell to the pistol in a holster at his waist and hidden beneath his untucked T-shirt, even as a glint from atop a low rise—a flash of sunlight reflected off something metallic—caught his attention.

A split second later, before he could react, the sand in front of the bike kicked up as a bullet slammed into it, inches from his front wheel. Chava flinched as a second bullet buried itself into the front tire of his bike. Then, before he had time to react, a third shot rang out, sending Chava tumbling off the bike.

# TWENTY-FIVE

WHEN THE BLACK HAWK landed at Naval Air Facility El Centro, a pair of desert camo painted Humvees were waiting on the tarmac along with four machine gun toting Marines who were apparently accompanying them into the desert.

"That's a lot of firepower, considering we're taking a jaunt on navy land in the middle of California," Rory said, eyeing the men as they made their way toward the waiting vehicles.

"Just a precaution," said Cade. "We may have to spend the night out there, so I want to be prepared. The Humvees are loaded with everything we'll need, including tents, rations, water, and survival backpacks for each of us, just in case. As for the Marines, hopefully, all we'll need them for his muscle to move sand and get inside the *San Isidore* once we find it."

"After what you told us about the map and logbook being stolen, I'm happy to have some firepower along for the ride," said Decker. "We might be in the middle of California, but that doesn't mean we're safe. With alien technology up for grabs, there are plenty of hostile governments who won't think twice about making a play for the orb, even on US soil."

"Which is why there's no time to waste," Cade replied as

they reached the Humvees. "We have to get out there right away."

"I agree," said Decker. "But I'd like to make a phone call first."

"Mina?" Rory asked.

"U-huh. I want confirmation that we're supposed to be working with these guys before I climb into one of those Humvees," Decker replied. "After all, they did abduct us at gunpoint, and we only have Cade's word that Mina agreed to any of this."

"Our intervention was a necessary course of action," Cade said, "for which you have my apologies. Please feel free to confirm our arrangement with your superiors. You have five minutes, and not a moment longer."

Decker nodded and stepped away from the group. He took out his phone and dialed.

Mina answered almost immediately. "I was wondering how long it would take you to call me."

"About as long as it took to get my phone back," Decker replied. "I assume you know where we've been since our arrival in Palm Springs?"

"Not at first," Mina admitted. "I was concerned when I heard from the pilot of your jet saying you had been intercepted and taken away in another aircraft. But then I received a call from Commander Cade on a secure line known only to certain high-ranking individuals within the Pentagon and the government, who explained to me in no uncertain terms why we could not pursue the orb on our own."

"Then he's telling the truth. We're working together."

"He left me with little choice. Since our mission was blown and he had all of you in his custody, it was the only way to salvage the situation without walking away, which I was not prepared to do under the circumstances."

"And the orb?" Decker asked, even though he already knew the answer. "Who gets that?"

"Again, I had no choice but to go along with Commander Cade and let him have it, at least for now."

Decker glanced over his shoulder to make sure that Cade was out of earshot. "You realize he has an intact flying saucer, right? Once he makes it fully operational with that orb, he'll wield a technology literally light years beyond anything in the possession of any other nation on earth. There's no way to tell how dangerous that technology could be in the wrong hands."

"I'm aware of the implications." Mina did not sound happy. "That's precisely the reason we have withheld the orb recovered from the U-boat, despite pressure to hand it over. We'll just have to hope that Commander Cade and whichever shady branch of government he works for are *not* the wrong hands. At least until we can find a way to either obtain the orb so that it cannot be used or remove it from the equation permanently."

"You mean destroy it?"

"If it becomes necessary, yes."

"And in the meantime, we're working for these people."

"No, we're working *with* them on equal footing as per our agreement. There is a difference."

"You sure about that?"

Mina sighed audibly on the other end of the line. "I know it's not ideal, but you'll just have to go along with this for now, John. At least until I can figure out exactly who we're getting into bed with and how much influence they have."

"Judging by what I saw last night, they have a lot of influence." Decker glanced over his shoulder to where the others were waiting next to the Humvees. Cade looked impatient. "Do you even know where they took us?"

"Not officially, but I can hazard a guess," Mina replied. "There are only so many places to hide a UFO."

"Right." *More like a whole bunch of UFOs*, Decker wanted to say. But he didn't, because Cade had forbidden them from talking about what they had seen, and he didn't know if that included keeping it from the members of his own organization.

"Is there anything I should know about Cade and his associates before I hang up?"

"Nothing that comes to mind," Mina replied. "Mostly because we know nothing about them. I'd watch your backs, though. I've met people like him before, and you're only safe while you're useful. Once his need for you expires . . ."

"Yeah. I figured as much. I'll check in with you again soon as I can."

"Understood . . . and good luck." The line went dead.

Decker slipped the phone back into his pocket. She had sounded calm, but he had detected a hint of stress in her voice. Mina was more worried than she was letting on. Whether that meant that she really did know something about their newfound colleagues but was keeping it to herself, possibly for the same reason that Decker hadn't mentioned the hangar and Area 51, or whether she just didn't trust Cade, he couldn't be sure. But he knew one thing. Mina was right. Cade wasn't any less dangerous because they were all supposed to be on the same side, and once they located the orb, all bets were off.

# TWENTY-SIX

CHAVA HIT the ground hard and rolled, even as another shot rang out, the sharp crack reverberating across the dusty landscape. Sand flew up into his face and he swore, scrambling sideways to find cover. His arm hurt like hell and his shirt sleeve stuck to him, wet and slick. He had been hit, but there was no time to check how badly he was hurt, because even a moment's hesitation could mean the difference between life and death.

The derelict fuselage of the helicopter, which he had given little thought to moments ago, now became his refuge. He rolled behind it, pulling the gun from his belt at the same time and firing off several quick shots toward where he'd seen the muzzle flash.

When there was no return fire, he glanced around the fuselage and caught sight of movement atop one of the low sandy hills at the base of the mountain. It wasn't much—just a slight tonal shift against the background of the hill—but it was enough to tell him that whoever was up there was still very much alive and probably wearing desert camo. He couldn't see the gun, which meant that it was also painted to match the barren terrain, or maybe the shooter was using a camouflaged fabric wrap to disguise the weapon.

Chava cursed again. Whoever had shot at him was not military because they wouldn't have started shooting without warning the moment he showed up. Instead, they would have identified themselves and instructed him to leave. And the shooter was on high ground, which meant they had probably seen him coming from a mile or more away and set up a sniper's nest in anticipation of his arrival. And like a fool, he had walked right into the trap. Not that he would ever have expected to encounter such a lethal reaction to his presence in a location like this. He had been more worried about ending up on the wrong side of a live fire exercise, and given what he was sheltering behind, it was a valid concern.

Another shot pinged off the fuselage near his head. Chava flinched and shifted further behind the helicopter, then peeked through the empty frame where the vehicle's side door had once been. From this angle, he had a partial view up and past the cockpit window toward the spot on the hill where he had seen the sniper. Then he waited. The man might be lying low, but when he took another potshot at the helicopter, the flash of his gun's muzzle would once again betray his exact location.

A minute passed with no sign of the sniper, then another, and Chava started to think that his assailant had made their escape, but then, just as he was contemplating a dash for the bike, the gunman on the hill took another shot.

And there was the muzzle flash Chava was waiting for.

He quickly took aim and squeezed off a couple of shots.

From high on the hill, there was a flurry of movement as the bullets smacked into the soft earth close to where he'd seen the muzzle flash. More return fire hailed down upon him. Several shots that peppered the skeletal helicopter.

Chava rolled away from the gunfire, found himself peering under the cockpit window.

This was getting out of hand. He checked his weapon, saw that he was down to one round. He had only brought the gun as a precaution. Now he wished he'd brought more firepower with him.

One round.

If he missed again, he would be dead.

Chava closed his eyes, centered himself. He focused upon his opponent with his mind's eye. Sensed him up on the hill, crouched in a dip behind a scraggy bush with his rifle aimed down toward the helicopter, waiting for Chava to reveal his location.

Chava drew in a long, calming breath, prayed that his gift of second sight had not failed him. Then he opened his eyes, stood up quickly, and aimed toward the bush at the same time. Pulled the trigger.

The pistol went off, its last projectile flying toward the spot where Chava had sensed his adversary, even as he ducked back down and waited for the return fire that would tell him he had missed.

But there was none.

Instead, there was more movement on the hill. But this time it wasn't his assailant shifting position but rather tumbling down toward the jeep.

Chava watched the man roll until he came to rest next to a low dune, but he didn't move to investigate. Not yet. Because he couldn't be sure that the man was truly incapacitated, and he also wanted to confirm that there wasn't a second shooter lying in wait. Instead, he cast a brief glance down to his arm, and his shirt sleeve, which was already stained with blood. He undid the shirt, then slipped the sleeve down and away from the wound. To his relief, there was no entry or exit wound, but rather a raw scrape across the side of his bicep. The bullet had only grazed him.

Nonetheless, he removed a pocketknife and cut the sleeve off at the seam, then used it to wrap around the wound, tying it tightly. Closing the knife and slipping it back into his pocket, he raised his head and peeked back up toward the slope. There was no sign of anyone else, either waiting for him to move or hurrying down to aid their stricken companion. That meant nothing. Whoever had opened fire upon him had done so with ruthless intent. They clearly had no qualms about taking a life, which meant that if there was another shooter, they would be more interested in killing him than checking on their fallen comrade. But he doubted a second gunman would sit idle while his comrade did all the work. Besides, he couldn't hunker down behind the junked helicopter forever, especially now that he was out of ammo and had no way to return fire. And his bike was lying on the ground too far away to be of any use.

There was only one course of action open to him.

Heart racing, Chava stood up and stepped into view.

# TWENTY-SEVEN

THE HUMVEES BARRELED across the desert terrain, bumping over sand dunes. Decker and Cade occupied the lead vehicle, along with two of the Marines, while Rory and Abby followed behind with the other two. After he finished talking to Mina, Decker had rejoined the group, and Cade had pulled out an iPad and finally shared the results of the satellite GPR flyover. There were several anomalies that Cade's analysts back at Area 51had identified, but they had dismissed most of them as rock formations under the sand and had narrowed it down to three likely candidates. Of those, one looked especially promising. An elongated area of darkness that stood out against the lighter landscape around it. And the anomaly was in the right place, tucked up close to the southern edge of Superstition Mountain, which would be exactly where a ship might have come aground if the surrounding land had been underwater at the time.

Rory was especially excited, because he had used GPR during previous archaeological excavations, and he declared that it was one of the best hits he had ever seen. The anomaly was shaped like a galleon, with one end pointed and the other flat. There was even what looked like the line of a fallen mast. However, it wouldn't be so easy to see from the ground. The galleon had been there for hundreds of years and was no doubt buried under many tons of sand. It could take days, or even weeks, to excavate. And if it turned out to be nothing more than a uniquely shaped rock, then they would be back to square one.

Cade had not been so pessimistic. "It's the ship, I'm sure of it," he had said. "My analysts are some of the best in the world. If they say it's there, then I believe them. I'm confident that we've found the *San Isidore*. It's the only anomaly that even looks like a ship."

"Still doesn't mean we can reach it easily," Rory had grumbled. "We had all the necessary equipment to excavate the ship waiting for us in Palm Springs before you got in our way. How do you propose that we move that much sand without it?"

"We have our own equipment," Cade had replied. "It's being flown in and should arrive not long after we get there."

"What kind of equipment?" Rory didn't sound convinced.

"A small backhoe. Everything else we need is in the back of the Humvees. Shovels, pickaxes, a wheelbarrow for moving sand when the backhoe becomes too cumbersome. We also have tents and enough food and water to keep us going for at least a week. That should be enough time to find and excavate enough of the *San Isidore*, don't you think, Professor McCormick?"

"It's Mr. McCormick."

"But you are a professor, right?"

"I hold the necessary education, but I prefer not to use the title. It sounds stuffy," Rory had replied. "And as for excavating the galleon . . . I'm not sure that even a month would be enough time, given the enormity of the task. You know how large a Spanish Galleon actually is, and the archaeological significance of discovering one in the Colorado Desert?"

"We don't need to excavate the entire ship," Cade shot back. "We just need to move enough sand to get inside and find the orb. After that, you can liaise with the Navy and the Bureau of Land Management for permission to excavate the rest of the vessel on your own time."

"And how do you propose we keep treasure hunters out of the ship in the meantime?" Rory had asked. "Put up a polite sign asking them not to steal all the Aztec gold?"

"I'm sure the Navy has adequate resources to protect the site until you can arrange for a full excavation." Cade sounded weary. "And anyway, this is all hypothetical. We haven't even found the ship yet. Why don't we see what we've got before we start making decisions about its future?"

Rory had fallen silent after that, and Cade had wasted no time bundling everyone into the Humvees. Now, almost an hour later, they were closing in on the site.

Decker peered through the Humvee's windshield, watching the low hulk of Superstition Mountain growing bigger as they approached. He still hadn't completely managed to wrap his head around the idea that a European ship from the 16th century could end up in such a strange location. He understood Rory's explanation that the vessel had sailed up the Gulf of California and navigated a wide estuary that led into what the mariners believed to be a large inland sea, only to become trapped when the tidal bore that had created the estuary retreated, but it still sounded more like a treasure hunters' myth than hard fact. But the ground penetrating radar images didn't lie. There was definitely something buried under the dunes at the base of the mountain. But if there was a ship under the sand, it was even more incredible that no one had found and excavated it already.

Or maybe it had been found, because as they drew closer to the mountain, a low rumble shook the vehicle, and a dusty plume billowed into the sky ahead of them, obscuring their view and bringing them to a jarring halt.

# TWENTY-EIGHT

WHAT THE HELL?" Decker leaned forward and peered through the windshield at the swiftly expanding cloud of sand and dust. "That was an explosion. I thought there was no activity planned for this part of the bombing range while we're out here."

"There isn't," Cade replied, pulling his door open and climbing out of the Humvee.

Decker jumped out behind him. He shielded his eyes against the glaring sun and looked toward the mountain just as the boom from another explosion rattled across the landscape and sent even more debris up into the air. "Sure looks like *someone* is having fun blowing stuff up."

"If they are, it has nothing to do with us. We may have arrived too late." Cade turned to one of the Marines and barked an order to get on the radio and report the situation, then turned back to Decker just as Rory and Abby came running up from the other vehicle.

"So much for the Navy protecting the galleon," he said, glaring at Cade. "Unless your people just decided to go ahead and blast their way to the ship without waiting for us to arrive."

"As I've already explained to your friend, those explosions are not our doing."

"Then who is doing it?"

"My money's on whoever broke into that research facility in Sacramento and stole the ship's log and the map," Decker said.

"Russians," Abby muttered under her breath.

Cade squinted toward the sand plume. "Maybe, or maybe not. Like I said earlier, there are plenty of bad actors out there who would love to get ahold of that orb."

He had barely finished speaking when a third explosion rang out.

"Damn it." Rory's face twisted with anguish. "They keep doing that, and they'll destroy the galleon."

"I'm not sure they're worried about that," Cade said. "All they want is the orb, and they don't care if they end up blowing the *San Isadore* to pieces in the process."

"Animals," Rory muttered. "So much for us being the only ones who know the exact location of the ship."

"There's only one way they would know where to blast," Decker said, his eyes on Cade. "They must have seen the GPR scans."

"That's impossible." Cade shook his head. "Those images were taken by a top-secret US military satellite. We are the only ones who had access to them."

"Then your security has been breached," Decker said. "Someone within your organization must have leaked the images."

"Or maybe it was someone within *your* organization," Cade shot back. "After all, it was your people who co-opted a satellite they should not have known about to take the images in the first place."

"No one at CUSP would do that," Rory said.

"It certainly wasn't us," Cade replied. "My men are hand-picked and highly trained. They don't sell out to foreign adversaries. I would suggest that—"

"Enough." Abby stepped between Decker and Cade. "We can blame each other later. There are more pressing concerns right now. We need to stop whoever is out there."

"And quickly," Rory said, as yet another blast shook the earth. "Or that ship will be nothing but kindling by the time they get there."

Cade turned toward the Humvee and the Marine, who was still fiddling with the radio. "Well?"

The Marine shook his head. "We're being jammed. Both VHF and UHF. Radio is useless. So is the sat phone."

"Then we've got no choice but to deal with this on our own, at least for now," Cade said. He turned back to the Marine. "Corporal Walsh, go back to El Centro and let them know what's going on."

Walsh nodded and climbed back into the Humvee.

Cade motioned to Decker, Rory, and Abby. "The three of you should go with him. I'll continue on with the other Marines to the target site in the second Humvee and see what we're dealing with."

"Absolutely not," Decker said.

"Right," Abby agreed. "We're staying here with you."

"You are civilians," Cade countered. "It's dangerous and you're under my protection. I can't risk any harm coming to you."

"We're not civilians," Rory said, "as you already pointed out back at the hangar last night. And I can assure you that we are more than capable of taking care of ourselves."

"You'll do as I tell you."

"I might remind you that we are not your underlings," Decker said. "And this is a joint operation."

Cade rolled his eyes. "Fine. Whatever. We don't have time to argue about this." He started toward the second Humvee. "Come on."

"How are we all going to fit in there?" Abby asked. "There was barely any room with the four of us."

Cade snorted and held the door open for her. "You're the ones who wanted to come along. It'll be a tight fit, but we'll manage."

As he climbed in, Decker glanced over his shoulder at the other Humvee, which was already speeding back in the direction of the naval air facility. Moments later, they were barreling in the other direction, but instead of taking a direct route toward the target site, as they had been doing before, the Marine behind the wheel steered them parallel to the low rise of Superstition Mountain, circling around the location of the galleon so that they would not be so easily seen upon their approach.

Abby's concerns about space were founded. It was cramped. But unlike the vehicle he and Cade had previously ridden in, which only had four seats, this one had been outfitted for troop carrying and had sideways bench seats mounted in the rear of the cab. Decker could still see the other Humvee through the small rear window as it raced back across the desert toward the distant airbase to fetch help. But then he saw something else. A bright streak arching across the sky. A streak that homed in on the retreating vehicle with deadly precision and slammed into it, sending an enormous fireball belching into the air. Debris flew in every direction, even as a thunderous boom reverberated across the landscape. And as he watched, the Humvee reduced to smoking wreckage, and Decker came to a terrifying realization. Whoever was out there blasting away at the sand dunes to reach that ship was aware of their presence. Worse, they were heavily armed and intent upon defending their position with lethal force, which meant that the vehicle he was now riding in would soon meet a similar fate.

# TWENTY-NINE

CHAVA LOOKED up at the mountainside, half expecting another shot to ring out from a second assailant somewhere else on the slope. When nothing happened, he breathed a sigh of relief. His intuition had been correct. There was only one shooter. But it might not stay that way for long, because he doubted the gunman was out here all alone. He was probably a sentry, placed there to make sure that no one discovered what was going on out here. Because Chava was worried he might be too late. That someone else might already have found the Spanish Galleon, and the precious cargo it contained. There was no time to lose.

Warily, Chava made his way to the slope and scrambled up to the prone body of the man who had been shooting at him. He looked dead, but Chava checked his vitals anyway, just to be sure. Then, satisfied he was no longer in immediate danger, he examined the man, noting the lack of insignia or patches on his desert camo, which blended so perfectly with its surroundings that it was no wonder Chava hadn't seen the man hunkered above him on the hillside until it was almost too late. If the man had been a better shot, or if he had bothered to put the M-16 rifle lying at his side into either burst or full-auto mode, things would have ended differently. But his gun was in semi mode—one round per squeeze of the trigger—which reinforced Chava's hunch he was not a professional soldier. He was also not a skilled marksman. He had possessed the advantage of surprise and still failed to notch the kill. His ineptitude had directly led to his demise.

From somewhere close by, a boom reverberated across the landscape. Chava flinched and almost threw himself to the ground until he realized that it wasn't more gunfire. It was an explosion. And if he needed any more proof, the cloud of sand and dust rising into the air somewhere further along the mountain to his left no doubt.

He needed to move quickly if he was going to get the orb, assuming it wasn't already too late. Chava kneeled and searched his dead adversary, checking the man's pockets for any clue regarding his identity, or that of whoever was blowing holes in the mountainside.

He found nothing. The man was carrying no identification and had no personal effects that might give away who he was and where he had come from. All Chava discovered was a half-empty packet of cigarettes, a cheap plastic lighter, and the keys for the jeep that was sitting halfway between the wrecked helicopter fuselage and the base of the slope.

Chava ignored the cigarettes and the lighter but took the keys to the jeep, slipping them into his pocket. It seemed like a fair trade considering that his bike was now out of action with a flat tire thanks to the man who lay dead at his feet. Not that he had any intention of taking the vehicle right now. Given that he was almost certainly outnumbered and outgunned by whoever had put this man here to guard their activities, stealth was his only advantage. The last thing he wanted to do was announce his presence by driving around in a noisy, lumbering vehicle. But that didn't mean it wouldn't be useful later. Like if he needed to make a quick getaway. The jeep was just as suited to the rough desert terrain as his bike but would leave him less exposed.

There was one thing he intended to take right now, though. The M-16 assault rifle.

He discarded his useless pistol—it wasn't registered to him anyway and keeping it would only be a liability—then scooped up the M-16 and gave it a quick inspection and was pleased to see there was plenty of ammo left. He put the gun in burst mode, then stood up and looked around. A narrow path weaved around the mountain in the direction of the explosion he had heard, climbing steadily higher as it went. Returning to low ground would not be smart because it would make him vulnerable to another attack, whereas the path would give him a good view of whatever was going on with less risk of discovery. Chava gave the corpse at his feet one last glance and started toward the path.

At that moment, another boom rang out, sending a faint tremor through the ground under his feet.

A plume of dust rose into the air, pinpointing the exact location of his destination. Chava picked up the pace, hurrying along the path and keeping an eye out for any further assailants. By the time a third blast rocked the landscape, he was high above the desert floor with a bird's-eye view of his surroundings.

And that was when he saw it.

The broken mast of a ship sticking up out of a towering sand dune a couple of hundred feet below him, at the base of the mountain. Nearby, exposed and baking under the hot desert sun for the first time in hundreds of years, was the partially uncovered bow of the Galleon.

The *San Isadore*.

And inside the stranded galleon, somewhere deep in her hold, would be the orb. Now all he needed was to figure out a way to get in there and stop anyone else from getting their hands on it. Which would not be an easy task, because he counted at least twenty men near the ship, frantically moving the sand away from her hull. And it wouldn't take them long to find a way inside.

Then he saw something else.

A pair of Humvees speeding in opposite directions. One away from the mountain and the other toward it. Hurrying to intercept them were a pair of jeeps just like the one that belonged to the man he had killed.

One of the vehicles came to a halt. The door opened, and a man exited. He raised a long metal tube to his shoulder that Chava realized was a rocket launcher. Then he aimed and fired. A moment later, one of the Humvees erupted in a ball of orange flame. The other Humvee was still barreling toward the mountain, but it too had come under fire, from the other jeep.

Chava had no idea who the newcomers were, or even if they would survive long enough for him to find out. But he knew one thing. The situation had just gotten a whole lot more complicated.

# THIRTY

"THAT WAS A MISSILE." Rory stared through the rear window at the smoking wreckage. "They're firing at us!"

"I can see that." Cade was sitting in the front seat next to the driver. "We need to find cover."

The Marine needed no urging. He was already swinging the wheel hard to the right and flooring it, kicking up dust as he abandoned their circuitous route in a bid to find shelter. The mountain, which was really nothing more than a large, craggy hill, loomed ahead of them, growing ever closer.

"Where did it even come from?" Abby asked, glancing nervously through the side window toward the still burning wreckage of the other Humvee, which was now sending a thick cloud of black smoke up into the air.

"That's a good question." Cade was craning his neck, scanning the barren landscape surrounding them. "I don't see any firepower in the air, so it must be a ground-based system. My guess is something small and easily transported, like a shoulder-fired portable missile launcher."

"How would someone get a weapon like that on a military base?" Rory shifted in his seat, clearly uncomfortable.

"This isn't a Navy base. It's a bombing range, which means it isn't actively guarded. It's also surrounded by public land used by hikers and dirt bikes. All someone would have to do is smuggle it here in the back of a truck. Pretty easy." Cade turned to the Marine at the wheel of the Humvee. "Corporal Saunders. Can we go any faster? Where there's one missile, there's probably more."

"Going as fast as I dare," the man replied. "A couple more minutes and we'll be at the mountain."

"Incoming!" Rory shouted over the rumble of the Humvee's engine; his voice shrill and high. He flinched away from the window and ducked as the ground to their left exploded in a shower of sand with a deafening whomp.

The Humvee lifted on two wheels, teetering for a moment as if it was going to roll over, before its left side slammed back down onto the ground with a jarring thud.

"That was too close." Decker reached up and grabbed a strap.

"We're lucky it wasn't a guided missile, or we'd be a pile of smoldering wreckage right now," Cade said.

"I don't feel very lucky," Rory replied.

"Uh, guys, we've got company," Abby said as a jeep appeared over a low rise.

The vehicle came to a halt several hundred feet away.

A figure stood up from the seat next to the driver, aiming what looked like a long tube towards them.

There was a flash and a puff of smoke.

The Humvee's driver swung the wheel hard and swerved. A fraction of a second later, a second missile slammed into the ground, this time to their right.

Sand and debris rained down around them.

The jeep started forward again, closing the gap between them at an alarming rate.

"Saunders, bring us around and come to a halt." Cade ordered the driver, then he turned and barked at the two Marines riding in the vehicle with them, one in the front passenger seat and the other in the back, next to Decker.

"Sanchez. McDonnell. Take out that jeep before they have a chance to reload and fire again."

"Yes, sir," they said in unison as Corporal Saunders slammed on the brakes.

The two Marines threw the doors open and dismounted almost before the vehicle had come to a stop. They raised their rifles, took aim, and fired a series of short bursts at the approaching jeep. The sound of bullets pinging off metal echoed through the air. A moment later, the jeep drifted to the right, rode up a small sand dune, and toppled onto its roof, wheels still spinning.

Decker shifted sideways to make room as the Marines hopped back into the Humvee and they started moving again.

It wasn't long before Abby shouted a warning. "There's another one."

Decker turned to see a second jeep barreling across the desert towards them. "How many of these people are there?"

"Too many," Cade replied as a third jeep appeared, bearing down on them from the other direction.

Gunfire erupted, peppering the desert floor in their wake.

One of the Marines leaned out of the window and returned fire, but the vehicle was bumping so much that his aim was wide.

When a return volley strafed the side of the Humvee, he ducked back inside quickly.

"Yow." Rory pulled his feet up when a bullet smashed through the Humvee's outer skin and buried itself in the floor. "Aren't these things supposed to be armored?"

"Not this one. It's meant for shuttling personnel around the range, not combat," Cade replied.

"At least they don't appear to have another rocket launcher," Decker said. "Or we'd be toast by now."

The Humvee was riding hard now and losing forward momentum.

From the driver's seat, Saunders said, "That last volley of

bullets took out our tires. We're dragging in the sand. I don't know how much longer we can keep going."

Abby was staring out the window at the jeeps. "They're gaining on us."

"There's a pass up ahead," Decker said, leaning forward to peer through the windshield at the low foothills of superstition Mountain rising ahead of them. "We reach that, and we'll find cover."

Saunders was gripping the wheel so tightly that his knuckles were white. "It's too narrow for the Humvee."

Cade cursed as another burst of gunfire narrowly missed them. "Just do your best to get us there. We'll need to abandon the Humvee and head for high ground."

"You mean on foot?" Rory asked, incredulous. "That's crazy. They'll pick us off in seconds."

"Not if we keep our heads down and move fast."

Decker nodded in agreement. "It's our only chance."

Cade leaned forward. "I don't suppose our radio works yet?"

Sanchez, occupying the front passenger seat, shook his head. "No, sir. They're still jamming us."

"There goes any hope of rescue," Rory said. "Unless someone back at base notices the gunfight happening on their doorstep."

"Not likely," Cade told him. "We're miles out in the desert, and even if anyone did hear, they wouldn't think twice about it. People shoot at things all the time out here. They would just assume that it's an exercise."

"Just wonderful." Abby pulled a face. "I guess we're on our own, then."

"You're the one who wanted to come along on this trip," Decker said. "If you hadn't twisted our arms, you be safely back at your dig site in Arizona right now."

"Fair point." Abby conceded, then closed her mouth.

The Humvee came to a jarring halt in the shadow of the low mountain. The Marines threw the doors open and jumped out quickly, rifles in hand, and took up defensive positions.

"Grab your packs and let's go," Cade said, motioning for Decker, Abby, and Rory to move. "Keep your heads low and head for the pass."

"You got any plan beyond that?" Decker asked as one of the Marines took a couple shots of the approaching jeeps.

"Find a defensible position and see if we can hold these people off—whoever they are—until someone misses us and comes looking," Cade said.

"Doesn't sound like much of a plan," Rory grumbled as they sprinted toward the narrow desert pass with the Marines falling in behind them. "It could be days before anyone notices that we didn't return."

"Agreed." Cade said as they reached the pass and ran between a pair of towering rocks that felt almost like a natural gateway.

Two of the Marines Held back, taking up defensive positions near the entrance. The third soldier, Sanchez, accompanied them.

The mountain blocked the sun ahead of them, casting a long shadow through the narrow groove in the landscape. A fresh chapter of gunfire erupted behind the small group as they hurried to higher ground. Their pursuers in the jeep had obviously arrived at the entrance to the pass. But that wasn't the only problem. Because up ahead, standing on a low rise, was a solitary figure with an assault rifle, which he was pointing down into the pass.

Then, before anyone had a chance to react, he opened fire.

# THIRTY-ONE

DECKER THREW himself sideways as the rapid tat-tat-tat of gunfire echoed through the narrow pass. He landed hard and rolled behind a small outcrop, expecting to hear a return volley from the Marine who was accompanying them. But he didn't.

Rising to his knees, he glanced sideways, praying his companions would not be dead.

They weren't. Rory and Abby had taken shelter behind a larger outcrop of rock on the other side of the pass. Cade was hunched down near a jagged boulder that looked like it must have come loose from higher up the mountain at some point. Rivera was behind him, his gun trained on the figure who had appeared in front of them.

At first, Decker couldn't figure out why he hadn't returned fire, but then he glanced around and saw two men in desert camo crumpled on the ground further down the pass. He didn't recognize either of them, which meant they had probably come from the jeeps. They wore no insignia or any other identifiable markings. He wondered what had happened to the Marines guarding their rear. He hoped they weren't dead but considering that their assailants had made it into the pass, it didn't look good.

They would be dead too if it wasn't for the stranger standing on the mountainside ahead of them.

"You can come out now," he called out in a heavy accent. "It is safe, for the moment."

"Everyone okay over there?" Decker asked, glancing over at Rory and Abby.

"I think so," Rory replied.

Abby nodded. "I'm not loving how everyone keeps shooting at us."

"Please do not delay. We don't have time." The stranger motioned for them to join him. "There will surely be more dangerous men on the way."

Cade squinted up at their savior. "No offense, but how do we know you won't shoot us the moment we show our faces?"

"If I wanted to do that, you would all be dead now."

"He has a point," Decker said to Cade. He stood up, brushed himself off, and stepped back into view. Then he started forward again. "Let's go."

They made their way through the pass and started up the steep slope toward the stranger. Now that they were out of the shade the heat was brutal. Sweat dripped from Decker's forehead, stinging his eyes. When he glanced down toward their stricken Humvee, he saw several bodies strewn on the desert floor. From so far away, he couldn't tell if any of them were the two Marines who had hung back to guard their escape.

When they reached the ridgeline, the stranger extended a hand in greeting. "You are Americans, yes? From the military installation?"

Decker studied the stranger. He was dark-skinned with shoulder-length black hair that was transitioning to silver. His rugged, deeply lined face bore testament to a harsh life. "And you are?"

"My name is Chava."

"That's it? Just Chava." Cade raised an eyebrow. "No

explanation of what you were doing wandering around a restricted area with an assault rifle?"

"I am looking for something that is lost. Something that belonged to my people and was stolen a very long time ago."

"The orb," Rory blurted out. "You're looking for the orb taken from the Aztecs by the conquistadors."

Chava nodded. "I assume that you are here for the same reason?"

"I'm not permitted to disclose that information to a civilian," Cade replied.

"I shall take that as a yes."

"You can take it however you want," Cade said. He glanced down toward the dead men in the pass. "You have any idea who those guys were? The ones you took out."

"I do not know," Chava replied. "Except that they are not friendly."

"Yeah. We found that out already." Cade nodded toward the weapon in the newcomer's hands. "The rifle, if you please."

"I don't think so." Chava held the gun close to his chest.

Cade grimaced. "Rivera, please relieve our new friend of his weapons."

Rivera stepped forward and snatched the M-16 out of Chava's grip. He offered the M-16 to Cade, who took the gun.

Chava glowered but said nothing.

"That's better. I don't know if we can trust you, and I'd rather not take a bullet to the back."

Chava didn't look pleased, but he nodded. "Now, please. We must move if we are going to stop them. They have found the ship already and will soon gain entry to her hull. We cannot allow that to happen."

"They've found the *San Isadore*?" Rory asked.

"Yes." Chava started along the ridgeline in the direction of the blasting they had witnessed earlier. Whoever was setting off explosives had fallen silent now, either because they had noticed the Humvees approaching and didn't want to draw further attention to themselves, or worse, their task was complete.

"Not so fast." Cade hadn't moved. "I still have men out there. I won't leave them behind."

Chava turned back to face him. "If they didn't join us once the gunfire stopped, then they are dead."

"Not good enough." Cade shook his head. "We leave no man behind. I'm going back to look for them."

Chava observed him with narrowed eyes. "Don't be foolish."

"Now listen to me, I'm responsible for those men." Cade took a step toward him, anger glinting in his eyes. "I'm also in charge here, so how about—"

"Wait." Decker stepped between the two men, because he had seen movement on the trail behind them. A figure hurrying in their direction that he recognized as one of the missing Marines.

Cade visibly slumped with relief. "Saunders. Where's McDonnell?"

The soldier shook his head slowly as he approached. "He didn't make it."

"Dammit." Cade turned away briefly, his lips pressed together, then he swiveled abruptly and pushed past Chava. "Let's go get that orb."

# THIRTY-TWO

CROUCHING LOW BEHIND A SMALL RISE, Decker peered down at the incredible sight below him. A Spanish Galleon firmly trapped in the clutches of a vast sand dune and stranded miles from the closest body of water. Until this moment, he hadn't quite believed that the *San Isadore* would really be here despite the compelling circumstantial evidence of the ship's logbook and prospector's map. Even the GPR images were not solid proof. Just because something looked vaguely like a buried ship on ground penetrating radar scans did not mean it would turn out to be true once they started digging. It was more likely that they would find a natural rock formation, or even nothing but an area of denser ground. But here it was, large as life. A 15th-century ship in the middle of the Sonoran Desert, right where the legends said it would be.

"This is unbelievable," Rory said in a hushed voice. He was hunkered down next to Decker and staring at the partially uncovered vessel with wide eyes. "I've never seen anything like it. She's fully intact."

"It's a miracle they didn't damage the ship with all that blasting they were doing," Abby said, peering over Rory's shoulder.

"She won't stay that way for much longer," Decker said, because a makeshift base camp had been set up near the sand dune and it was a hive of activity. He could see men unloading equipment from a truck—jacks, chainsaws, winches, and other assorted tools—to cut through the ship's hull and gain access to her cargo area. Once that was done, they would probably reverse a truck up to the ship and quickly loot not just the orb, but all the other valuables contained within. "We have to get down there and find a way inside, secure the orb before they do."

"And how are we going to do that?" Abby asked, motioning toward the hostiles below them. "Those people have already tried to kill us once. If we show our faces, they won't hesitate to do it again. I don't want to end up on the wrong side of a missile."

"They won't fire a missile at us," Decker said, with more conviction than he felt. "An uncontrolled explosion like that could bring half the mountain down on that ship and they would never risk burying it under tons of rubble after they went to such trouble uncovering it."

"You sure about that?"

"It wouldn't be a smart thing to do," Cade said, sounding equally unsure.

"They still have guns."

"So do we," said Cade. "And Mr. Decker's right. We can't just sit up here and let them plunder the *San Isadore*. Rivera and I will go down to the ship with Mr. Decker. If there's a way inside that ship, we'll find it. The rest of you stay here out of sight."

"I am coming too," said Chava. "That orb belongs to my people, and I intend to return it to them."

"That orb belongs to an alien spaceship that crashed here hundreds of years ago," Cade replied. "It's not some mystical trinket that you can claim as part of your cultural heritage. You stay here with the others."

"I cannot do that. If you don't let me come, then—"

"Then what?" Cade's hand fell to the pistol in a holster at his waist. "I appreciate what you did back there, but you have no authority to demand anything. This is Navy land, and you are trespassing." He turned to the second Marine, Saunders. "Make sure he doesn't try to follow us or do anything to alert the hostiles down there of our presence. You have permission to use whatever force is necessary."

The Marine nodded. "Yes, sir."

Cade turned his attention back to Chava. "Are we good?"

Chava's eyes were nothing but narrow slits. He spoke through gritted teeth. "I will stay here . . . for now."

"Fantastic. Then we understand each other." Cade motioned to Decker. "You ready?"

"Any chance of a weapon?" Decker asked, eyeing the pistol in a holster at Cade's waist. "If we get into a scuffle with those guys down there, I'd love a way to defend myself."

Cade hesitated a moment, then motioned to Rivera. "Give him your pistol."

"Thanks." Decker took the weapon, noting that Cade wasn't willing to sacrifice his own firearm event though he also carried a rifle.

"Don't make me regret this," Cade said after the transfer was complete.

"You have my word." Decker glanced down toward the galleon, and the steep slope they would need to traverse. "There isn't much cover between us and that ship."

"We'll need to move fast and keep low." Cade moved to the edge of the rise. "On my mark."

Decker didn't reply. He was too busy concentrating on how they were going to navigate so much open ground without getting themselves killed in the process. All it would take was for one of those men preparing to enter the ship to glance up, and they would be sitting ducks. He only hoped that they were too busy with the task at hand to notice what was happening above them.

If a similar thought was running through Cade's mind, he

didn't show it. Instead, he raised an arm, then dropped it in a silent signal to move, before launching himself out into the open, and starting down the slope toward the Galleon.

Decker took a deep breath, gripped the pistol tightly, and followed.

Loose sand and gravel shifted under his boots as they scrambled down the side of the mountain. The men below were still unloading the truck and hauling gear up toward the ship's hull, oblivious to their presence. Another few minutes, and they would be standing on the deck of the *San Isadore*. If they were lucky, they would find a way inside and swipe the orb from under their adversaries' noses before they even knew what had happened.

But then, just when he thought they were going to make it, Decker sensed a movement to his right. He glanced around to see Rivera, who was a couple of steps behind him, lose his balance and pitch forward on the treacherous slope. His legs went out from under him, and he landed hard, sliding out of control down the slope toward the ship, hands grasping at the loose material on the mountainside in a futile attempt to stop himself. He kicked up a cloud of sand and dust as he went that was quickly snatched upon the breeze. He came to rest further down the mountainside and pushed himself back up, regaining his feet.

At first, Decker thought that the mishap had gone unnoticed. But soon a shout went up.

The men below broke into a frenzy.

Before he knew what was happening, bullets were flying, both from below and from above. Decker dropped to the ground in a desperate attempt to make himself a smaller target. Then, to his horror, he heard something else. A mighty whoosh amid the chatter of gunfire. A moment later, there was a loud boom somewhere higher up the mountain and the ground shuddered and buckled. Sand and blasted rock rained down.

So much for not firing a missile at us, thought Decker, as the mountainside under his feet shifted, gave way, and began to slip. Then he was tumbling head over heels in a cascade of debris that swept him inexorably down into oblivion.

# THIRTY-THREE

DECKER FELL for what seemed like an eternity. Grit flew into his eyes, blinding him. Rocks pummeled his body. Then he landed hard on something flat and unforgiving even as more debris rained down around him. From the ridge above and the desert below, he could hear the firefight continuing. At least the missile hadn't killed Rory and the others.

He stayed where he was for a short while, fearful of catching a bullet, then he wiped the sand from his eyes and took stock of his situation. He was on the deck of the ship. The gun Cade had given him was gone, lost during the fall. He was defenseless. But at least he was shielded from the deadly barrage of gunfire and invisible to the hostiles below, who probably thought he had perished in the explosion. That they were willing to launch a missile was proof of their recklessness. They had no qualms about damaging or even destroying the ancient vessel upon which he was now laying. Of course, he knew that already, thanks to the heavy equipment he had seen them preparing. The hostiles only cared about one thing. Looting the *San Isadore* for the contents of her hold, including the orb, which he had no doubt was their primary mission objective.

His own objective had not changed despite the perilous way

in which he had ended up on the ship's deck. He needed to find a way inside the vessel and get the orb before it fell into the wrong hands. Thankfully, other than a few cuts and bruises, he didn't appear to be hurt. But what about Cade and Rivera? He looked around and was relieved to see the commander further down the deck toward the bow of the vessel, next to what remained of the ship's mast, which appeared to have been partially destroyed in the explosion. The mast's top half now lay shattered on the deck between them, tangled in remnants of rigging that had somehow survived the ages.

He didn't see Rivera.

"You all right?" Decker asked, crawling along the deck toward the commander. He didn't dare stand up for fear that he would make himself an easy target for the hostile marksmen who were still engaged in a heated battle with the rest of his group on the mountain ridge above them.

Cade grimaced, rubbing his shoulder. A trickle of blood seeped from a cut on his forehead. "Mostly. Lost the M-16 in the fall and my pride has taken a beating, but other than that I'm good." He looked around. "Where's Rivera?"

"Don't know." Decker hoped the man wasn't buried under a pile of debris dislodged from the mountainside that had landed toward the ship's stern, burying the back end of the vessel under tons of rock and sand. If he was, the Marine was surely dead.

"Crap." Cade squinted and looked further up the mountain toward the spot where Rory and the others were hunkered down. From their lower vantage point on the deck, it was impossible to see them. He grimaced. "This is turning into one hell of a mess."

"Which is why we need to get inside the ship, and fast," Decker said. "Once we have the orb, we can get out of here."

"That might be easier said than done," Cade replied as a stray bullet pinged off a nearby rock. "Those people down there aren't going to let us go without a fight."

"Let's worry about one thing at a time." Decker was studying the ship, looking for any access to the vessel's interior. His gaze settled on a small door toward the stern behind the ruined main mast. Rory had showed them a plan of the *San Isadore* while they were on their jet, before they landed in Palm Springs and Cade waylaid them. The door led onto the *San Isadore's* main deck, which housed the officers' and captain's quarters. Above that would be the quarterdeck, and finally the poop. It was impossible to tell how much of those structures had been crushed by the avalanche of falling rocks, but if his recollection of the ship's plans was correct, there would be a ladder somewhere beyond that door leading down to the gun deck. Below that would be the orlop, where supplies like food and barrels of water would have been stored, along with cordage and ballast. Finally, at the ship's lowest point, was their destination. The hold. Decker pointed toward the door. "That's our way in."

"Then what are we waiting for?" Cade started toward the rear of the ship, bent low to remain out of sight. When they reached the door and tried the handle, it wouldn't open. He tried again, putting his shoulder into it this time, but still got nowhere. "Crap. It's jammed."

Decker stood with his back against the bulkhead, sheltered from the hostiles below them. "This ship has been buried here for hundreds of years, with tons of sand pressing down upon her. I'd be surprised if any of her beams are still true."

"We still need to get in there," Cade said, taking a couple of steps back. He drew his pistol and aimed it at the handle, then fired off a couple of quick shots, the sound masked by the gunfire still raging around them.

The door around the latch disintegrated. Splinters of wood and chunks of metal flew in all directions.

Decker flinched and turned away at the last moment. "You could've given me some warning."

"No time." Cade put his shoulder against the door again, and this time, it creaked open to reveal a dark and musty space beyond.

Fetid air belched from the doorway, released from its centuries-old prison.

Cade returned the gun to its holster and came away with a small flashlight that must have been secreted somewhere about his person and aimed it through the doorway. The beam lanced through the darkness to reveal a tight corridor with cubicles on each side covered by heavy curtains. These would be the officers' quarters, just large enough for a narrow bed but granting the luxury of privacy on a ship where pretty much everyone else would have slept below decks in hammocks they were forced to share with at least two other men, sleeping in shifts.

Beyond the officers' quarters, the deck opened up into a small space that contained a couple of long tables with benches. The officers' mess, maybe? Somewhere further back, at the very rear of the vessel, would be the captain's quarters. The most luxurious accommodations on the *San Isadore*. But it was the narrow hatch and steep staircase leading down into the bowels of the ship that caught Decker's eye. This was where they must go, even if that thought filled him with dread. Because he had no idea how stable the decks below them were, especially after the barrage of blasting inflicted upon the vessel. Not to mention the missile that brought half the mountain tumbling down upon it. But what bothered him most was the realization that if the men who had fired upon them managed to board the ship, he and Cade would be trapped and outgunned, with no means of escape. In short, the *San Isadore* would become their tomb.

# THIRTY-FOUR

THEY DESCENDED into the depths of the ship. The centuries-old stairs creaked and groaned under their weight, and Decker was afraid they would collapse, but the two men soon found themselves on the gun deck.

It was even darker down here. The beam of Cade's flashlight roamed over cannons that lined each side of the vessel, their barrels pointing aft and starboard toward rows of gun ports as if waiting for a battle that would never come. Hammocks, dozens of them, were slung between the support posts that supported the decks above, occupying every available free space. They were in such good condition thanks to the arid desert climate that Decker half expected the ghosts of long dead sailors to appear out of the darkness and reclaim their sleeping births at any moment. He could only imagine what it would have been like to spend months or even years crammed on a ship like this with hundreds of other sweaty mariners and soldiers. There would have been no privacy. Nowhere to bathe or wash your clothes. Even answering the call of nature must have been a chore.

Decker suppressed a shudder and nudged Cade. "Let's keep moving, shall we?"

The commander needed no urging. He moved forward, sweeping the flashlight beam across the floor ahead of them to make sure they didn't fall through a hole or rotten timber. "There should be another set of stairs somewhere around here that leads to the orlop deck. After that, we should be in the hold."

"There." Decker pointed to a rectangular opening near what looked like a smaller mast that pierced the deck toward the ship's bow. "That must be it."

They hurried forward, ignoring the groaning timbers beneath their feet.

When they reached the opening, Cade shone his flashlight down to reveal another staircase, narrower than the first.

Cade went first, testing each tread to make sure it would bear his weight. They were deep inside the ship now and the sound of gunfire had faded to the point that Decker wondered if it had stopped, or if they just couldn't hear it anymore. The air was still and heavy. It pressed around them like a living thing, as if eager to greet the only humans to set foot here in half a millennium.

Decker fought back a wave of claustrophobia, partly due to the all-consuming darkness, and also because of the low ceiling that provided barely enough room to walk upright. But it was nothing compared to the cramped space that awaited them one more deck below in the hold.

Hundreds of barrels and crates pressed in on all sides, stacked floor-to-ceiling against the steeply curving sides of the ship, with only a narrow walkway left between them to navigate. There were neat piles of what looked like bolts of fabric in several places. At the bow, where the ship narrowed to a point, smaller open-topped crates contained wine bottles.

Looking at the vast amount of cargo, Decker was overcome by the futility of their task. "How are we ever going to find the orb among all of this?"

"Beats me." Cade lifted the lid from a nearby crate. The contents glinted a metallic yellow under his flashlight. Rows of roughly cast gold ingots. He touched one, letting his fingers roam gently across the surface of the ingot. "If the rest of the crates are like this one, there must be millions of dollars-worth of gold down here."

More like hundreds of millions, Decker thought. But they weren't here for treasure. "They wouldn't put the orb in a crate like this along with the gold. If the legends are true, if the orb is what we suspect, its value would be immeasurably more to the conquistadors than all the other treasure in this hold. We should look for a box or other container that reflects the orb's unique nature."

"That could take days," Cade replied, his flashlight playing across the hundreds of stacked crates and other items clogging the hold. "We don't even have hours. And there's only one flashlight, so we can't split up."

"I know that." Decker wished that Rory was there with them instead of pinned down on the mountainside above. The archaeologist might have some idea of exactly what they were looking for, and where it would be. But it was too late now.

He followed Cade as he picked his way through the ship's hold, examining the crates as he went, removing lid after lid only to find yet more tightly packed ingots. But there was nothing that looked like it might contain a more precious cargo than gold. And all the while, Decker was aware that the minutes were ticking away, and that whoever had ambushed them—blown up the Humvee and brought the mountainside crashing down with them on it—might breach the ship at any moment and find their way into the hold. The only thing that stood in their way was the lone Marine on the ridge above, and the enigmatic stranger named Chava, who had shown up out of the blue. He was afraid they might already be dead, along with Rory and Abby. His worst fears were confirmed when the thud of heavy footsteps reached their ears from the deck above. At least two people and probably more, making their way through the ship and heading in their direction.

Decker froze even as Cade snapped the flashlight off, plunging them into darkness.

He turned toward the front of the ship, and the narrow staircase they had descended into the hold. He sensed Cade beside him, coiled like a snake ready to strike, pistol pointed into the swirling black void in front of them. Decker didn't know how much ammunition the commander had left his gun, but he was sure it would not be enough.

Then, moments later, the beam of another flashlight carved a narrow swath of illumination down through the hatch. There were boots on the stairs. And they were not alone in the hold anymore.

# THIRTY-FIVE

DON'T SHOOT." A familiar voice echoed through the darkness.

Decker's shoulders slumped with relief. It was Rory.

Cade turned on his flashlight again and aimed it forward.

The stranger, Chava, was standing at the foot of the stairs next to Saunders, the only remaining Marine. To their rear, he could see Rory and Abby.

"What are you doing down here?" Rory asked.

"What do you think we're doing?" Cade replied, his voice laced with irritation. "Looking for the orb. More to the point, what are *you* doing here?"

"We got flushed off the ridge," Saunders replied. "The hostiles sent a contingent through the canyon and up the path from behind in an attempt to trap us in the crossfire. We had no choice but to abandon our position."

"So you came here?" Cade didn't sound any less annoyed.

"It was either that or abandon you and take our chances on the mountainside. I wasn't about to fail our mission or leave you behind. Also, the galleon provided the best chance of cover from which to repel further attacks."

"Fair enough." Cade glanced up toward the decks above. "Why aren't we under attack right now?"

"I barricaded the door leading below decks."

"He did a pretty good job," said Rory. "It will take them a while to break through, but we shouldn't stay here too long. The orb won't be in the hold."

"What?" Cade frowned. "Why not?"

"Because the orb would have appeared like magic to those conquistadors. Given its size and enormous power, the captain would have wanted to keep it close at hand until he could deliver it to the king."

"Like in his quarters," Decker said.

"Which are all the way back up at the top of the ship," Cade said. "We walked right past them on our way down here."

"We don't have much time," Rory said. "That door won't hold forever. We need to get there before those people who were shooting at us."

"And then what?" Abby asked. "Even if we find the orb, we're still trapped in the ship. They aren't going to let us just stroll out of here with it tucked under our arm."

Cade was already making his way back to the stairs. "We'll worry about that when the time comes. Right now, our only concern is securing the orb."

---

They climbed back up through the ship. When they reached the main deck, Rory led him past the narrow corridor and the officers' accommodations, toward the captain's quarters on the other side of the mess. From somewhere behind them, Decker could hear their attackers trying to break through the barricaded door.

He turned back toward the captain's quarters just in time to see movement ahead of them. A figure appeared in the doorway.

Cade raised his gun, but then lowered it again quickly, a

smile spreading across his face. "Rivera. We thought we'd lost you."

"Not a chance, sir." Rivera's wide, muscular frame filled the doorway. "I ended up buried under all that sand. Took a while to dig myself out, then I came looking for you."

"And now you've found us." Cade hurried toward the Marine.

"I found something else, too." Rivera held up a small wooden box. He opened a door on the front to reveal a metallic object about the size and shape of a baseball, or perhaps a little bigger. The surface was smooth and tinted metallic gray. Cade's flashlight played across the orb, and when Decker looked at it, he had the strange sensation that it was both reflecting and absorbing the light. Under different circumstances, he would have marveled at this strange and clearly alien object, but he had seen it before. Or at least, another one very much like it. A couple of years before, he had encountered this same technology powering a dimensional drive on a sunken World War II U-boat. That adventure had almost cost him his life and also those of the U-boat's original crew, who were trapped in a flat and featureless alternate dimension, if he hadn't volunteered to activate the device and rescue them. This orb had found its way to earth centuries before the one he had encountered back then, yet he could still sense the energy emanating from it. The air around them felt thicker, as if the orb had somehow changed its very composition.

"Where did you get that?" Rory asked, taking a step forward.

Rivera glanced back over his shoulder. "I found it sitting on a desk in the cabin behind me. Figured it must be what we came here to get."

"Good work, Marine," Cade said. "Now, let's find a way out of here."

"That might be easier said than done." Abby was looking back through the corridor and past the officers' quarters to the barricaded door their attackers were still trying to break through. The door was shaking more with each successive blow they dealt. A heavy wooden beam had been dropped into sturdy brackets on each side of the door—a barricade system which had probably been meant as a last resort to protect the captain and officers if the ship was boarded—but after so many centuries, the nails holding the brackets in place had corroded and were giving way to the incessant pummeling from the other side of the door.

"That won't hold for much longer," Decker said.

As if on cue, the door gave one last mighty shake, and then one of the brackets finally gave way and the wooden beam clattered to the floor. The door flew open. Then the corridor was full of men and the bullets started flying.

# THIRTY-SIX

THE CORRIDOR WAS A BOTTLENECK, barely wide enough for one man to traverse at a time, which gave them an advantage, at least temporarily. But it was slim. Cade had his pistol, but only Saunders still carried a rifle. Even so, Cade was able to pick off the first man through the door, dropping him before he had made it more than a couple of feet along the corridor. Saunders did the same in quick succession with the man following up the rear. But that only alerted the men behind them of the danger. Instead of rushing blindly forward, they opened fire.

Decker threw himself sideways to avoid a hail of bullets, landing heavily next to a table.

He looked around to see that Abby and Rory had already taken shelter in the captain's quarters, along with Rivera, who was still holding the box containing the orb. Saunders and Cade were hunkered down behind another table that they had turned on its side and were returning fire. He couldn't see Chava.

Cade rose quickly from behind the table and got off a couple of shots, managing to score a hit on another assailant, who was doing his best to push through the door. The man dropped to the floor, screaming and clutching at his side. Another assailant appeared behind him and peppered the table, causing Cade to duck back down.

"We need to retreat," he hollered, glancing sideways at Decker. "The captain's quarters. Go. We'll cover you."

Decker wanted to protest. He hated to turn tail, leaving others to fight his battles, but he was unarmed and, therefore, useless. He gauged the distance from the table to the door and figured it was about twelve feet. Not a long way to go under normal circumstances, but it might as well be a mile right now. But there was no choice. He steeled his nerves, then launched himself at the opening, even as a volley of bullets followed behind, tearing up the floor in his wake. He crashed through the door and landed hard on the floor, rolling sideways out of view. He rose to his feet in time to see Cade and Saunders barrel through the doorway and slam the door, then grab a piece of ancient furniture that looked like a sideboard, and heave it across the opening. There was no way the flimsy piece of 500-year-old furniture would stop the men intent upon killing them and taking the orb. At least, not for very long, but it was better than nothing.

Then he remembered Chava, the stranger who had saved them back in the canyon. At first, he thought the man hadn't made it, but then he saw him standing near a desk upon which sat an inkwell and quill pen next to a pile of rolled up maps that looked like they might disintegrate into dust at any moment. Behind the desk was another large piece of furniture with glass doors. A bookcase stuffed with old volumes. Who knew how much all of this stuff was worth, but they probably wouldn't live to find out.

"We can't stay here," Rory said, echoing Decker's thoughts.

"What about the windows?" Abby asked, looking toward the row of lead paned windows at the back of the cabin. They would once have looked out upon the ship's wake as it traversed the ocean, but now there was only darkness beyond them. And Decker thought he knew why. Because the ship's stern was still buried under the shifting sands of the Anza-Borrego Desert. There would be no escape that way.

Even though he didn't want to admit it, Decker could see only one way they would make it out of this situation alive. He turned to Rivera. "Give me the orb."

"What are you doing?" Rory asked, his eyebrows shooting up in alarm.

"Getting us out of here." Decker waited for Rivera to open the box, then he reached in and removed the orb. When he cupped it in his hands, the metal felt warm under his touch. It pulsed gently, as if reacting to him.

"You can't be serious," Rory said, turning pale when he realized what Decker intended to do. "You don't know where it will take us."

"You're right, I don't. But I know that staying here is a death sentence. There's only one other way out of this room and we're outnumbered and outgunned. We don't stand a chance."

"This is a bad idea." Rory shook his head. "The last time you used one of these, back on that U-boat, it didn't just take *you*. It took the vessel, too. The entire U-boat shifted dimensions. That's how they were able to escape so easily after attacking Allied ships back in the war. The sub would blink out of existence only to reappear tens of miles away. At least, until it malfunctioned. How can you be sure this orb won't do the same thing now?"

"Because the Germans had integrated their orb with the U-boat. This one isn't wired into anything."

"Do you even know how to use it?" Abby asked.

That was a good question, but Decker had a feeling the orb would do his bidding, because he could sense a presence inside his head, and it was speaking to him in a vague, sibilant whispering that filled his mind in a language he didn't understand. A strangely unsettling language nothing like any that had ever been spoken by a human. It was almost like the device was reaching out, connecting with him in a way that went beyond technology and bordered on sentience. Was that how the Aztecs were able use it? Had it reached out to them, too?

"Well?" Rory shuffled closer to Decker. "Can you operate that thing or not?"

"I guess we'll find out," he said, because bullets were ripping into the cabin door now, shredding the ancient wood and reducing it to sawdust. Linking arms with Rory, Decker looked around the group. "Hold on to each other. I don't want anyone to get left behind."

Then he concentrated on the orb, focusing all his mental power on being somewhere else—anywhere else—even as the cabin door flew apart and half a dozen heavily armed men barged into the room. But they were too late, because the cabin was already fading from view. The orb glowed and pulsed, sending out rays of ethereal light that swallowed everything in its brightness.

At that moment, Decker sensed movement from the corner of his eye.

Chava was reaching out. He placed his hand on the orb and pried it from Decker's grasp. Then, before Decker could react, he was overcome by a sense of weightlessness, followed by another flash of blinding white light.

An instant later, they were no longer aboard the *San Isadore*.

# THIRTY-SEVEN

DECKER OPENED his eyes and at first, all he saw was a hazy glare. He squinted against the brightness, and waited until they adjusted, to discover that he was lying on his back staring up at a cerulean sky beyond a towering ring of trees with smooth, slender trunks, and twisting, almost serpentine branches that reached out and wrapped around each other to form an interlocking canopy.

His head hurt, a throbbing pain that quickly diminished to a pulsing ache. A soft, whispering breeze carried a sweet, almost nutty fragrance. He inhaled deeply, noting how the air tasted . . . different. A sharp tang of citrus layered beneath an earthy musk danced at the back of his throat. Decker had never experienced a sensation quite like it before. It was heady. Exotic. It ignited his senses and filled him with energy. After a few breaths, the pain in his head faded away to nothing.

He sat up and looked around.

The orb was lying next to him, nestled on a bed of fallen leaves. He appeared to be alone. There was no sign of Cade, Rory, or the others. Had the alien device transported only him, leaving everyone else to face certain death back on the *San Isadore*? He hoped not, but right now, there were other concerns.

Like figuring out exactly where the alien device had brought him.

He knew one thing. This certainly wasn't his intended destination of Maine. It Wasn't the Anza-Borrego Desert, either. Exactly the opposite. He was in a verdant forest, surrounded by tall trees of a species he didn't recognize. Plants grew here and there between them in thick clusters, their stalks topped by huge red flowers with curving red and yellow spotted petals that almost seemed to move on their own. Above the canopy, towering hundreds of feet above against the unnaturally intense blue sky, was an enormous step pyramid that looked decidedly Aztec. Was he in Mexico?

Tearing his gaze way from the huge structure, he watched an oversized insect that looked a bit like a cross between a dragonfly and a wasp stray too close to one of the blooms. A thin tendril shot from the center of the flower and wrapped around it, snatching the hapless insect from the air and dragging it back into the plant where it was quickly overwhelmed by dozens of smaller, red-tipped filaments.

Decker shuddered. If this was Mexico, it wasn't the Mexico of *his* earth. And if the plants in this world were carnivorous, who knew what else might be out there in the forest looking at him the same way that plant had viewed the wasp?

"Man am I glad to see you," said a familiar voice from somewhere to Decker's rear.

It was Rory. He wasn't alone after all. That, at least, was a small mercy.

Taking the orb, he stood up, noting how cold it was. When he turned around, Rory was walking toward him through the forest with Abby at his side. The rest of the group was conspicuous by their absence.

"Where are we?" Rory asked.

"You're guess is as good as mine." Decker thought back to the last moments before the orb transported them. He had been focusing on a safe place to go. CUSP's headquarters in Maine.

Then Chava had grabbed the orb right at the last moment. Had he hijacked the device? Made it do *his* bidding instead of Decker's. There was an obvious way to find out. "Where's everyone else?"

"Don't know," said Rory. "One moment I was in the captain's quarters on the *San Isadore*, and then I was here, wherever *here* is. I was afraid no one else had made it, that the orb might have left the rest of you behind, but then I found Abby."

"And in the nick of time," Abby said. "Because there was something moving around in the trees above me. I have no idea what it was, but it sounded big and decidedly unfriendly. I was convinced it was going to attack me before Rory came along."

"Then we shouldn't stay here," Decker said. An image of that plant snatching an insect out of the air rolled through his head. Apparently, he was right to be concerned. There were other dangers in this forest. "Whatever you heard might come back if it decides we aren't a threat."

"And go where?" Rory asked, glancing around.

"There." Decker nodded toward the pyramid rising out of the forest. "Seems like the obvious choice. After we find the others, of course."

"Or you could do whatever you did before with the orb and get us back home."

"Love to, but I have a feeling it's done all the dimension hopping it's capable of for the moment." Decker held the orb up to show them. "Completely inert. Either we broke it escaping those men back on the galleon, or it needs time to start working again. Either way, it amounts to the same thing. We're stuck here for the time being."

"That's just great," Abby muttered under her breath. "Talk about *out of the frying pan*."

"Decker did what he had to," Rory told her sharply.

Abby frowned. "Cool it, okay? I wasn't complaining. I just don't want to end up as a light lunch for whatever is out there."

"Neither do I." Decker took a deep breath, sucking in the

strangely redolent air. "We should find safe shelter. I have no idea where we are, or if this is even Earth. But I know we can't stay here. Once we're out of harm's way, we can wait for the orb to do whatever it does."

A look of alarm flashed across Abby's face. "What do you mean, *if this is even Earth*? Are you saying we might be somewhere else entirely?"

Rory nodded. "The orb was designed as a star drive, to carry its inventors across vast distances in space. We have no idea if it shifted us to another dimension, took us to another planet, or both."

Abby groaned. "I'm beginning to wish you hadn't convinced me to come along on this expedition."

"Um, who convinced who?" Decker asked.

"Okay fine. I wanted to come. But now I've changed my mind." Abby glanced around nervously. "If you can't get the orb to work again, we could be stuck here forever."

"I'm hoping it won't come to that," Decker said. "This device has spent centuries on that ship buried under the sand, and it still worked just fine. I'm sure we just need to wait a while."

"That's what I like about you, man," Rory grumbled. "You're always so confident."

"It's worked for me so far." Decker flashed a broad smile, even though he was anything but happy. "Now, how about we go find the—"

Decker never got a chance to finish what he was saying, because at that moment, a figure erupted from between the trees. A man wearing tan colored desert camo and carrying an assault rifle. Then, before anyone could react, he raised his gun, took aim, and fired.

# THIRTY-EIGHT

A BURST of gunfire ripped through the air.

Decker tensed, waiting for the bullets that would surely slam into him. Instead, they whizzed harmlessly above his head, even as the gunfire was abruptly silenced, to be replaced by a panicked, warbling scream.

The reason was as terrifying as it was fortuitous.

A shadowy form plunged from the tree canopy above them and scooped the man up, clutching him with razor sharp talons. It writhed through the air, an enormous serpent-like creature that twisted and undulated, more like a snake than anything possessed with the ability to fly. Its long, scaly body and lashing tail shimmered in hues of blue and green, the colors shifting and rippling like oil on water. Batlike wings beat the air, translucent flaps of leathery skin woven with veins that pulsed with black viscous ichor. Its head was narrow and angular, with cold ice-blue eyes and a terrible gaping mouth crammed with pointed, sharp teeth.

It swooped back into the treetops with its squirming prey, a plaintive cry rising over the man's horrified shrieks. A chittering, high-pitched wail with a whistling keen that vibrated all the way down to Decker's bones. Then, as quickly as the creature had appeared, it was gone. And so was their attacker, his dying screams becoming fainter until they were abruptly silenced, which was somehow worse.

Decker stared at the branches above him in shocked disbelief.

"It took that man," Abby said, her voice small and fragile. "Just dragged him off like he was nothing."

"I wouldn't feel too bad. He was about to kill us," Decker said, finally lowering his gaze. The man's rifle lay on the ground, dropped in his terror. Decker slipped the unresponsive orb into his backpack, then hurried forward and picked the gun up, checked the magazine. It was high capacity, probably a hundred rounds. Much larger than the standard military issue rifles Cade's men carried. He estimated it was still at least half-full. "And we're armed now, which makes me feel a whole lot better."

"What the hell was that creature?" Rory's face was drained of blood. He took a step closer to Decker, as if that would somehow protect him.

"Who cares what it was?" Abby said. "We have to do what Decker said and figure out why the orb isn't working. Fix it and get the hell out of here before that thing comes back."

"That's not quite what I said," Decker replied. "With any luck, the orb will start working again on its own. But if it doesn't, I have no idea how to fix it."

"What? Why not? You've used one of these things before. You told me that when we were back on the plane. How can you not know how it works?"

Decker grimaced. "I activated an orb one time when it was hooked up to a German U-boat, and even then, I was winging it. It's not like I've read the user manual or anything."

"Wonderful. You activated that device without having a clue what it would do or where it would bring us." Abby folded her arms, a scowl creasing her face. "That's freaking awesome."

"Hey, give the man a break," Rory said. "The alternative was getting riddled with bullets."

"In case you hadn't noticed, we almost did anyway. If that . . . that thing . . . whatever it was, hadn't swooped down out of nowhere, we'd be dead right now."

"We still might be, if we don't get out of here," Rory said, glancing nervously toward the spot where the serpentine creature had dragged the screaming man away. "Even if that creature doesn't come back, there's probably more of them out there."

"I agree," Decker said. There were probably other lifeforms just as dangerous as the batlike creature prowling the forest. In fact, he was certain of it, and next time, they might not be so lucky. "Let's find the others, then make our way to that pyramid. We need a safe place to figure out our next move before anything else decides to have a go at us."

"How do you know the pyramid is safe?" Abby asked.

"It has to be safer than here," Rory told her. "It's going to get dark at some point, and I suspect that's when the really bad things will come out to play."

"Hey," called a voice from somewhere between the trees.

Decker turned to see Cade striding toward them, with Chava and the two Marines at his rear.

"Am I glad to see you guys," Cade said as he drew close. "We heard screams and thought something had happened."

"It did, but not to us," Decker said. "One of the bad guys from the galleon somehow came along for the ride and tried to kill us."

"At least until something ate him," Abby said.

"What do you mean, ate him?" Cade looked around nervously.

"Exactly what I said. Some kind of winged serpent swooped down out of the trees and carried him off."

"Which is why we can't stay here," Decker said. He turned and glared at Chava. "Wherever *here* is, because it sure isn't the safe place I intended to go before you interfered. It's not even earth. At least, not *our* earth."

A faint smile touched Chava's lips. "This is Omeycan, the Place of Duality. The highest of the Thirteen Heavens. The place of rest and balance."

"Great. A bunch of superstitious mumbo-jumbo." Cade threw his arms in the air. "For a moment there, I thought you might actually have something to contribute."

"Do not dismiss the legends of my people. The Extlahualtin Teotl was also myth—an orb with the power to transport whoever wields it to another plane of existence—yet here we are."

"So let me get this straight," Rory said with a scowl, "of everywhere we could go—New York, Vegas, Rome—you decided that another plane of existence would be a better idea?"

"I did what was necessary," Chava said. He turned to Decker. "Those people would have killed us, and I could not be sure you had the mental strength to command the orb and get us off that ship. And even if you did, I was not convinced you could be trusted any more than those men who were on the other side of the door."

"So you stepped in and brought us to this forest," Decker said, remembering how the sibilant whispering in his head had quieted the moment that Chava had touched the orb.

Chava nodded. "I had no choice. The orb is my destiny. It is what I was born to protect. I cannot allow it to fall into the wrong hands."

"Well, I don't know about the rest of you," Cade said, his voice heavy with sarcasm. "But that just about clears everything up for me."

"I know you are angry, and I do not blame you. But you also have to understand that I am the last in a long line of Watchers. Descendents of the Aztecs who first discovered the orb and realized its immense power, and the danger it would present if improperly used. The Spaniards who stole it understood nothing but their own greed. They took it and sailed away, never to be seen again. Ever since that time, certain men and women, those possessed of the right abilities, have stood ready to reclaim the orb should it ever reappear." He shifted his attention back to Decker. "Do not feel bad, friend. My power to communicate with the orb is stronger than your own."

"Perfect." Rory folded his arms. "Then how about you communicate with it right now and take us back to where we belong?"

Chava shook his head. "I wish that I could, but the orb will not work again until it absorbs more power."

"And how is it going to do that?"

Chava glanced toward the structure towering above the trees. "We must go there. The pyramid is a vast source of energy. If we place the orb on the cradle at its apex, it will absorb the power necessary to open a portal back to our world, just like it did centuries ago when my people moved back-and-forth between the realms."

Cade snorted. "This is getting more ridiculous by the minute."

"No. I've heard about this," Rory said. "There are people who believe that the great pyramid in Egypt might once have acted like a giant battery capable of producing wireless energy. Nikola Tesla was obsessed with the pyramids for that very reason. The Aztec pyramids must have fulfilled a similar function. This is awesome. If we can prove that Tesla was right and the pyramids were built as power plants, it will change history."

"I don't care about changing history," Cade said. "I just want to get out of this place." He turned to Chava. "You're sure the orb will work again if we get to the top of that pyramid?"

Chava nodded. "I am sure."

"Fantastic." Cade clapped his hands. "Let's go climb a pyramid."

# THIRTY-NINE

AN HOUR after they started walking toward the pyramid, pushing through a dense jungle that became ever more impassable as they drew closer to the towering structure, they found a ruin. A broken piece of wall fashioned from stone blocks. At one time, centuries ago, it had probably been part of a larger building, but now there wasn't much left. The jungle had done a good job of tearing the ancient structure apart and reclaiming the toppled stones, covering what remained in thick, twisting vines and spongy moss. In fact, if it hadn't been for Rory, they might have walked right past it without ever realizing.

"This is incredible," he said, staring at the crumbling wall. "The craftsmanship. The construction. It looks very much like Aztec ruins found in Mexico." He reached out and ran his palm along the surface of a block.

"Look, there's more," Abby exclaimed excitedly, pointing toward a set of flat slabs stacked one upon the other poking from the ground several feet away. "It's a set of steps, or at least, what's left of them."

"What does it mean?" Decker asked.

"We're getting close to the pyramid," Rory told him. "These must be the remains of the city it served. I bet there are all sorts of ruins here."

"Really?" Cade looked around. "All I see are trees."

"That's why the ruins in Mexico went undiscovered for so long," Abby said. "Even the pyramids were covered in so much vegetation that they were almost impossible to find. They just looked like mounds in the jungle."

Cade didn't look convinced. "If this used to be a city, then where did all the people go?"

"That's a good question," Chava said, his voice heavy with disappointment. "When the conquistadors stole the orb, the portal between the worlds closed, trapping thousands of my people on this side. I expected them to still be here."

"You're only telling us this now?" Cade observed Chava with narrowed eyes. "You were going to walk us right into the arms of a bunch of Aztecs who have been trapped here for five hundred years?"

"They are my people, like I said. They would have helped us."

"Or they would have killed us, taken the orb, and used it themselves." Cade shook his head. "I knew we couldn't trust you."

"It is not a matter of trust. It is a matter of necessity. I do not trust any of you, either."

"Great. We're all on the same page. We don't trust each other," Decker said, growing tired of the back-and-forth. "It doesn't matter whether the people of the city would have helped us, because they aren't here, and the city is gone. What matters now is getting to the top of that pyramid with the orb. It's the only way we're going to get home."

"We shouldn't wait too long," Cade said, glancing toward the sky. "The sun is getting low on the horizon. It will be dark soon, and I don't want to find out what happens in this forest at night."

They started walking again, picking their way through the trees toward the pyramid. As they drew close, they found even more ruins. And something about them worried Decker. They didn't look like they had simply collapsed over time. Many of the stones bore what looked like the scars of a great cataclysm. They were shattered. Broken into pieces and charred by fire. At one point, he stopped and examined what must've once been a large public building, but was now nothing more than an overgrown rubble pile.

"Something bad happened here." Decker turned to Rory. "What do you make of this?"

"I agree. There was definitely a disaster of some sort." Rory pulled vines and foliage from one of the destroyed blocks. "You can see where the stones have been scorched by fire."

"But it must have happened a long time ago," Abby said. "Hundreds of years, by the looks of it."

Rory nodded. "I agree. Maybe that's where all the people went. They were killed during whatever tragedy befell this place."

Decker cast a quick glance toward Chava, but the man remained silent.

Cade, however, did not. "This is all very interesting, but it doesn't help us. I don't give a damn how or why those Aztecs died. We need to keep moving." He pushed past Rory and Abby and continued on through the forest, toward the pyramid that now towered so high above them that it blocked out the swiftly sinking sun.

Rory let his fingers linger on the stone for a moment longer, then stepped away, his gaze boring into the commander's back. "The more time I spend with that man, the less I like him," he hissed. "And it wasn't a very high bar to begin with."

"He's not wrong, though," said Decker, turning to follow Cade and the Marines. "We can't stay here."

They pushed through the forest for another thirty minutes before coming upon the pyramid. It looked even more daunting now they were at its base, constructed of enormous stone blocks placed one atop the other to create a series of huge platforms that only a giant could navigate. Here, too, there were signs of abandonment. The pyramid had avoided becoming totally overrun by the twisting vines and vegetation that had swallowed the ruins that surrounded it, but it had not escaped whatever cataclysm destroyed the rest of the city. Just like the ruins they had previously discovered, the stones here were blackened by ancient soot and scarred by deep gouges. Decker stared up at the towering structure. It appeared impossible to scale, at least until he saw a set of smaller steps ascending toward a square building atop the pyramid that he assumed was a temple, just like its counterpart in Mexico.

Cade had noticed it too and was already making his way toward the steps. At the bottom, he paused and glanced back at Decker. "Bring the orb. The quicker we reach the top, the faster we'll get back home." Then he started climbing.

"Now, there's something we actually agree on," Rory said, walking at Decker's side.

"I'm surprised you don't want to stay awhile and explore these ruins."

"Yeah, no thanks." Rory shook his head. "After what I saw back there, how that creature swooped down out of the trees and dragged that guy off, I think I'm good."

"Me too," said Abby. She squinted up toward the top of the structure as they reached the base. "Wow. That's a lot of steps."

"If this pyramid has the same dimensions as the one at Chichen Itza, there will be ninety-one of them," Rory said.

"Fantastic." Abby scowled. "I haven't eaten anything since breakfast—which feels like a whole world ago—I'm wicked dehydrated, and now I have to climb almost a hundred steps."

"It won't be that bad." Rory nudged her with his elbow and put his foot on the bottom step. "Race you to the top."

Abby watched him start to climb. "The minute we get back, I'm looking for another job."

"You're the one who wanted to come with us," Decker said, stepping past her and starting up the side of the pyramid.

"Yeah." Abby hurried to catch up. "You don't need to keep reminding me."

# FORTY

BY THE TIME they reached the top of the pyramid, Decker was drenched in sweat. With no forest canopy to provide shade, it was brutally hot, even though the sun was making its final descent toward the horizon and the land would soon be drenched in darkness.

The temple building was larger up close than it had looked from the ground. It was constructed of the same large blocks and ringed by a narrow walkway. There were two entrances into the structure, one on each side, leading into a dark and murky interior. The air within was stale and heavy.

Decker waited for his eyes to adjust to the gloom, then looked around.

An altar occupied the center of the space. Or at least, it would have had it not been toppled at some point in the past, possibly during the same event that destroyed the rest of the city. The heavy oblong altar stone was cracked into three pieces, one of which had toppled onto its side. Next to it, smashed on the floor, were the remains of a stone column with a flat top.

"This was where the people who built this pyramid would have made sacrifices," Rory said, approaching the broken altar stone.

"You mean like human sacrifices?" Cade asked, looking at the stone with a mixture of disgust and awe.

Rory nodded. "They would have held the victim down on this altar and cut out their beating heart." He ran his fingers along a narrow groove carved into the top of the stone. "This was a channel to siphon off the blood. Even after so many centuries, you can still see the dark stains."

"Animals," Cade muttered. "Superstitious, foolish—"

"Please, do not judge my people," Chava said. "Your own descendants are hardly free from superstition and sin. It wasn't too long ago that your people were burning witches and desecrating corpses in case they came back as vampires."

"You have a point," Cade admitted grudgingly. He glanced around. "How about you tell us what we need to do with the orb so we can turn it back on and get the hell out of here?"

"There is nothing you can do," Chava said. "The pyramid is broken."

"I'm sorry?" Cade took a step toward him. "You said that if we came up here, that if we placed the orb on its pedestal, that it would absorb the power of the pyramid and reactivate."

"I did say that." Chava didn't flinch as Cade got close enough that for a moment, Decker thought the commander might land a blow upon him. Instead of backing away, the Mexican merely pointed to the smashed stone column nine next to the altar. "But I was wrong. The pedestal has been destroyed."

"Then we just put it back together. It's just a few bits of broken stone, after all. How hard could it be?"

Chava's reply was calm and even-toned, as if he was explaining to a young child. "It is not that simple. Even if we could repair the pedestal, which we cannot, my people are not here. Without them, we cannot perform the necessary ritual."

"What ritual?" Cade didn't look convinced. "You never mentioned a ritual."

"The pyramid is a great conductor of energy, but it can only be unleashed with a specific ritual performed within this temple. A ritual performed in this temple."

"This temple was used for human sacrifices," Cade said, pointing to the broken altar stone. "Rory already confirmed that."

"Correct." Chava nodded. "My ancestors believed the orb was a gift from the gods, and that those gods demanded a price for its use."

"This is ridiculous." Cade almost spat the words. "The orb wasn't given to your people by some higher deity. It's part of an alien spacecraft that crashed on Earth hundreds of years ago. It doesn't need blood, and neither does the pyramid."

"I think there's a bigger question here," Decker said, turning to Chava. "If you think that the only way to get the orb working again is through a human sacrifice, which one of us did you have in mind?"

"I never said that a sacrifice was required. I told you what my ancestors believed."

"And you also said that without them to perform the ritual, we can't unleash the power necessary to get the orb working again."

"That is true," Chava said. "But not because of human sacrifice or the words of a ritual. As we have already discussed, this pyramid is a power plant and the people who knew how to use it are no longer here. Without the knowledge buried within their superstition, we are helpless."

"I refuse to believe that," Cade said. "The pyramid isn't some piece of complex machinery. It's a pile of stones. If it has the ability to somehow concentrate power and recharge the orb—and frankly, I'm skeptical—then all we need to do is wait."

Chava shrugged. "Maybe. Maybe not. Either way, we aren't going anywhere in the foreseeable future, so I suggest we make ourselves comfortable here in this temple, where it is safe, and wait until morning. If the orb isn't working by then, we can decide what to do next."

"If the orb isn't working by morning, then . . ." Decker let the thought trail off, because to say it aloud was more than he could bear. After being stranded for more than a year in the past and losing hope that he would ever see Nancy again, he had finally made it home to her. Now he was lost again, this time on an alien world in another dimension. And he only had himself to blame.

# FORTY-ONE

WE NEED to find food and water," Decker said. "Otherwise, it won't matter whether or not the orb works again."

"I agree. We need to keep our strength up," Cade replied.

Rory nodded. "We should light a fire, too. If we find water, we can boil it to make sure there are no viruses or parasites. Who knows what microscopic nasties are on this world, and I don't particularly want them inside of me."

"And the flames will keep predators away," Cade agreed. "There must be animals in this forest. I'll take my men, and we'll find dinner. We'll also look for water."

"Good idea," Decker said. "I'll come with you."

Cade shook his head. "You're the only one who knows how to use the orb. At least, the only one I trust. We can't risk anything happening to you." He pointed at Chava. "You can come with us. You seem to understand this place better than anyone else."

Chava looked uneasy.

It didn't go unnoticed.

"You have a problem with that?" Cade asked.

"No. I do not have a problem. I will go with you."

"Good." Cade eyed the M16 rifle in Decker's hands. "You comfortable using that?"

Decker gave him a curt nod.

"In that case, let's go." Cade started toward the temple entrance with the two Marines and Chava at his heel. He stopped and turned, looking back at Decker. "We'll do our best to be back before dark. I suggest you find some fuel for the fire at the base of the pyramid and get it lit ASAP. If the sun sets, the fire will act like a beacon."

"It will also act like a beacon for anyone else who's out in the forest," Rory said.

"The Aztecs who built this place died centuries ago, and if anyone else followed us through the portal, we would know about it by now. We'll be fine. Build the fire!" With those parting words, Cade turned and started back down the side of the pyramid with the two Marines and Chava at his rear.

Decker watched them go with a faint sense of unease. He hated the idea of splitting up, but he also understood that with only a few guns between them, it would be much too dangerous for the entire group to go traipsing through the forest, especially when they could stay in the relative safety of the temple atop the pyramid. That many people would also make it hard to find anything to eat. On their trek through the forest, he had seen several small bushy trees heavy with a bright orange fruit that looked like a cross between a banana and a mango, but there was no way he dared to pick it without knowing whether the fruit was safe to eat. The same would be true for anything else they found growing here. Which meant they would have to catch their dinner, and a small group stood more chance of doing that than a large one. Of course, consuming meat was also a risk, but probably less so than vegetation.

He stood at the entrance to the pyramid and watched as the small group of soldiers turned hunters reached the bottom of the steps and started across the small clearing surrounding the pyramid until the densely packed trees swallowed them up.

Above the forest, in the distance, a faint black shape swooped through the air, silhouetted against the sky. He could make out the barest impression of a flicking tail and beating wings. Was it the same creature that had dragged their attacker to his death? It was impossible to tell from such a long way off, but he was fine with that. The creature was far enough away that it would not bother them.

"You think Chava really believes what he said?" Rory asked, joining Decker at the entrance. "That we need some ancient ritual to get the pyramid to do whatever it does and energize the orb?"

Decker shrugged. "Your guess is as good as mine. But it seems to me that if the pyramid needs to be activated, there must be a more logical way to do it than performing a ritual."

"Right. I was thinking the same thing. There are all sorts of fringe theories about the pyramids in Egypt. About how they have undiscovered chambers inside that somehow created a chemical reaction that produced hydrogen gas which was then used to power some sort of generator. There are even theories that they used obelisks as wireless transmitters for that energy. None of this has been verified, or accepted by mainstream science, I hasten to add, but even if the theories are nothing more than pseudoscience, they do not stray into the realm of the supernatural. Nowhere does it state that the ancient Egyptians were using rituals or incantations to create energy. Likewise, I highly doubt that we need a ritual to get the pyramid we are currently standing on to create energy."

Decker turned away from the entrance and went to his pack, which was sitting on the floor near the shattered altar. He unbuckled it and removed the orb, examining it for a moment. The metal was smooth and cold to the touch. There was no warmth. No vibration. No hint that anything was going on within the object. It was dead. He returned the orb to the backpack and stood up again.

"Still nothing?" Abby asked. She was sitting across the small room with her back against the wall and her knees pulled up to her chest. She looked small and scared. Nothing like the confident, overeager young woman who had muscled her way onto this expedition.

"No. Still nothing." Decker pushed his hands into his pockets. Chava's claim that the orb would not work again until it had absorbed energy from the pyramid didn't make sense to him. As Cade had pointed out, the orb was not a gift from the gods. It was part of a crashed alien spacecraft recovered by the Aztecs, who misunderstood its origin. There was no reason to believe that a crashed star drive would require the meagre power generated by a stone pyramid to continue operating. For a start, like Rory said, pyramids being used as power plants was nothing more than a fringe theory, with no hard evidence to support it. That was a sobering thought, because if the pyramid and orb were connected only by superstition, it would not matter how long they stayed atop the structure. The alien device in his backpack would either start working again under its own steam, or it wouldn't, and right now, all evidence pointed to the latter.

Decker pushed the grim thought aside and turned to the others. "Come on. Let's find some wood and light a fire before it gets too dark."

# FORTY-TWO

CHAVA FOLLOWED Cade and the two Marines through the forest. He suspected the commander had ordered him to come along on this hunting expedition, more to keep an eye on him than for any knowledge he might possess of this world. Not that it mattered, because Chava was beginning to wonder if everything he had learned from the stories passed down through the centuries was even accurate. After all, he had expected to find a thriving community of Aztecs here. The descendants of men and women who had been trapped on the wrong side of the portal when the conquistadors stole the orb. People who would understand what must be done and help him. But there was no one. The pyramid and the city surrounding it were in ruins, and it had clearly been that way for a very long time. Even though the city was empty, Chava couldn't shake the feeling that they were not alone in this place. There was something here, a presence he had noticed the moment they arrived. At first, he had thought it was just his imagination, but he could still sense it, dark and hostile, reaching into the deepest corners of his mind.

The seer had been right. There was an evil here, and Chava knew he had made the right decision when he reached out and took control of the orb. Brought them all here. Because whatever was in this place had to be kept here at all costs. It could not be allowed to escape into their world, which he knew was its ultimate goal. Thankfully, the orb remained inert—he could achieve that much—but it wouldn't stay dormant forever. Which meant he needed a new plan, and quickly. Thankfully, an idea had occurred to him. And if at least some of the ancient knowledge passed down through the ages was correct, he could implement it that very night.

# FORTY-THREE

CADE and the others didn't return until sunset. They stepped into the abandoned temple at the top of the pyramid as a night blacker than any Decker had ever seen descended upon the forest. Between them they carried the carcass of a creature that looked a bit like a wild boar, except that it was smaller and leaner, with thick and silky orange fur and a horn-like protrusion on its snout. They had also found a fast-flowing river about half a mile from the pyramid from which they filled up a couple of five-quart collapsible canteens. In the morning, Cade said, they would refill them if necessary.

Decker, Rory and Abby had built a fire, which now crackled in the center of the small space, the smoke rising though a small hole in the roof that had probably been used to vent the temple during ceremonies when it would have been lit by torches.

Cade wasted no time building a makeshift tripod above the fire with longer pieces of wood, then boiled the water in an aluminum pot provided by one of the Marines, who was carrying a portable stove kit in his pack.

They cooked the meat from their catch on wooden spits and sat around the fire eating hungrily and washing it down with freshly purified water that was still warm. But no one cared, because they were all dehydrated after their ordeal of the past twelve hours. To Decker, it tasted like some of the best water he'd ever drank.

When the meal was finished, Cade told them that he and the Marines were going to keep watch throughout the night—just to be safe—taking turns and rotating every few hours so each of them got a few winks of sleep. Although Decker wondered just how much rest they would all actually get, since they would be bedding down on a hard stone floor with only their packs for pillows. He stood up and walked to the temple entrance, stepping outside and sitting on the top rim of the enormous building and staring out over the landscape below. He strained to see through the inky blackness of the alien night. He figured that if any anyone had survived on this world after the conquistadors stole the orb, he might see the dim glow of another distant fire, or maybe the faint light of a settlement. But there was nothing.

The moon had risen and hung low in the sky. Or rather, *two moons* had risen—a pair of crescents, one large and glowing with an ethereal yellow light, within which the faint pockmarks of ancient craters were visible, the other a smooth pale blue and sitting at a much further distance. Together, they cast enough light for Decker to see the treetops as they stretched to the horizon. It was breathtaking and also drove home the fact that he was further from Nancy than he had ever been before. Because even when he was trapped in the early 1900s, she was still there, waiting for him in a future he knew would eventually arrive. He might not have survived long enough to come home to her, given the large span of years that separated them, but he could at least send her a message, let her know where he was, and that he would always love her. He had put that plan into action, giving Mina—who would have barely aged by the time the 21st century rolled around—a letter which she had thankfully not needed to deliver. This was different though. There would be no letter this time. No love note across time and space. He would simply have vanished into the Anzo Borrego desert, never to be seen again.

"I can guess what *you're* thinking about," Rory said, leaving the shelter of the temple and settling next to him on the edge of the pyramid with his legs dangling off the side.

"Like you aren't?" Decker cast him a sideways glance. "How is Cassie, by the way?"

Cassie Locke was Rory's girlfriend. They had met in the Amazon jungle during a mission to rescue a tv production company making a show about cryptids who ended up coming across the real deal with deadly consequences. They had been together ever since, even though she now had her own show and travelled at least half the year.

"She's good," Rory said. "Still hosting the supernatural TV show. She's been in Egypt for the last couple of weeks filming an episode about a high priest named Amenmosep in the temple of Sekhmet, who was rumored to drink blood to absorb the life force of his victims and live forever. I guess people claim that he's still around to this day."

"He's not," Decker said, thinking back to the Titanic and the bloodthirsty ancient Egyptian vampire that had almost cost he and Mina their lives.

Rory looked at him with narrowed eyes, perhaps waiting for Decker to elaborate, but it wasn't going to happen. The details of what had happened to Decker and Mina in the past, including their passage on the ill-fated ocean liner, was known only to a select few. CUSP operatives did not engage in idle chatter about past missions. When and if Rory ever needed to know about Amenmosep's true fate, he would be told by either Adam or Mina. Until that time, Decker was not at liberty to comment.

After a few moments, Rory turned his attention to the forest beyond the pyramid. His gaze drifted up to the double moons. "I guess this proves we're not on some alternate Earth."

"Or at least, not one that formed in a solar system similar to our own," Decker said.

"I don't want to die on this world," Rory said after a brief moment of silence. "I don't want Cassie to think I just vanished. I don't want her to spend the rest of her life wondering."

Decker said nothing. He had only moments ago been contemplating the same thing about Nancy. He could feel the tension in the air. He wanted to reassure Rory, tell him that they would get home, but he didn't want to lie. There was every chance they were stuck on this world for good. Thankfully, at that moment, Chava stepped out and approached them, carrying three aluminum mugs, which must have come from the stove kits in the backpacks.

"Here. I brought these for you," he said, offering them two of the mugs.

Decker took one, saw that it contained a light brown liquid. "What is this?"

"A special herbal tea made from an ancestral recipe. My people have consumed this tea for hundreds of years. It will build stamina and refresh the senses. Please, drink."

"Are you sure it's safe?" Decker eyed the concoction with a mixture of curiosity and suspicion. "Where did you even find the ingredients?"

"My ancestors brought the plants necessary to make this tea with them when they came here centuries ago and must have grown them in the city near the pyramid. I found some while we were out looking for food and water."

"I'm not sure about this." Rory sniffed the concoction warily.

"It is good, I assure you." To prove his point, Chava drank deeply from the third mug. "See?"

Decker hesitated a moment, then took a sip.

The tea had a lemony bitterness but there was also a hint of sweetness on the tongue. It was like nothing he had ever tasted before. But it wasn't bad, and it quenched his thirst. He drank some more.

Rory watched him for a moment, then did the same.

Chava's gaze shifted to the forest and the pair of alien moons in the star filled sky. "I can't believe that I'm actually here in Omeycan. It's even more breathtaking than I imagined it to be." He looked back down and smiled at Decker. "I'm home."

Decker wanted to say that none of them should be here. That wherever this might be, it was not home, but he couldn't articulate the words. And he was tired. In fact, he could hardly keep his eyes open.

Next to him, Rory yawned and mumbled something unintelligible.

Decker tried to lift himself up, to get back to the temple and warn the others that something was terribly wrong, but his legs were like lead. Then the darkness closed in.

# FORTY-FOUR

DECKER AWOKE to scratching sounds in the darkness. He was groggy and his head hurt.

From off to his right, Rory groaned. "What the hell happened?"

"I don't know." Decker pushed himself up. They were still atop the pyramid, outside the temple and close to the edge. The last thing he remembered was drinking the tea Chava had brought them. The cup lay on the cold, hard stone next to him, tipped over. The moons were no longer in the sky, and behind him, the fire had died down to nothing but glowing embers. He had no idea how long they had been out. "I think we were drugged."

"Crap. I knew there was something off about that tea."

More scratching sounds. Closer this time. Like nails on stone . . . or talons.

Decker stood and peered over the edge of the pyramid into the darkness beyond. He could make out the faint outline of the closest steps, but that was about it. "There's something down there."

Rory scrambled to his feet. "You. mean, like an animal?"

"No. More like several animals," Decker replied, because

now he could see the glint of eyes in the gloom, at least four pairs. They were close, too. He swiveled on his heel, started toward the temple. "Come on. We have to warn the others."

"What's going on?" Cade appeared in the doorway. He was bleary eyed. clearly he had also been drugged.

"Creatures. They're climbing up the pyramid toward us." Decker stepped inside the temple. The two Marines stood to one side, both looking the worse for wear. Abby was there too, crouching by the remains of the fire. There was no sign of Chava. He was gone. Decker resisted the urge to go to his backpack and check on the orb. There were more immediate concerns, like defending themselves from whatever was out there in the darkness.

"What kind of creatures?" Abby was on her feet now.

"I don't know, but I'm guessing they won't be friendly." Decker looked around for the rifle he'd picked up after the man who attacked them back when they first arrived in this strange place had been carried off by a winged beast but didn't see it. Chava must have taken the gun after he drugged them. But at least Cade and the Marines still had their pistols—although Cade was probably low on ammo—and Saunders carried a rifle. It was scant defense but better than nothing.

"Look." Abby's eyes flew wide. She pointed to the temple door, or rather, the ledge beyond it, where a dark, muscular form was pulling itself up over the lip of the pyramid.

Saunders raised his gun and stepped forward, positioning himself between the rest of the group and the creature.

Cade pulled his pistol from its holster and joined him.

Rivera took up a position on the other side.

All three aimed at the temple door.

The beast drew closer, skulking slowly forward with wary confidence.

Decker's blood ran cold.

Even on all fours, the creature was five feet tall at the shoulders, a stocky mass of rippling muscle beneath a scaly dark hide, with a large, bulbous head, and red eyes that seemed to possess an inner fire. Its pointed snout above a set of powerful jaws filled with triangular, serrated teeth reminded Decker of a shark.

The beast hunkered down in the temple doorway, observing them even as three more creatures appeared over the rim of the pyramid behind it. Then, with a high-pitched squeal, it leaped.

# FORTY-FIVE

GUNFIRE SPLIT THE AIR. Saunders stumbled back with a grunt as the closest beast breached the temple entrance. The creature made it a few steps inside, before a hail of bullets tore into it, sending the monstrosity crashing to the ground.

But the danger was far from over.

A second beast leaped over the corpse of its fallen comrade and was met with an equally vicious round of gunfire, even as a third made it into the temple and rolled sideways to avoid the lethal barrage, only to be cut down by Saunders, who turned his weapon upon the creature before it could pounce.

Decker felt useless without a gun of his own. All he could do was usher Rory and Abby to the other side of the temple and watch as a fourth beast appeared in the doorway, lips pulled back in an angry snarl.

Cade took aim, but his gun clicked harmlessly. He cursed. "I'm empty."

"I got your back." Rivera fired off several shots, scoring several direct hits on the beast even as Saunders turned the rifle back upon it. A moment later, the creature's legs gave out and it fell to the ground, dead.

A silence descended.

The acrid stench of blood and gunpowder hung in the air.

For a long moment, nobody moved, their eyes fixed upon the door.

When it became clear that the attack was over, that no more beasts were going to come charging at them, Cade holstered his pistol and wiped a bead of sweat from his brow, shoulders slumped. "That was fun."

"What the hell were those things?" Saunders walked over and looked down at the closest creature. He nudged it with his foot, then staggered back with a yelp and almost fell over the corpse of another beast when the creature's leg contracted.

Rivera couldn't help laughing. "Jumpy much?"

"It was just an automatic reflex." The relief on Saunders face was clear.

"Remind me again how you got into the Marines?" Rivera said with an amused snort.

Saunders flipped him the bird. "Who was it that killed three of these beasties to your one?"

"Who has the bigger gun?"

"That's enough," Cade said. "Fun's over." He took a step toward the dead beasts.

At that moment, Decker sensed a movement from the corner of his eye. A stirring of the shadows up toward the ceiling. There, wedged in the opening of the chimney, holding itself in place with huge claws curled into the stonework, was another creature, this one larger than the others. There was no time to shout a warning. Before Decker could even open his mouth, the creature let go.

It dropped with the agility of a cat, twisting mid-air to better find its prey, then hit Rivera square in the back, its jaws sinking into his neck.

Rivera screamed and fell to his knees, the sound quickly cut off as the beast tore out his windpipe.

Saunders raised his rifle and fired a quick volley, even as the creature released Rivera from its grasp and turned toward the rest of them. It bucked and shuddered as bullets slammed into its thick, scaly hide. But it wasn't done yet. It swiveled, fixed its gaze upon Abby, then dropped low, preparing to leap. Its jaws opened wide, thick, drooling saliva dripping to the floor.

Saunders walked forward, calm as could be, and placed the gun's muzzle against the back of the creature's head, his eyes nothing but narrow slits. "Go back to hell."

Then he pulled the trigger.

Skull and brains erupted in an explosion of viscous gore.

The beast, at least what remained of it, swayed once, twice, then toppled sideways to the ground.

Saunders rushed forward, ignoring the still twitching beast, and dropped to his knees next to Rivera, head bowed.

"He's dead," Abby said, between gut-wrenching sobs. She turned to Rory, flung her arms around him, and buried her face in his shoulder. "That monster. It . . . it . . ."

"I know." Rory hugged her tight.

Decker looked at Cade. "We should check the perimeter. Make sure there aren't any more of those things."

For a moment, Cade didn't answer. He observed the fallen Marine with glassy eyes. Then he seemed to pull himself together. "Let's go."

Decker started toward the entrance, but Cade stopped him. "Wait. We're not going out there without weapons." He crossed to the Marines, took the rifle from Saunders, then bent down and picked up Rivera's fallen pistol.

He held it out.

Decker looked at the weapon, at the blood smeared barrel, the grip. He hesitated, just for a moment, then he took the gun and kept going.

They stepped out into the cool early morning air as the first rays of dawn were painting the distant horizon in fiery shades of red and yellow. The sky was a deep cobalt blue, almost black, but not quite.

A cloud of what looked like huge, oversized bats swarmed

overhead, racing back to wherever they waited out the daylight hours.

Decker shuddered and turned to follow the ledge that ran around the exterior of the temple, keeping his gaze lowered toward the sides of the pyramid in case there were more creatures climbing up toward them. Cade went in the other direction, and they met up again on the opposite side of the structure.

"Anything?" Decker asked.

Cade shook his head. "This is exactly why I wanted to post a guard."

"It wasn't your fault. Chava drugged us."

"It was entirely my fault. I should never have accepted that drink from him. Now one of my men has paid for that mistake with his life." Cade's face was thunder. "When we find him, there's going to be hell to pay."

Decker agreed with the sentiment, but right now, there were other concerns. "We should go back to the temple. I need to check something."

Cade nodded and started back toward the front. "There's only one reason why Chava would do this."

When they entered the temple, Decker went straight to his backpack and opened it.

"Well?" Cade hovered over him.

"It's gone," Decker said, standing up. "Chava took the orb."

# FORTY-SIX

"WE HAVE to go after Chava. Find the orb and get it back," Rory said. "He can't have gotten very far."

They were standing outside of the temple, partly because no one wanted to get caught unawares in a confined space again, and also because they didn't want to look at Rivera's body. It was full daylight now, and the temperature was already rising. The sounds of animals reached their ears from the jungle below. Weird chattering sounds and whooping cries. The occasional bloodcurdling shriek. Birds wheeled in the sky high above them, silhouetted black against the sun's glare.

"He could be miles away by now," Cade said. "We were out cold for hours. Besides, in this terrain, we wouldn't see him if he were standing five feet from us, and we have no idea which direction he went in, or where he's going."

"Why would he do this to us?" Abby asked, a slight tremble in her voice.

"I have a suspicion," Decker replied. He thought back to what Chava had said when they first arrived in this jungle. That he had reached out and taken control of the orb, told it to bring them here, because he couldn't be sure if Decker would be able to use the device to get them off the ship before they were killed.

Which made sense . . . sort of. But at the same time, if all Chava wanted to do was escape the predicament they were in and keep the orb from their attackers, he could have done that by taking them anywhere else on Earth, instead of an alien world in what might be an alternate universe. It didn't add up. There was only one logical explanation. Chava had brought them here specifically because it was the only place he thought the orb would be safe from falling into the wrong hands. And Decker suspected that he included no one but himself in that category. Which meant there was only one place he could take the orb to guarantee that it would be secure. "He brought us here to make sure that the orb would never again be found."

There was a moment of silence.

Cade stared at him, then nodded slowly. "All that stuff about bringing the orb to the pyramid so it could recharge itself was nothing but a load of bull. He never had any intention of letting us get back to Earth."

"Right."

"I saw his face when we found the ruins of the city," Rory said. "For a second there, he looked shocked, like he was expecting something else."

"Uh-huh." Decker folded his arms and stared out across the jungle. "He thought that his people would still be here. That they would help him. Welcome him and the orb with open arms."

"And probably kill the rest of us," Rory said. "The question is why?"

"That's not something we'll get an answer to until we find him," Cade said. "And we *will* find him, because if we don't, then this world will be our tomb."

"And how exactly do you propose we do that?" Rory asked. "Like we already discussed, he could have gone in any direction, and I'm pretty sure it's not safe to just wander aimlessly around here."

"It's not safe to stay here either," Cade said, glancing back toward the temple. "As Rivera already found out."

"So you're suggesting . . ." Rory let the question trail off.

Cade's shoulders slumped. "I don't know what I'm suggesting. We're between a rock and a hard place, as the saying goes. We only have two working guns, and not much ammo for either of them. There's barely any food and water to go around. And unless Chava returns of his own volition, which I think we all agree is highly unlikely, it will be almost impossible to track him and take the orb back."

"And even if we do somehow get the orb," Decker said. "We'll still be stuck here, because it isn't working."

"Which brings up another interesting question," Rory said. "*Why* isn't it working? After all, it's alien technology far in advance of anything the people who built this pyramid could have understood. It must possess vast amounts of power in order to rip open a portal between dimensions. It seems unlikely that using it once would drain it to the point of obsolescence."

"I agree," Cade said. "Which means that Chava knows more about the orb than he was letting on."

"Are you saying he could have switched it back on and taken us home at any time?" Abby asked, sounding deflated.

"I'm saying it's a distinct possibility. Maybe Chava did something to sabotage the orb."

"Like what?"

"Again, that's a question we will only be able to answer when we find him." Cade walked to the edge of the pyramid and looked down into the jungle. "Anyone got any ideas?"

There was stony silence.

"That's not very encouraging," Rory said, when it became clear they didn't.

"Trying to chase Chava into the jungle when we don't know where he went is pointless and will only result in more problems. We need a better strategy than that," Decker said. "In the meantime, there's a task that has to be done."

Cade nodded. He didn't need to say anything, because it was

on all of their minds. Rivera. Since there was no way to return home with his body, the Marine deserved a proper burial.

Saunders held his rifle out to Decker. "The commander and I will bring him down to the jungle and find a suitable resting place. Perhaps you could watch our backs."

"You've got it." Decker took the weapon, even as another inhuman shriek echoed through the forest beneath them.

Cade hesitated a moment, his gaze drifting in the direction of the unnerving sound, then he took a deep breath and turned back toward the temple. "Let's be quick about it. This jungle is decidedly unfriendly, and I'd rather not be next on the list to bury."

# FORTY-SEVEN

CHAVA MADE his way through the jungle with the resolve of a man who knew exactly where he was going. It was daylight now, which made the trek easier, but already the temperature was soaring, and despite his ability to easily tolerate hot climates, it would still take a toll.

He would be fine, though.

Earlier, after mashing the leaves he had found the previous day in the jungle, boiling water over the fire, and making the tea used to drug everyone else, he had gone through their packs and transferred every item he thought would be useful to his own backpack, including their canteens. He had also relieved Decker of the orb. Finally, he had picked up the M16 and slung it over his shoulder. He had considered taking the other weapons, too, but had stopped himself. While he was prepared to abandon these people to a wild and dangerous jungle in a place far from home, he was not willing to leave them completely defenseless. It would be no different than if he had put a gun to their temples while they slumbered and pulled the trigger, executing each of them in turn. But while he may have been a lot of things, Chava did not consider himself a murderer. That he was almost certainly condemning them to death anyway was not his concern. He had left them with the means to defend themselves, and that was all that mattered. Whether they succeeded or failed was beyond his control.

Honestly, he had expected his plan to fail. The burly commander, Cade, clearly did not trust him, and neither did the man named Decker. But they were also tired, dehydrated, and afraid, which had all played to his advantage. He had told them that the tea was made from an ancient recipe used by his people, and that the principal ingredient had been brought here centuries ago when the city was built. And he had not lied. The drink was made from the leaves of a plant known as pipiltzintzintli, which had powerful psychotropic properties that his ancestors had used in ceremonies to enter an altered state of consciousness. But ingest too much of it, and you would pass out before the plant's hallucinatory effects had time to kick in.

It was not surprising that he had found the plant growing wild here amid the ruins of this city. His Aztec ancestors had cultivated a variety of entheogenic plants for use in their spiritual ceremonies, and they would have been unlikely to stop that practice when they arrived in Omeycan. If anything, just the opposite. To them, this was a place much like the Christian heaven that their conquerors from across the ocean believed in, except that they knew there were seven such divine realms, of which Omeycan was the highest. Here, in what they thought to be the physical manifestation of that highest heaven, they would want to be closer to their gods than ever.

Still, there had been an awful moment when Decker refused to drink. Thankfully, Chava had made a much weaker version for himself by diluting the concoction with water, which he had used to assuage Decker's distrust, and that of his companion. The watered-down tea had not been enough to have much effect, but he had still suffered a series of mild and vaguely unpleasant hallucinations in the hours that followed. They were easily dismissed, although had he consumed much more, he might have rendered himself incapable and scuttled his own plan.

Now, after many hours of fighting his way through dense jungle vegetation, he was almost at his destination. Initially, when they had arrived in this place, he had been disappointed to find the city in ruins. But even though he kept it to himself, Chava knew his people were not gone. He didn't know how, but he could sense them calling out to him. A faint whispering at the back of his mind that urged him to come join his brethren at their new city in a fertile valley many miles to the south. And when he got there, once the orb was safely out of their reach, he would send help back to Decker and the others. This was a promise he had made to himself, which he intended to keep. They might never leave this place, but at least they would not die alone and afraid in the jungle . . . if they managed to stave off the monsters that prowled here for long enough.

# FORTY-EIGHT

THEY BURIED Rivera under the shade of a large tree that looked a little like someone had mashed together an oak and a pine with thick, snaking branches and needlelike leaves.

Actually, buried wasn't correct. They had no tools with which to dig and probably would not have gotten very far anyway given the tangled mass of roots that snaked everywhere across the jungle floor. Instead, they laid him to rest within a natural depression in the ground, then covered the grave with stones from the ruined Aztec city. Finally, Saunders cobbled together a crude headstone in the shape of a crucifix made from two fallen branches, lashed together with thin vines pulled from the trunk of a tree. He held the fallen Marine's dog tags. One was on a chain, which Saunders had removed from around his colleague's neck. This he looped around the makeshift headstone so that it would hang there is a memorial. The other dog tag had been tied into the laces of Rivera's left boot. He pocketed this one for the Marine's family, assuming they got back home.

When their solemn task was completed, they made their way back to the pyramid.

But as they approached the edge of the jungle, where it gave way to the clearing within which the huge structure sat, Cade brought them to a halt with a raised fist. "Hold up."

"What is it?" Rory asked.

"Look." Decker nodded toward the base of the pyramid, where a group of three men stood. They wore the skins of an animal Decker didn't recognize and carried long wooden weapons with shards of dark-colored stone embedded in them. They looked like clubs but were at least three feet long. More weapons hung from belts around their waists. A curved dagger on one side, and a sword on the other. The men were talking excitedly among themselves, but it was impossible to hear what they were saying.

"I guess the people who built the city aren't all dead, after all," Abby whispered, pressing herself flat against a tree trunk out of sight.

"Question is, what are we going to do about them?" Rory said. "All of our stuff is at the top of the pyramid."

"Maybe they're just passing through," Cade said, although from the tone of his voice, he didn't believe it. And he was right. Because soon two more men appeared. They exited the temple at the top of the pyramid and started down toward the warriors waiting at the bottom.

Decker was dismayed to see the men were carrying the backpacks they had left there. "So much for passing through."

"This is so bad," Abby said sourly. "We lose those backpacks and we're done for."

"She's right. We have to get them back." Cade was watching the proceedings with narrowed eyes. His hand moved to the pistol in its holster on his belt, even though the weapon was empty.

"What are you suggesting?" Decker asked, alarmed.

Cade glanced sideways toward him, his gaze settling on the M16 rifle that Decker was still carrying. "I think you know."

A chill ran up Decker's spine. "We're not shooting those men."

"I agree . . . unless we have to. Hopefully, a couple of warning shots will be enough to convince them that we mean business."

Rory shook his head. "I wouldn't count on it. These people have been here for hundreds of years, cut off from Earth. They've probably never even seen a gun."

"Which is why we might have to use deadly force. Kill one of them, and the others will probably fall in line. One way or another, we're going to get our gear back."

"That's horrid." Abby stared at Cade with a look of horror on her face. "Do you even hear yourself?"

"Do you have a better idea?"

"How about we try being friendly first? Just ask them for it."

Rory nodded. "I agree. And besides, in case you forgot, we need to find Chava and get the orb back so we can get out of here. Making enemies of the locals won't exactly help us in that regard."

"And what makes you think these people will let us have the orb even if we find it?" Cade asked. "Don't forget, the orb belonged to them before the Spanish stole it. They're just as likely to kill us and keep it for themselves as help us."

"I'm aware of that." Rory looked glum.

"Then what are we going to do?" Abby asked.

Decker was still watching the warriors. It looked as if they were preparing to leave. "We stay out of sight. Follow them back to wherever they came from. After that, we can reassess the situation. Make a more informed decision."

From somewhere behind them, there was a rustle of leaves.

"Um, guys?" Rory turned in the direction of the sounds. A look of panic flashed across his face. "I don't think that's going to be an option."

Decker swiveled around, bringing the rifle up.

Standing among the trees, watching silently, were more warriors. At least a dozen of them, holding wicked-looking metal tipped spears that were pointed in their direction.

# FORTY-NINE

IT WAS early afternoon by the time Chava reached his destination. He didn't know how he had found it, only that the closer he got, the more insistent the whispering in his head had become. Actually, whispering was not really the right word, he now realized. It was more like a vague coherence breaking through a sea of background noise, much like the occasional snippet of disjointed chatter piercing the static of a radio tuned to the swirling emptiness between stations.

He stood at the edge of the forest and looked down onto a sprawling metropolis nestled in the valley below. It was Aztec. Or at least, how that civilization might have evolved on Earth had invaders from across the sea not wiped it out. There were wide central avenues that ran parallel to the length of the valley, lined with one- and two-story buildings constructed of a golden-hued stone that almost seemed to radiate the light of the sun above. Smaller avenues crisscrossed the valley in the other direction, intersecting with even more roads to form neat city blocks of smaller, one-story structures made of what looked like adobe brick that spread out all the way to the edges of the valley. Toward the center of the metropolis, the buildings got taller. Four and five stories. They surrounded an enormous central square anchored at each corner by a large step pyramid as big as the one within which he had sheltered with Cade, Decker, and the others before making his escape. And at the center of the square, the biggest pyramid of all. It dwarfed every other structure in the city, rising what Chava estimated to be a staggering six or seven hundred feet, nearly three times the size of the Great Pyramid of Cholula, the largest such Aztec structure on earth, and even more impressive than the Great Pyramid of Giza in Egypt. He could only imagine how much ground the structure consumed, but it had to be half a dozen football fields and maybe more. At the top, on a platform at least a couple of acres in size, was the most stunning temple he had ever seen. It almost seemed to glow under the rays of the sun, glittering so brightly that at first he had to squint when he looked at it. And then he realized why. The entire temple was completely clad in gold.

Chava could hardly believe what he was looking at. It was beautiful. Awe-inspiring. It was overwhelming. It felt like the home he had yearned for his entire life. Maybe on some higher level, he had always had a connection with this place. Certainly, he had never felt fully connected to those around him back on Earth. To the places he had lived. He had been a loner. A soul adrift. Maybe that was why he was so suited to being a Watcher. His consciousness straddled two planes of existence. His ancestors had believed in the fundamental duality that permeated all facets of their lives. Chava was the living embodiment of that belief. And now, he was about to fulfill a destiny that had been predetermined before he had even been born. But there was still one thing left to do.

Feeling lighter than he had in years, Chava started down toward the city, even as the whispering in his head grew clearer and more insistent.

# FIFTY

THEY HAD LEFT the ruined city behind many hours ago and were now being marched through dense jungle under the brutal heat of the afternoon sun, hands bound behind their backs with thin strips of vine that were much stronger than they looked. At first, after their captors had appeared, Decker thought Cade might resist, but apparently the commander knew a hopeless situation when he saw one, and had allowed the warriors to take their weapons. But Decker suspected there was another motive for Cade's swift acquiescence beyond the obvious—that they were hopelessly outnumbered and would never have been able to shoot their way out of the situation before being impaled by spears. Chava was gone, and so was the orb. He had left them stranded and condemned to a certain death once nightfall came and the creatures that had killed Rivera returned. Because there was no way they would be able to fight off another such attack with their limited amount of ammunition. Allowing themselves to be captured by these warriors was not so much an admittance of defeat as it was a tactic for survival.

"Who are these guys?" Abby asked, stumbling along next to Rory.

"If I had to guess, the men we saw at the base of the pyramid are Jaguar Warriors," Rory said, keeping his voice low even though their captors didn't appear to care if they talked among themselves. "They're dressed in animal skins and carry clubs inlaid with what looks like a volcanic glass similar to obsidian. I've read about the Jaguar Warriors, even worked on an excavation down in Mexico and uncovered Jaguar Warrior artifacts, but it's incredible to see them in the flesh."

"And the other guys?" Abby glanced toward the spear-carrying warriors. Unlike their animal skin clad counterparts, these men wore breastplates and tunics adorned with white feathers, and a red sash around their waists. Their helmets were fashioned to represent the head of a bird with vibrant colored plumage, and a beak curving down over their foreheads. They carried shields similarly decorated with feathers and carved with the same bird motif as their helmets.

"Eagle Warriors," Rory replied. "Although those feathers on their uniforms are much too large to have come from any eagle. This is living history that we are experiencing. It's incredible."

"That's not quite how I'd put it," Cade said. "I don't suppose you speak their language?"

"No." Rory shook his head. "But I wish I did. Imagine what they could teach us about the culture from which they evolved back on Earth."

Cade sounded disappointed. "I was thinking more like finding out what their intentions are toward us. If we can't talk to them, we won't know what they plan to do with us. I'd hate to end up at the top of one of those pyramids getting my heart cut out as an offering to their gods."

"I'm sure that . . . I mean . . ." Rory sounded flustered. "Actually, you probably don't even want to know."

Cade glanced back over his shoulder at the archaeologist. "I have a feeling that I do."

Rory took a deep breath. "Eagle Warriors had a very specific role in the Aztec military. Namely, capturing prisoners to be used in their ceremonies as human sacrifices. In fact, you couldn't even become an Eagle Warrior until you'd captured twenty prisoners for sacrifice."

"That doesn't bode well for us."

"If it makes you feel any better, they might not kill us right away," Rory said. "And they won't necessarily cut out our hearts. They killed people in a variety of fun ways, including drowning, impaling, and flaying. They even pitted prisoners against each other in gladiatorial-style combat, depending on the deity receiving the sacrifice."

"Let's hope it doesn't come to that," Cade said with a scowl. "There must be a way to communicate with these people. Make them understand we mean no harm."

"Good luck," Decker said. Other than shouting commands and poking them with spears, the warriors had shown little interest in bridging the language barrier.

"I'm not sure it would do any good, even if we could communicate with them," Rory said. "Eagle Warriors were single-minded in their devotion to capturing prisoners for sacrifice. These men probably don't care how friendly we are."

"Where do you think they're taking us?" Abby asked, looking around as they walked.

"Wherever it is can't be too far away," said Rory, studying the small contingent of Jaguar Warriors who were taking the lead as they hacked their way through the jungle. "These men are traveling light. They only have small animal-skin canteens of water hanging off their belts. No food, no extra weaponry, nothing. They aren't on an extended scouting or hunting trip."

A horrible thought occurred to Decker. "They were looking for us. We lit a fire in the temple at the top of the pyramid last night. It would have been visible for miles. They must have seen it."

"And that got them wondering who was out there in a city that was supposed to be abandoned," Rory said. "We should have been more careful."

"We made an error of judgment," Decker said. "We found

that ruined city and assumed that whoever had built it was long gone, and that we were alone here, which is clearly not the case."

"We should not have advertised our presence, it's true," Cade said. "But our error might yet prove to be a fortuitous one."

"I don't see how," Rory said.

"It's simple. Chava was expecting his people to still be here. My guess is that he intended to hand us over to them." Cade glanced around, studying the faces of the warriors to see if any of them were paying their prisoners any attention. When he realized that they were not, he continued in hushed tones. "When he realized the city was nothing but a ruin, and his people were not there, he drugged and left us for dead, then stole the orb."

Decker realized what Cade was saying. "You think Chava suspected his people were still out there somewhere, and he went looking for them."

"That's exactly what I think. It's the only logical conclusion. What would be the point of incapacitating us and stealing the orb just to wander aimlessly in a jungle on a world he knows nothing about? It would be as much a potential death sentence for him as his betrayal could have been for us."

"But why?" Abby asked. "The orb doesn't even work anymore."

"I'm not so sure about that," Decker said. "I've been giving it some thought, and I don't know how, but I suspect it was Chava who stopped the orb from working. He gave us that story about it needing to recharge at the top of the pyramid, but as we've already discussed, that doesn't make any sense given the alien origin of the technology."

"He lied so that we would go with him to the city," Rory said.

"Yes. At least, if my theory is right."

Abby shook her head. "That still doesn't explain *why* he did it."

"Because his people have been trapped here for hundreds of years, ever since the conquistadors stole the orb." Cade's face was dark as thunder. "I assume he wants to bring them home."

"He didn't have to betray us to do that," Decker said. "He could have just told us the truth."

"I'm not sure it's that easy," Cade said. "We have no idea how large the civilization on this planet has become since their forced exile. There might be hundreds of thousands, even millions of people here. An entire population like that suddenly returning to Earth would cause havoc. And they would probably want their old lands back. It would be a bloodbath. He knew we wouldn't allow him to give them the orb, just like we cannot allow him to do so now."

"That's why you let us get captured, isn't it?" Rory said. "You figured they would lead us to him."

"Yes."

"How do you propose we stop Chava and get the orb back even if we *do* find him?"

"I have no idea," Cade admitted. "At least not yet."

"You'd better think fast," Decker said, because ahead of them the jungle thinned out, and beyond it was a lush valley within which lay a sprawling city with an enormous golden pyramid at its center. "Because I think we are at the end of our journey."

# FIFTY-ONE

UPON ENTERING THE CITY, they were marched straight toward the central pyramid, passing through narrow streets and then along a wide main avenue to the base of the massive structure. Decker was surprised at how quiet the place was. The streets were empty, even though it was still afternoon. There were no merchants going about their business. No children playing. None of the hustle and bustle he would have associated with such a large metropolis. The city felt deserted, but Decker knew that it wasn't, because as they were herded past low one-story dwellings, he saw gaunt faces peering out at them from the darkness behind the windows. Men and women who looked almost like ghosts, watching with an expression that Decker could only describe as fear.

Soon, they reached the pyramid. But they did not climb the steps leading to the glittering temple of gold sitting atop the enormous structure. Instead, they entered through a small door at the base of the structure and descended into the bowels of the building along a narrow tunnel lit only by flickering torches. After a while, they reached a larger square chamber, where they were handed over to grim looking men dressed in leather tunics who cut the cords of vine that bound their wrists, then forced them down another narrow corridor, only wide enough for them to pass in single file, which ended in a set of steep steps that looked like they had been carved from bedrock, at the bottom of which was a much larger space with at least half a dozen prison cells on each side. The cells were constructed of thick stone blocks and had doors with bars fashioned from what looked like iron. The air was heavy and stale and carried a faint odor of decay. They were separated into two groups, with Decker, Rory and Abby forced into one cell, while Cade and Saunders were hustled into another. After locking the doors with large keys hanging from their belts, their captors retreated, leaving them alone.

Decker looked around. The cell was dark, illuminated only by weak light that spilled through the bars from torches burning in the central area. But it was enough for him to see two stone ledges fashioned from large blocks, one on each side of the small room, which presumably served as places to lie down even though there were no mattresses, blankets, or any other concessions made to the comfort of those held within the chamber. A wooden bucket setting the corner, from which wafted a foul stench of excrement that provided a clue to its reason for being there. And it was cold. Freezing, in fact, which led Decker to believe that they were not merely inside the pyramid, but some distance beneath it and underground. For all intents and purposes, they were in a dungeon.

"This is pleasant," Rory said, wrinkling his nose. "The food here had better be good, or it's not getting more than two stars from me."

"We've been in worse," Decker said.

"Have we, though?" Rory crossed to one of the stone ledges and sat down as far from the rank-smelling bucket as possible.

"How can the two of you be so flippant?" Abby asked, pacing the small cell with clenched fists.

"Because getting ourselves worked into a panic won't do any good," Decker told her. He went to the door and peered out through the bars toward the cell opposite, where Cade and Saunders were being held. "You guys okay over there?"

"Yes," came the answer. Cade's face appeared at the bars. "For now, at least. Did you notice how quiet the city was?"

Decker nodded. "It was unnatural. I saw some people looking out through their windows, and they looked scared."

"Thoughts?"

"I don't know. But my gut is telling me that something is very wrong here." Decker grabbed hold of the bars, tested the door. It felt solid. He reached around and explored the lock and keyhole with his fingers. If he had possessed anything with which to pick the lock, he might have been able to release them, but he didn't. Giving up, he turned and walked to the ledge, then sat down next to Rory, resting his head against the wall.

"What are you doing?" Abby asked, a note of panic creeping into her voice. "You're just going to sit down and give up?"

"I'm not giving up," Decker said. "I'm waiting. It's not like there's much else we can do until those guards come back."

"And then?"

Decker shrugged. "Your guess is as good as mine."

# FIFTY-TWO

SEVERAL HOURS PASSED before the guards returned carrying metal bowls containing a thin porridge, and cups of water, which they pushed through narrow slots in the bottom of the cell doors. When he saw the guards, Decker jumped up and raced to the bars where he tried to engage them, demanding to see whoever was in charge, but his pleas fell on deaf ears. Or, more likely, ears that didn't have a clue what he was saying. On a whim, he mentioned Chava, hoping to elicit some glimmer of recognition, because if their double-crossing companion had made it to the city, he was certainly not languishing in this dungeon. But this too failed to garner a response, and he watched helplessly as the guards turned and left without uttering a single word, leaving behind the food and water.

Rory picked up one of the bowls and sniffed it warily.

"Doesn't smell too bad," he said, taking the spoon that stuck up out of the soupy gruel and trying some.

"Stop. What are you doing?" Abby jumped to her feet. "For all you know that stuff might be poisoned."

"Relax," Decker said. "If they wanted us dead, there are more direct ways to do it than locking us in a dungeon and then surreptitiously poisoning our dinner."

"I suspect that they *do* want us dead," Rory said, dipping the spoon into the porridge again. "But not at this moment. We were captured by Eagle Warriors, which means that our eventual fate will be much grislier than being killed by tainted food." He took another mouthful and nodded appreciably. "You should try it. This isn't actually all that bad."

"You're only saying that because we've barely had a thing to eat in two days," Decker said, picking up the other two bowls and handing one to Abby, while keeping the other for himself. "But regardless, we should eat, because we need to keep our strength up."

"I think I'll pass if it's all the same with you," Abby said, sniffing the concoction with obvious disdain.

"John's right, you need nourishment," Rory said. "Just imagine that it's a nice bowl of oatmeal with maple syrup on top."

"Is that what it tastes like?"

"Not in the least."

"That's what I thought," Abby shot back, but even so, she picked up the spoon and took a tentative bite, then started to eat, slowly at first and then with more gusto.

"Thought you weren't going to have any of it?" Decker asked, bemused as he finished his own bowl.

"Yeah, well, like you said, I need to keep my strength up." Abby picked up a cup of water and drank deeply. "Doesn't mean that I enjoyed it." She set her empty bowl back on the floor and returned to the ledge, where she sat down and closed her eyes.

Several more hours passed, although it was impossible to tell how long because their cell contained no windows or any other means with which to gauge the passage of time. Decker had conversed briefly with Cade across the open space between their cells, but there wasn't much to say, so he sat back down and was soon overcome by a deep weariness. They had been walking all day, and he was exhausted. He yawned and closed his eyes and soon fell into a fitful sleep despite the uncomfortable nature of their digs.

He dreamed of being lost in an endless jungle at night, and stalked by dark, shadowy creatures with glowing red eyes and gaping maws. They chased him through the undergrowth, gaining with every passing moment even as he struggled to escape on legs that felt as heavy as lead. Finally, he came to a huge crumbling pyramid overgrown with vines. With nowhere else to go, he started to climb, pulling himself up the steep stone steps leading to the top of the pyramid, and the temple at its summit, while behind him, the creatures drew inexorably closer.

Decker pulled himself over the rim, drenched in sweat, chest heaving. He looked back down, expecting to find the creatures snapping at his ankles, but instead they had come to a halt and were now waiting on the steps below, hunkered down and silently watching. First, he didn't know why, but when he turned and stepped into the temple, the reason became clear. He wasn't alone. A dark figure stood facing away from him and staring through a window at the vast jungle below. A black outline silhouetted against the window frame that almost seemed to weave and shift in the darkness as if it were made of pure smoke. It reeked of malevolence. Thick. Tangible. Terrifying.

At first, he wondered if the figure realized he was there, but then a voice echoed in his head, deep and resonant. Full of menace. "You have my gratitude. I have waited so long to be free."

Decker stepped into the temple. "What are you?"

The figure ignored him.

"Answer me."

For a moment, he received no response, then the figure spoke in a voice that seemed to reverberate all the way down to Decker's bones. "I am the destroyer. The eater of souls. I am chaos."

The figure shifted and undulated. Fingers of smoke wafted

around it in wispy curls. It twisted and writhed in a furious maelstrom of coiled strands. Then, before Decker could react, the figure exploded toward him with a chilling screech . . .

# FIFTY-THREE

JOHN!" Rory's voice cut through Decker's nightmare, jolting him awake. He sat up quickly and looked around, realizing that he had been lying on the stone ledge in their cell.

"What is it?"

"Something's going on."

From beyond the cell, there was a commotion. Several guards had entered, dragging a partially limp body between them. They went to the cell next to the one in which they had put Cade and Saunders and opened it.

Decker jumped up in time to see them dragging their captive inside, and he recognized the man immediately. It was Chava. And he looked dreadful. His shirt and shoes were gone, and his pants were bloody. There were deep lacerations across his chest, and what looked like cuts on the soles of his feet. But it was his face that shocked Decker the most. He had a split lip, and his nose was clearly broken. One eye was swollen shut.

"It looks like they tortured him," Rory whispered, peering over Decker's shoulder. "I guess they weren't as friendly as he thought they would be."

"Apparently not." Decker watched as the guards dumped Chava unceremoniously on the floor of the cell and retreated, slamming the cell door behind them and locking it. One of them turned back and spoke through the bars, but Decker didn't understand what he said.

Somewhere within the cell, came a mumbled reply in the same foreign tongue.

*At least he's not dead*, thought Decker with relief, because right now, Chava was their only hope of opening a line of dialog with their captors.

The guards turned and left, ignoring their other prisoners.

Chava's prone form was barely visible in the dim light, sprawled on the floor of the cell. For a short while, he lay still, then he moved, dragging himself forward until he reached the door and grabbing hold of the bars to pull himself up to a sitting position.

After a few moments, he gathered the energy to talk, his voice heavy with pain. "I don't suppose I am exactly in your good books right now," he said quietly to no one in particular.

"You drugged us, stole the orb, and left us to die," Cade replied. "What do you think?"

"I am sorry, my friend," Chava said. "I truly am. I meant no harm to any of you and planned to send help back for you once I found my people and the orb was safe."

"Yeah, well, your people found us on their own," Abby said. "And for the record, they aren't exactly friendly."

"Judging by his condition, I think he's already found that out," Decker said to her, before turning his attention back to Chava in the cell opposite. "What happened?"

"And start at the beginning," Cade said. "We need to know everything if we're going to get out of here."

"Very well." Chava shifted position, turning slightly so that he could look out of the cell toward Decker. "There is a legend among my people. A story about an orb sent to us as a gift from the gods, that had the power to open a gateway to Omeyocan, the highest of the thirteen realms of heaven. It was a verdant world abundant with gold. My ancestors built a city called

Aztlan with a magnificent pyramid at the center and built a temple on top to hold the orb. It was from that pyramid that they opened the gateway to Omeyocan and mined the gold. But in the year 1524, the conquistadors found and sacked the city after witnessing huge amounts of gold flowing through the portal. They didn't understand how it worked or what it was, but that didn't matter. They decided to steal the orb, take the orb back to the king of Spain, so that he could enrich himself. But they got greedy and decided to keep on sailing up the Sea of Cortez, now known as the Gulf of California, looking for more treasure. Back then, the Sea of Cortez connected to the Salton Sea at certain times of the year. When they couldn't find a northern passage out into the Pacific Ocean, they turned around only to find that they were trapped because the estuary connecting the two bodies of water had retreated. The ship ended up beached and lost to the sands, while the men she carried presumably died of thirst in the desert."

"Okay, maybe not start quite so far back," Rory said. "We know this part. I know Cade said to start at the beginning, but you can skip the history lesson."

Chava coughed. "Very well. My people vowed to get the orb back. There was only one problem. They didn't know where it was. To that end, they created a sect called the Watchers. Men and women with the power of second sight who would know when the orb was found and make sure the prophecy was fulfilled."

"What prophecy?"

"In order to mine the gold, my people built a city here in Omeyocan that grew to house tens of thousands, including large contingents of both Jaguar and Eagle Warriors. When the conquistadors attacked Aztlan and closed the portal, stole the orb, they trapped those people here with no way to get home. The prophecy says that once the orb is found, and the portal reopened, those warriors will flow through and reclaim the lands stolen from them by the Spanish."

"So what happened to the city on this side of the portal?" Decker asked. "You said that the conquistadors attacked Aztlan, but the city we found here was also ruined, so how did it get that way? Was there a war at some point?"

"No. Not a war. When the conquistadors, who had no idea what they were doing, closed the portal on their side, it caused a cataclysm that destroyed much of the city here on this side and almost wiped out the people living there. The survivors relocated to this valley and built a new civilization. There was one problem. The void between worlds is not empty. A powerful entity resides there and yearns to escape its isolation. My people realized this soon after the orb first arrived and found a way to contain the entity and to keep it sated."

"Human sacrifices," Rory said. "And lots of them."

"Yes. After the cataclysm, the portal didn't completely close on this side, so my people here continued the tradition. It was the only way to keep the entity at bay."

"What kind of entity?" Decker asked, an icy chill enveloping him.

"We call it Tezcatlipoca," Chava said, his voice strained. "The God of Chaos."

# FIFTY-FOUR

DECKER'S THOUGHTS flew back to the nightmare he was having just a few brief minutes before—the shadowy figure in the temple at the top of the pyramid—and his stomach twisted in knots.

*I am the destroyer. The eater of souls. I am chaos.*

Was it possible that Chava was describing the same entity that he had dreamed about? There is only one way to find out.

"Tell me more about this God of Chaos," Decker said.

"Very well. As I told you, I am a member of an ancient sect called the Watchers. There are only a handful of us left, and all but a few are now of an advanced age. One of those elders, a powerful seer, received a vision of the orb being found in the California desert. He warned me that the ancient prophecies were not correct. That something had changed, and that if the orb fell into the wrong hands, a great evil would be unleashed upon the world. I thought he meant the men who attacked and almost killed us. They surely did not have pure intentions for the orb. But I was mistaken." Chava lowered his voice, even as his words to, somber tone. "It was not the men back there in the desert that we had to fear, but these people, the descendants of my own ancestors. Like I said, when the Spaniards stole the orb, they did not close the connection between worlds correctly and created a tear in the fabric of space-time on this side that would not heal itself. The rift was small, and for centuries the people here contained Tezcatlipoca in the void between dimensions. But eventually, the rift grew too large, and he escaped his interdimensional confinement and forced those who live in this realm to do his bidding. But Tezcatlipoca was not satisfied with the meager offerings on this world. They could not offer enough human sacrifices to keep him sated without depleting their numbers to the point of unsustainability. He yearned for more. He knew that one day, someone would find the orb, and the gateway between worlds would open once more. And then, he would have access to a world of billions instead of thousands."

"You're talking about Earth," Rory said.

"Yes. An entire world waiting to be subjugated, and a limitless supply of souls upon which to feast. But I made a terrible mistake. I thought that bringing us to Omeyocan would save humanity. That if I brought the orb here, it would be beyond the reach of those who would accidentally unleash Tezcatlipoca's scourge upon the Earth. Of course, it meant that none of us would ever return home, but it was a small price to pay for saving humanity."

Cade snorted. "You were going to leave us stranded here forever?"

"I made a decision in the heat of the moment. I could not let those men back aboard the *San Isadore* kill us and take the orb. Likewise, I could not trust Mr. Decker to secure our escape. His control over the orb might not have been strong enough. I did what was necessary for the greater good."

"How's that working for you?" Cade said, his voice laced with anger.

"Not so well. Tezcatlipoca sensed it the moment we arrived here. After we found the ruined city, he reached out to me. Spoke in my mind. Told me to bring the orb here, to the new city my ancestors built after the cataclysm. That is why I drugged you and stole the orb."

"You thought that bringing the orb to the entity that wants to destroy humanity was the best course of action?" Cade asked.

"I was deceived. I thought it was my people who were reaching out, but it was really Tezcatlipoca, who has my people under his full control. The moment I arrived here, they arrested me and took the orb, but they could not get it to work."

"Well, that's something at least," Rory said. "I guess the orb really is broken."

"No. Not broken. The orb exists in dimensional flux. It has the capacity to be in multiple realities at the same time or to be nowhere at all. It can exist outside of its physical form or cease to exist completely within the linear flow of time. After we arrived here, I sent it away and blocked its energy from inhabiting this realm so that it could not be used to go back to Earth."

Abby looked perplexed. "I don't understand. You didn't send the orb away. It's still here. I've seen it."

"What you saw is the physical representation of the orb within our observational reality," Rory said. "But the essence of the orb, the part of it that connects with whoever is operating the device, is on another plane of existence entirely."

"Huh?" Abby didn't look any less confused. "So the orb is here, but it's also not here?"

Chava's voice drifted across the open space between their cells. "That is correct. I sent it to the liminal space between dimensions and have been keeping it there through the force of my will. When Tezcatlipoca realized what I had done, he ordered me to be tortured. He thought that inflicting unbearable pain would force me to release my hold upon the orb."

"That's horrible," Abby said.

"It was distinctly unpleasant, but I was able to endure through the pain, at least so far. But I am sure they will come back and take me again, and then I might not be so fortunate."

"Torture has never been an effective method of getting a

prisoner to do what you want, despite its widespread use throughout the ages," Cade said. "It also doesn't make sense in this situation. This Tezcatlipoca creature, or whatever the hell it is, doesn't need information. It wants you to relinquish control of the orb. It could accomplish that simply by killing you."

"But he can't," Chava said. "Tezcatlipoca is afraid that if I die, and my mental connection to the orb's essence is abruptly severed, it will stay where I sent it, forever beyond his reach. He will not take that chance. That is why he paused my torture. But they will take me again, and this time, I am not sure that I have the stamina to keep resisting."

"Is that true?" Abby asked. "That if you die, the orb will never work again?"

"I don't know," Chava replied in a voice barely above a whisper. "But neither does Tezcatlipoca."

# FIFTY-FIVE

"WHAT EXACTLY ARE we dealing with here?" Decker asked, looking at Rory.

Chava had fallen silent quite some time ago and now appeared to be sleeping with his back pressed up against the bars of the cell opposite. Or maybe he was unconscious. It was hard to tell. Decker hoped the wounds inflicted upon him by his torturers would not prove fatal. Otherwise, they really might be stranded here forever.

"I've heard of Tezcatlipoca," Rory said. "He was one of the most important deities in Aztec religion and was associated with all sorts of things, like obsidian, hurricanes, divination, temptation, sorcery, the night sky, and warfare. He had his own festival called Toxcatl, which, like many Aztec festivals, was centered around human sacrifice."

"Kind of a jack of all trades," Decker said.

"Right. But just like the rest of the Aztec gods, he wasn't real, of course. Not in a literal sense. Like all civilizations, they were trying to explain the world around them in ways they could relate to. Find reason in the chaos."

Decker shuddered when Rory said that word. He remembered the dark figure in his nightmare uttering that word.

Was it possible that his sleeping mind had somehow interacted with the consciousness of a real-life god? After what Chava had told them, it certainly appeared that his nightmare had been more than a disturbing fantasy. But he decided not to mention that.

At least, not yet. "If we believe what Chava said, then Tezcatlipoca is absolutely real."

But Rory wasn't so sure. "Whatever escaped into this world and is now apparently controlling the people of this city isn't Tezcatlipoca. The concept of him, along with all their other gods, predates the arrival of the orb and any encounters they might have had with an entity in the void between dimensions. I suspect that they simply projected the idea of their God onto a real and dangerous entity that then saw the opportunity to manipulate them."

Cade had been listening. His voice drifted from the opposite cell. "If it isn't an ancient Aztec god, then what exactly *are* we dealing with?"

"That's the million-dollar question," Rory said. "It might be a life form from another dimension that somehow got trapped inside the void, or maybe a being that originated in the space between dimensions."

"Or it might have been put there deliberately," said Abby. "Because if the space between dimensions is the entity's natural habitat, then why would it want to escape so badly?"

Rory nodded. "You mean like a cosmic prison cell."

"Exactly." Abby was talking fast now, the words tumbling over each other in a breathless stream.

"Whether it came from the void, or was imprisoned in the void, makes no difference," Decker said. "It has escaped and apparently has the people living in the city under its thrall."

"And if the entity gets its way, it will use the orb to go somewhere with richer pickings," Rory said. "Namely Earth. The question is how do we stop it? Chava won't be able to hold out forever."

Decker thought about this for a moment but did not come up with an easy answer. Destroying the orb—assuming it was even possible—would trap the entity in this dimension forever. But it would also mean that they could never return home, and it would doom the people here to a lifetime of servitude and misery, neither of which was an acceptable option. But when Chava finally relinquished his control of the device, which would surely happen at some point given his weakened condition, the entity would get its way, and the seer's vision would become reality. The Earth, and its billions of inhabitants, would end up as nothing but cattle to be consumed by a creature that was clearly ancient, and might be as old as the universe itself. There was only one acceptable solution. "We have to force Tezcatlipoca back into the void and close the portal."

Rory stared at him. "Great. Do you have any idea of exactly how we accomplish that? Because I'm pretty sure that asking nicely won't do the trick."

Decker sat down. He leaned his head back against the wall. "If I did, I'd tell you."

Rory sat down on the opposite ledge. "That's what I thought." He sounded defeated.

Decker closed his eyes, but this time he was determined to stay awake. The last thing he needed was another encounter with an entity that had the ability to enter the mind of anyone it desired, and if what Chava said was correct, control them, too. But there must be limits to the entity's power, because it had not been able to influence Chava's mind, perhaps because he had developed strong mental fortifications against such manipulation.

Several hours passed.

The guards returned with more bowls of the same thin porridge, which they ate in silence. Even Chava managed to force some down, although he soon dropped the bowl and appeared to drift back out of consciousness. Either his physical condition was getting worse, or the mental strain of resisting Tezcatlipoca was becoming too much.

After several more hours, the guards returned again, but this time they were not bringing food. They went to Chava's cell, unlocked the door and hauled him to his feet.

Decker stood at the bars of his cell and watched helplessly as they dragged him away. At one point, Chava lifted his head and made eye contact. And in those eyes, Decker saw not just pain, but also defiance. The stoic Watcher was not done yet. But who knew what fresh horrors awaited him in the hours ahead, and how long he would be able to hold out.

# FIFTY-SIX

HE WON'T SURVIVE another torture session," Rory said. "They'll either break him or kill him."

"There's nothing we can do about that," Cade said from across the common area between their cells. "Not unless you can bend iron bars."

This was a sobering thought. No one replied because there was no point. With no means of escaping their cells, they really were powerless. It was beyond frustrating. Decker returned to the ledge and sat back down.

An hour passed, then another.

It had been a while since they had last eaten, and Decker was beginning to think the guards had forgotten about them, or perhaps Chava had given Texcotlipoca what he wanted, and the guards no longer cared whether their captors lived or died. But then footsteps rang on the staircase leading to their dungeon.

Soon, four guards appeared, but they were not accompanying Chava. Neither were they bringing food. Instead, they crossed to the cell. They unlocked the door and stepped inside. Two of the guards Kept Decker and Rory at bay with the same clubs embedded with shards of obsidian that the Jaguar Warriors had carried back at the pyramid, while the other two grabbed Abby and hustled her toward the door, holding her tightly by the arms. They ignored her frantic struggles as they wrestled her out of the cell.

"Don't touch her." Rory tried to sidestep the guards still in the cell. At least, until one of them drove the end of their club into his stomach, causing him to double up in pain. He gasped and staggered backwards, his cheeks puffed out and his face red.

The other guard pointed his club at Decker. A clear warning not to try anything.

Then, both guards retreated quickly and slammed the cell door, locking it again.

Decker watched, helpless, as they dragged Abby away, kicking and squirming in their grasp.

Rory rushed to the bars and strained to look out. "Hey. Where are you taking her?"

The guards did not respond. They continued toward the stone staircase from which they had appeared minutes before. They passed through the door and manhandled Abby up the steps and out of sight. Before long, her terrified protestations faded, and the dungeon descended into morbid silence.

Rory took a couple of steps back, then rushed at the door, slamming his shoulder into it with all his might. He grunted and backed up again. Repeated his charge. The door shook in its frame but held firm.

When he retreated for yet another useless run at the door, Decker stood in his way. "Stop. All you're going to do is hurt yourself, and that will do nothing to help Abby."

"We can't let them take her!"

"And we can't stop them."

"He's right," Cade said. "Now be quiet. Someone is coming."

Decker went to the bars and looked out. Cade was correct. He could hear light footsteps on the steps leading down to the dungeon. After a moment, a figure wearing a hooded robe appeared and crossed to the cell door in front of Decker. The figure lifted his arms and lowered his hood to reveal a young man with tanned bronze skin, dark black eyes, and even blacker hair.

He placed a finger on his lips and produced a key, which he inserted into the lock. A moment later, the door swung open, and the young man moved silently back and motioned for them to step out, then turned to the cell containing Cade and Saunders and unlocked that door as well.

When everyone was free, he motioned again that they should follow him and started toward the steps.

Rory glanced at Decker. "Is this a jailbreak?" He whispered under his breath.

"I believe it might be," Decker replied as they reached the steps and started up.

The robed figure turned and pressed his fingers to his lips again with narrowed eyes. Then he resumed climbing the steps.

They reached the top and navigated the narrow passageway leading to the chamber where the vines tying their wrists had been cut when they first arrived. Other than that, the room was empty. They continued up through the pyramid and finally exited the enormous structure.

It was night. Above them, the twin moons hung in the sky, bathing everything in a silvery glow. The wide central avenue leading up to the pyramid stretched away for as far as the eye could see. But this was not where they were going. Their savior led them off the main thoroughfare and took them down a series of narrow side streets lit with flickering torches that cast long, dancing shadows. Decker tried to keep track of their route so that he could return there once they had secured some weapons and figured out a plan. Abby was out there somewhere, and he had no intention of leaving her to face whatever fate her captors had in mind. But it was pretty much impossible. They were moving fast, and every street looked identical to the last. After a while, he lost track of the twists and turns.

Finally, after walking for at least a mile through the mazelike back streets, they arrived at a nondescript one-story building constructed of adobe brick with small windows covered by closed shutters. The man in the robe knocked on the door twice with a clenched fist and muttered to whoever was on the other side in a language Decker didn't understand. There was a brief exchange and then came the sound of bolts being drawn back.

The door opened, and the robed man ushered them inside. The space beyond the door took up the entire footprint of the building in one large room. There were cots for sleeping along one wall and a large hearth that doubled as both a source of warmth and also a means of cooking food with a cauldron hanging on an arm. A sitting area took up the center of the room. Six people stood observing them with intense curiosity. Four men and two women. One of those, an older gentleman with silver hair and a deeply lined face, approached them. He opened his arms in greeting and said, "Bienvenido. Estás entre amigos."

Decker stared in disbelief. He hadn't understood a single word any of their captors had spoken since they first encountered the Jaguar and Eagle Warriors at the ruined pyramid. But he understood this, or at least he recognized it. The man standing in front of them was speaking Spanish.

# FIFTY-SEVEN

## NORTHERN MEXICO CIRCA 1524

JUAN CAVALLERO PLUNGED his sword into a Jaguar Warrior who towered above him on the steps of the pyramid at the center of the Aztec city. The man had swung his club in what would have been a stunning death blow if Cavallero had not dodged sideways at the last moment. The club had whistled harmlessly past mere inches from his face, leaving his attacker momentarily defenseless. And that was all it took. Cavallero thrust his sword forward, running his adversary through with lightning speed. The Jaguar Warrior dropped his club, looked down in shock as the conquistador withdrew his bloody weapon from the man's chest, then pitched forward and tumbled past him down the steps.

Cavallero wasted no time. He pressed forward toward the temple at the top of the pyramid. A few steps behind him, Captain Francisco de Alvarado, his second-in-command, was busy dispatching a warrior of his own. Around them, locked in furious battle, were a hundred of his men, some of whom were fighting their way to the top of the pyramid, while others defended from below, slaying any Jaguar or Eagle Warriors who tried to ascend behind them. At least a dozen of his men had already fallen to the ferocity of the Aztec warriors, but their superior training and weapons had provided a tactical advantage that had sent at least ten times that many Aztecs to meet their maker.

The sun was poking up over the top of the pyramid now, sending golden rays of light across the jungle below. Cavallero reached the top step, cut down another Jaguar Warrior and tossed his body aside. He could see the temple directly ahead. Stacks of gold bars stood piled neatly on the ledge outside, waiting to be transported to wherever the Aztecs took them to be fashioned into jewelry, ornaments, statues, and even plates. But it was the object inside the temple that held his attention. The orb he had seen from the ridge above the city earlier. The same orb that had somehow burst forth with blinding white light through which Aztecs had appeared carrying all those bars of gold. It still sat in its cradle on the altar, glowing faintly as if resting, and just waiting for him to snatch it up and take it back to Spain where he would present it to the king and share in the wealth that would surely flow through it. Not that he was leaving all the gold that had already emerged from it behind, even if he had to send a runner back to the ship for more men to carry their prize out of the jungle. Or even better, once he vanquished the Aztecs here in this city, he would enlist their help, and anyone who refused would meet the same fate as the steadily shrinking number of warriors defending their temple.

Cavallero made his way onto the platform, ignoring a temple priest, who scurried past him and down the steps, only to be summarily sliced open by one of Cavallero's men even though the priest was unarmed. It wasn't like the man was innocent after all. Who knew how many people the priest had sacrificed over the years, cutting open their chests and ripping out their hearts. It was a vile barbarian practice Cavallero loathed. The priest deserved no mercy.

"There it is," said De Alvarado, mounting the platform, his

sword still dripping with blood. He took a step toward the temple door, his eyes wide with anticipation. Or maybe it was greed.

"No." Cavallero put a restraining hand on the eager captain's shoulder. This was *his* expedition, and he should be the one to take the orb. "It's mine."

He stepped forward and entered the temple. Behind him on the steps of the pyramid, the screams and shouts of battle were fading as the last of the Aztec warriors met their end.

Approaching the altar, he reached out, was about to close his hands over the orb, but then he withdrew them. The air felt strange. Wrong. It was like putting his hands into a nest of invisible swarming insects. He steeled his nerves and tried again, reaching for the orb. But before he could close his hands upon it, the orb lifted from its cradle on its own and hovered as if by magic several inches above the altar.

Cavallero stumbled back, startled, and bumped into De Alvarado.

A deep, vibrating hum filled the air.

From somewhere behind him, Cavallero heard a gasp.

Several soldiers had arrived at the temple now and were crowding the doorway to see the spectacle within.

The hum got louder. It vibrated all the way down to Cavallero's bones. He had felt no fear back when he was on the rise overlooking the city and watching all that gold being produced out of thin air. He was sure he could tame the orb. That whatever witchcraft the Aztecs had used to produce so much gold could be bent to his will. But now that he was experiencing it up close and personal, his resolve had melted. All he wanted to do was turn and run. Flee this place and never come back. But he couldn't. And not only because a horde of gaping conquistadors blocked the doorway, but also because as their leader, he was unwilling to show his fear. Still, he wasn't going to get any closer to the orb. Eventually, he reasoned, it would become inert once more, and then he could take it. Or maybe he would let his captain have the pleasure of being the first to hold the orb, after all.

He turned to De Alvarado.

The order for his captain to pluck the orb out of the air danced on the tip of his tongue.

But before he could utter a word, the temple was engulfed in the same blinding white light that he had seen from their jungle vantage point earlier. Except now, they were in the middle of it. He felt a moment of weightlessness, coupled with a strange sensation of being pulled in a hundred different directions all at once. Then, just as quickly as the terrifying light had erupted, it faded away.

Cavallero lifted an arm and shielded his eyes against a sudden glare that came not from the orb, but from the sun. But not *his* sun, because when his eyes adjusted to the brightness, he saw the faint outlines of not one but two moons hanging in a deep and cloudless blue sky. He was still standing in a temple atop a pyramid, but this one was larger and looked much newer. He went to the door in a daze, looked out over a sprawling city that he did not recognize. Even the jungle had changed. High above them, swooping in the sky, was a gigantic beast with leathery wings and a long neck that Cavallero could only describe as a demon.

It was like something from a fever dream.

He couldn't help wondering if he had died in that strange explosion and was now in hell. But if that were the case, he hadn't gone there alone, because at least ten of his men, including De Alvarado, had been swept up in the burst of light and transported to this strange and unholy land along with him.

He felt a vague sense of relief.

But it was short-lived. Because, to his horror, Cavallero realized they were not alone. Aztec warriors were ascending the steps of the pyramid. Dozens of them, with clubs and spears at the ready.

Without a moment's hesitation, he turned to his second-in-command and barked a terse order to engage the enemy.

De Alvarado waved the men forward, then rushed at one of the Jaguar Warriors, who had made it to the platform atop the pyramid, and killed the man with the brutal sweep of his sword, thus proving that this was not, indeed, the afterlife.

Cavallero watched as dozens more Aztec warriors arrived on the platform and swarmed his men. Pulsing white light still filled the temple. And then he realized. The orb had somehow created a doorway to this place, and it was still open. All he had to do was walk through it, and he would be safe.

Cavallero glanced over his shoulder. His men were still battling the Aztec warriors. He briefly considered drawing his sword to help them. But that would be foolish. It was clear they were outnumbered and would soon be defeated. Better to withdraw and escape back to their own world. All he had to do was give the order, but he didn't. Because the Aztecs were almost upon the temple and might kill them all before they could do so. Or rather, they might kill *him*. No, better they keep fighting and allow him to escape. It meant his men would be stranded here, but their sacrifice was a small price to pay, at least in Cavallero's mind. His mind made up, Cavallero turned and walked into the light, and back to his own world, even as the portal shrank and closed behind him.

# FIFTY-EIGHT

## PRESENT DAY

FOR A MOMENT, Cade looked taken aback, then he replied to the man, also speaking Spanish. After conversing for a minute, he turned to Decker. "He wants to help us."

"That's great," Decker said. "But why is he speaking Spanish? The people on this world are descended from the Aztecs, not the conquistadors."

Rory nodded. "That's right. He should be speaking Classical Nahuatl." He turned to Decker. "That's the language of the Aztec empire. Variations of it are still spoken by scattered communities in rural parts of Central Mexico today, although none of those variants are the same as the classical tongue and most would probably be unintelligible to a fifteenth-century Aztec."

Decker nodded briefly. "Well?"

"He's speaking Spanish because he's descended from both the Aztecs and the conquistadors. His name is Cualli de Alvarado. His ancestor was stranded here centuries ago along with the Aztecs," Cade said. "But his lineage isn't important. Right now, all you need to know is that some of the inhabitants of the city have been able to resist the influence of Tezcatlipoca since he escaped the void and took control. But the entity has total control of their emperor, Yaotl. They have maintained a low profile until now, but they view our arrival as a good omen. A sign they should fight and reclaim the city."

"How did they know we're here?" Rory asked.

"They have eyes and ears inside the warrior class, and sympathizers among the nobility and high priests."

"Great," Decker said. "Does Cualli know where Abby was taken and why?"

Cade turned back to Cualli, and there was another brief conversation before he addressed Decker again. "He doesn't know. Not for sure. But he said no one ever leaves the cells under the pyramid and lives to tell the tale. If she was taken from your cell by the guards, then it probably means they intend to sacrifice her."

Rory went pale. "We have to stop them. This is all my fault. She's only here because of me."

Decker put a hand on his shoulder. "She forced her way onto the expedition through her own stubbornness. Whatever happens, you are not to blame." He turned to Cade. "That said, Rory is correct. We have to stop them."

"Easier said than done. The guards will have taken Abby to the temple on top of the pyramid to be prepared, but it will be almost impossible to reach her. The pyramid will be heavily guarded by Eagle Warriors. And it gets worse. There aren't supposed to be any ceremonies in the next few days. If they've taken her to be sacrificed, then the emperor must have decided to perform an unscheduled ritual, which hardly ever happens."

"I can only think of one reason why they would do that," Rory said.

Decker nodded slowly. "Chava."

"He looked dreadful when they dragged him off," Cade said. "It was only a matter of time before they either killed or broke him."

"I wonder which it was?" Decker mused.

"Impossible to say, but Tezcatlipoca was apparently worried that Chava dying would render the orb forever useless. I don't see him taking a chance like that."

"Neither do I," Decker said. Despite everything, he was relieved that Chava might still be alive. The man had betrayed them, but he had done so for noble reasons. In a similar situation, Decker might have done the same. In fact, if stopping Tezcatlipoca meant destroying the orb—assuming that was even possible—he would not hesitate, even though it would doom them to a life trapped in this strange world. Because the alternative was too awful to contemplate. He had to protect Earth and everyone on it . . . He had to protect Nancy. "If Chava was unable to hold out, Tezcatlipoca won't waste any time using the orb and opening a portal."

"I agree." Cade turned back to Cualli, but at that moment, there were two short, sharp knocks on the front door.

Everyone froze.

Cualli motioned to one of the other men, who approached the door and spoke in a low voice. There was a reply in the same undecipherable Aztec tongue that Decker had heard everyone except Cualli using. For a moment, he feared that their escape had been discovered, and they had been tracked to this home on the outskirts of the city. For all he knew, there was a contingent of Jaguar or Eagle Warriors waiting in the streets right now to drag them back to that dank, dark dungeon. But his fears were put to rest when the man who had approached the door pulled back the sturdy bolts holding it closed and swung it open. A young woman with large dark eyes, long black hair that had been tied tightly at the back of her head, and an attractive oval face stood on the other side. She wore a flowing white blouse made of a material that looked a little like silk, and a matching skirt secured with a purple sash. Glancing around nervously, she stepped inside and waited until the door was closed and locked before approaching Cualli. After a few moments of conversation, Cualli turned to Cade and spoke again, this time in Spanish.

"What is it?" Decker asked him when the brief exchange was over. "What's going on?"

"This woman is a priestess of the temple. Her name is Izel. Like Cualli and the others here, she has been able to resist the entity that calls itself Tezcatlipoca, but she has remained silent until now for fear of being put to death, as have most of the others who have resisted his control. But she can stand idle no longer, because Chava failed, and now Tezcatlipoca has gained control over the orb. There will be a ceremony during which he will open a portal to Earth and go through it."

Decker almost didn't want to hear the answer, but he had to know. "And Abby?"

"They're going to sacrifice her at dawn, as the first rays of the morning sun hit the altar, as an offering to sustain him on his journey." Cade clenched his fists. "Which isn't good, because that's less than two hours away."

# FIFTY-NINE

THEY MADE their way toward the pyramid under the cover of darkness. The curfew was still in place until dawn, so they split up into small groups of five or six and took different routes through the back streets where they were less likely to be noticed. There were three dozen of them, including Decker, Rory, Cade, and Saunders. The rest of the contingent were made up of men and women loyal to Cualli, and who were not under the influence of Tezcatlipoca.

In less than half an hour, the sun would rise, and one way or another, this would be over. Either they would be successful, or they would all be dead. Decker tried not to dwell on that unsettling thought, because if they didn't succeed, Tezcatlipoca would pass through the portal to Earth where he would feast on humanity.

Rory pulled at his clothing. Like Decker and the others, he was now wearing a dark-colored robe with a blue sash that Cualli had provided. Unfortunately, the garments were rough and itchy, but they were necessary. If someone spotted them on their way to the pyramid, they would simply look like residents of the city, which would not have been the case in their own clothes. Of course, they were still breaking curfew. "Do we actually have a plan?" He whispered, grimacing when his adjustments made no difference.

"Nothing I have any confidence in," Decker admitted. There had been no time to discuss strategy beyond arming themselves with swords that had been fashioned in the likeness of those the conquistadors had been carrying when they had become stranded here centuries before. Cualli had explained that the Aztecs still preferred their traditional weapons—heavy clubs inlaid with razor-sharp obsidian, which could inflict devastating injuries when swung at an enemy combatant, and wooden throwing spears, also tipped with obsidian. Spanish-style swords, he had told them, were more often used by the common classes because they were considered an inferior weapon, possibly because of their association with the conquistadors. Thankfully, Cualli had been stockpiling swords, which were easy to get and not tightly controlled by the Aztec military, for this very scenario, and quickly distributed the weapons among their group.

Decker was thankful for this, because if they didn't move fast, Abby would die. But it still wouldn't be easy. They had no idea what kind of resistance they would meet when they reached their destination. All he knew was that they would have to fight their way to the top, overpower the priests and any warriors who were present, capture the orb, and free Abby. After that, it was anyone's guess. Maybe they could destroy the orb—although Decker had his doubts given its alien origin—or send it into the void where it would be forever beyond the reach of Tezcatlipoca and his minions on this world. Of course, if stopping the orb from falling into Tezcatlipoca's hands were that easy, Chava would presumably have done so already.

All in all, it did not look good.

They turned down another dark side street under the shadow of the pyramid, following behind the man Cualli had tasked with getting them safely to their destination. Cualli himself had joined one of the other groups, saying that it would be best if they did not all travel together under the circumstances. For the same reason, he had assigned Cade and Saunders to one of the other groups. Now, they were approaching the rendezvous point at the base of the pyramid, where they would meet again and move on the temple at its apex as one unified force.

"Wait." Rory came to a sudden halt, pointing toward an intersection with a wider avenue a couple of blocks away. There, standing on the corner, was a small group of what looked like Jaguar Warriors.

For a moment, Decker thought the warriors might have seen them, but the men made no attempt to move in their direction. They shrank back into the shadows and pressed themselves flat against the closest building.

Several minutes passed.

The warriors still made no attempt to leave.

Were they stationed there to guard access to the pyramid? If so, it presented a problem. Somehow, they would need to get past these warriors in order to reach the rendezvous point.

More minutes ticked away.

The warriors still had not moved. They stood in a tight group, talking among themselves in low tones. One of them threw his head back and laughed, then slapped the man next to him on the back. It didn't look like they were on high alert, which was probably just as well, although it didn't make getting past them any easier. But then, thankfully, the men moved off, ambling down the street away from them, then turning and disappearing from view.

Decker breathed a sigh of relief. He looked up at the pyramid towering above them and the temple at its apex. The twin moons had slipped below the horizon, and a dense layer of cloud cover blotted out the heavens, but the pyramid was ablaze with light. Torches on poles stood on the steps all the way to the top on all four sides, and the temple itself radiated a warm yellow glow. He could see figures within, moving around as they prepared for the ritual that would begin at dawn. He wondered if one of them was Abby, but it was impossible to tell from such a distance.

They continued on for several minutes, drawing ever closer to the base of the pyramid, until up ahead, they came across another, larger group of figures pressed into the shadows ahead of them. But unlike the warriors they had encountered moments before, these people were friendly.

"Decker," Cade said in a voice barely above a whisper as they drew close. "We were getting worried. What took you so long?"

"Ran into some warriors. Had to wait them out."

"Well, you're here now, so that's all that matters." Cade motioned toward the priestess, Izel. "We have a plan to reach the top of the pyramid unnoticed, but it's risky."

"Tell me," Decker said.

Cade nodded and relayed the plan, talking fast and keeping it brief, because there wasn't much time.

When he was done, it was Decker's turn to nod. "That just might work." His gaze slipped toward the heavens, and his stomach tightened. The sky behind the pyramid had turned from black to a deep blue, and he could see the faint tinge of orange on the horizon. It was almost dawn. In another ten or fifteen minutes, when the first rays of the morning sun streamed into the temple at the top of the pyramid, Abby would lose her life, and Tezcatlipoca would open the portal and pass through it, dooming everyone on Earth.

It was now or never.

Decker's hand dropped to the sword in its scabbard hanging on his sash before he turned to Cade and the others. "Let's finish this."

Then he started toward the pyramid with grim determination.

# SIXTY

BY THE TIME they reached the base of the pyramid, the sky had lightened considerably. Decker hoped the priestess was right, and Abby would not be sacrificed until the first rays of the sun shone into the temple and touched the altar stone, which had not yet happened, but would not be far away. He also hoped the plan Cade had relayed to him would work, because it was their best chance of reaching the top in time. And they were about to find out, because a contingent of stern-faced Jaguar Warriors stood at the base of the pyramid guarding the stairs leading to the temple. He counted fifteen, but more warriors guarded the other approaches to the pyramid, and Decker was sure that if trouble broke out, others would not be far away.

Azel wasn't concerned. She marched up to the warriors, who apparently recognized her as a priestess, because they parted to let her past. But when the rest of their group approached, the guards closed ranks to forbid them passage.

The priestess turned and issued a terse command, pointing to their group, although Decker had no idea what she was saying.

For a moment, the guards hesitated, apparently confused by this turn of events. Then they stepped aside and allowed Decker and the others to continue, although they watched warily as the group passed silently by.

Decker breathed a sigh of relief. He was sure there would be more warriors atop the pyramid, but they had at least avoided one confrontation.

"I wasn't sure that would work," Rory said in a low voice once they were climbing the steps.

"Me neither," Decker admitted. Azel had taken an enormous risk by agreeing to help them reach the summit of the pyramid. She had told the Jaguar Warriors guarding the steps that he and the rest of their group were to be sacrificed to Tezcatlipoca, offering themselves willingly to ensure their place in the afterlife. The Aztecs, from whom these people were descended, had preferred to sacrifice prisoners taken in battle, but here in this new world, cut off from their home, there was no one to fight, so they had developed a system of willing sacrifice. Thankfully, the guards were so used to this that they thought nothing of a priestess bringing sacrificial victims to the temple. Of course, once they reached the top and their true motives were revealed, those same warriors would waste no time in rushing to aid their brethren. They had not so much avoided a battle as delayed one. Decker only hoped that by the time the Jaguar Warriors realized their error and reached the top of the pyramid, it would be too late. The orb would either be destroyed or sent somewhere far away where Tezcatlipoca could not use it. What happened after that was anyone's guess, but Decker suspected it would not end well for any of them, including the priestess. Still, if he had to give up his life to save those he loved back on Earth, then so be it.

They were approaching the top of the pyramid. And just in time.

The sun was starting to poke up over the horizon, illuminating the wide main thoroughfare leading to the pyramid and chasing the darkness away. A few more minutes, and sunlight would spill into the temple, dooming Abby.

Decker pushed himself to climb faster.

Above them, standing at the edge of the platform and guarding the temple, were more Jaguar Warriors. Azel motioned for their group to halt, then ascended the last few steps and spoke to the closest man. But this time, the guards did not stand aside. Instead, they blocked her path.

The conversation became more agitated.

"We might have a problem," Cade muttered under his breath.

"Let's just see what happens," Decker replied. His gaze moved beyond the guards, to the temple. Abby was laying on the altar stone, bound by her wrists and ankles. The clothes she had been wearing when they took her from the cell were gone, replaced by a white wrap skirt and blouse. She lay still, with only the faint rise and fall of her chest indicating she was still alive. Decker suspected she had been drugged. Chava kneeled nearby, hands tied behind his back. He looked worse than when they had taken him away and was clearly struggling to remain upright. A lone Jaguar Warrior guarded him, although it was unlikely that Chava had much fight left in him. On the far side of the altar, standing with his arms folded and head held high, was a man wearing a blue and white robe adorned with gold ornaments, long flowing cloak, and a feathered headdress. He was flanked by two warriors.

Rory leaned close to Decker. "That must be their emperor, Yaotl."

Decker nodded. It was a fair assumption, but there was someone else he was more concerned with. Standing at the head of the altar, brandishing a large dagger, was the high priest. Behind him, on a stone dais, rested the orb. Even from so far away, Decker could feel the charged energy emanating from it. And behind the orb, in the shadows at the back of the temple, something shifted and moved. An undefined shape that writhed and undulated like curling smoke. And in that moment Decker sensed an entity. Felt it touching the edges of his mind. Probing the darkest recesses of his psyche.

Tezcatlipoca knew they were there, and why.

He stepped forward to warn Azel of the danger. Tell her to get back. But then, so fast he barely registered the movement, one of the Jaguar Warriors drew a dagger from his belt and plunged it deep into her chest.

# SIXTY-ONE

NO!" Rory sprang to catch Azel as she fell, clutching her in his arms and lowering her gently to the ground.

Cade drew his sword and lunged forward, striking the Jaguar Warrior with a glancing blow that opened a long gash below his ribcage. He swung the sword again, toppling the man this time and sending him headfirst off the platform and down the side of the pyramid.

Shouts came from below. The men on the ground had seen the commotion and were racing up the steps toward them.

Decker touched his friend's shoulder. Azel's eyes were open, but the light had faded from them. "You can't do anything for her. She's gone. We have to save Abby now."

# SIXTY-TWO

FOR A MOMENT, Rory didn't move. But then he laid Azel gently on the ground and stood up, his face creased with determination. "Let's go get her."

Cade was already on the platform next to the temple with Saunders by his side. Despite the Jaguar Warriors' legendary ferocity, they were no match for the pair's superior skills. Cade easily dispatched another man. Saunders stepped nimbly aside as a guard rushed him, club held high. He dealt his attacker a slicing blow with his sword and toppled him down the steps toward the warriors who were swiftly making their way up from below.

Cualli looked at Decker, and a silent understanding passed between them, before he turned to face the warriors approaching from below, with his people falling in line to his left and right, weapons at the ready.

Decker stepped onto the platform, dodging Cade as he sent another Jaguar Warrior tumbling off the pyramid.

The temple was ahead of them now.

He started toward it, pulling his sword from its sheaf.

But then, from his rear, Rory shouted a frantic warning. "John, look out!"

Decker swiveled to see a Jaguar Warrior bearing down on him with a club in his hands. He twisted sideways as the man swung the club, but it still slammed into his arm and send the sword flying from his grasp. Unarmed and vulnerable, Decker did the only thing he could think of. He lunged forward and grabbed at the club. The obsidian blades embedded along its shaft cut into his palms, but he held on despite the pain, and yanked the weapon out of his attacker's grip, then tossed it aside.

The warrior wasn't done yet. He reached down to his belt, drew a long, thin bladed knife. Now it was his turn to lunge.

But Decker had tackled more than one knife wielding perp in his former life as a detective in New York. He deftly sidestepped and grabbed the man's wrist, looped his arm under the warrior's elbow, then jerked quickly down. The warrior howled and dropped the knife. Decker spun his body, spinning and extending his leg. Then he pulled the warrior by the shoulder and pulled the man forward over his extended leg, slamming him to the ground. Bending down, he scooped up the knife—a much better weapon to use at close quarters—and sprinted toward the temple.

The sun was above the horizon now. Rays of warming light spilled across the top of the pyramid and bathed the altar in a soft yellow glow.

The priest with the dagger stepped forward, closing his eyes and reciting a prayer.

The other priests joined him, praying fervently with their eyes closed and their hands raised.

Decker doubted that their god cared much about the priests' devotion, or about the Aztec emperor, Yaotl, who had joined the priests in prayer. Once the portal opened, he would leave them behind to fend for themselves.

The high priest opened his eyes, lifted the dagger high over Abby's chest.

He looked toward Yaotl, who nodded, a slight smile touching his lips.

Decker was inside the temple, a few steps from the altar.

The warriors flanking Yaotl moved toward him. One of them went to grab his arm, but Rory took him by the collar and jerked him away. He stumbled backwards, regained his balance, and made a move to attack a second time. But Rory had anticipated his movements. He barreled forward, grabbed the man around the waist, and drove him through the temple door, narrowly missing Cade, who stepped quickly aside, then rushed forward and ran his sword through the second warrior, who was already swinging his obsidian-tipped club.

Saunders ran through the door and made a beeline for the priest guarding Chava, but Decker paid him no heed. He was focused on the high priest and the dagger that was now slicing down through the air toward Abby's chest.

He launched himself into the air and over the altar, slamming into the priest, sending him crashing to the ground, even as the knife skimmed harmlessly past Abby.

Decker fell heavily, landing on top of the prone man.

Something hard and metallic slammed into his gut. The air rushed from his lungs. For a moment, Decker thought he had fallen onto the knife, impaling himself.

He rolled sideways, looked down at his stomach and saw blood.

Heart racing, he reached down, touched the wound. Except nothing was there. He pulled his clothes aside but saw no injuries. When he glanced sideways, he understood why. It was the hilt that had knocked the breath from him as he landed. The blade had firmly embedded itself in the high priest's stomach.

The man was clutching the handle with both hands, a look of wild panic on his face. He tugged at the knife, pulled it out, which only made him bleed even more. He pushed himself up, tried to regain his feet and finishes task. But he was too weak and collapsed back to the floor, dropping the knife.

Decker stepped over the dying priest and kicked the knife away. It clattered across the floor and ended up underneath the altar. From somewhere behind him there was a cry. He turned to see Saunders gripping his upper arm as he faced off against the Aztec warrior who was guarding Chava. Blood spilled through his fingers. He had lost his sword.

The warrior swung his club toward the stricken Marine, who jumped back and barely avoided a second brutal blow, and in doing so, ended up with his back against the wall.

The Aztec could smell victory. He advanced, raising the club.

Decker was still holding the knife he had taken from the Jaguar Warrior out on the ledge. He raised his arm, flicked his wrist, and sent the blade tumbling through the air in lazy arcs.

The warrior gripped the club with both hands, drew it back to deliver a deadly blow.

At that moment, Decker's knife buried itself in his back.

He howled in pain and dropped the club, twisting and thrashing as he tried to remove the knife.

Saunders saw his opportunity. He dodged sideways, snatched up his sword from the floor with his good hand, and plunged it into the warrior, finishing him off.

The Aztec emperor realized that he was now defenseless. He turned and ran for the exit, almost tripping over his own robes in his haste to escape.

Somewhere beyond the door, Decker could hear the sound of fighting as Cualli and his people held back the Jaguar Warriors who were advancing from below and trying to reach the temple. He had no idea if they would hold out, or for how long, but that wasn't his main concern. There was only one thing that mattered now. The orb. He turned toward the dais on which it sat, but then he stopped and stared.

Because the orb was no longer there. It was floating in the air, with wisps of ephemeral smoke twisting around it like elongated, curling fingers. And standing in the gloom behind the smoke was a dark figure Decker that recognized from his nightmare. If he hadn't known better, he would have thought the barely defined shape was nothing more than shadows moving as the sun inched higher above the horizon. But it wasn't. Tezcatlipoca had the orb.

They had failed.

# SIXTY-THREE

CADE RUSHED to the altar and tugged at the bindings restraining Abby to free her. The drugs were wearing off now, which was something, at least. She looked down at the high priest, her face creasing. "He was going to kill me."

"But he didn't." Decker never took his eyes off the shadowy figure holding the orb in its grasp.

Chava struggled to his feet and stumbled toward Decker. "I'm sorry. I have failed. He has control of the orb."

"I know." Decker wasn't sure what to do. Weapons would not work against the entity. That much was clear. He watched helplessly as Tezcatlipoca lifted the orb. Somewhere inside his head, Decker swore he heard the entity laugh. Certainly, it did not deem them a threat.

For a moment, everything became still. It was as if time had frozen in place. Then the orb pulsed with light. A strange hum filled the air, growing louder with each passing second. It sounded like a thousand crickets chirping all at once. Then, suddenly, the air in front of Tezcatlipoca exploded into a column of shimmering, silvery light that seared Decker's eyeballs and caused him to look away instinctively.

When his eyes adjusted and he looked back, the light had

expanded to fill the center of the room. In the middle was a jagged dark tear behind which he could see nothing but swirling darkness, as if the fabric of reality was being pulled apart at the seams.

Decker sensed someone beside him.

It was Chava. He reached toward Decker. "Everyone. Join hands."

"Why?" Cade looked confused.

"I don't have time to explain. Please, just do it."

Decker took Chava's hand, offered his other hand to Abby, who took it quickly.

Rory stepped forward and did the same, along with Cade and Saunders, to form a human chain with Chava at one end and the injured Marine at the other.

The light was expanding. The surrounding air crackled and shimmered. Decker's hair stood on end. He struggled to breathe, as if the portal was sucking the air from the room.

"Think of a place back on Earth. Somewhere you will all be safe," Chava said, looking at Decker. Then he stepped toward the explosion of light and reached out with his free hand.

Decker wanted to ask what he meant, because Chava's phrasing was odd. He had said, somewhere you will all be safe, not somewhere *we* will all be safe. Was it just a mistake because English clearly wasn't his first language, or was it something more?

But before he could say anything, Chava spoke again. "Whatever you do, don't let go."

His fingers grazed the outer limits of the pulsing column of light.

It was like someone flipped a switch.

One moment they were in the temple, and the next they were tumbling through an empty nothingness.

Decker's stomach flipped.

Abby screamed.

This was nothing like the last time they had passed through

the portal. Back then, they had endured only a few moments of mild discomfort. Now it felt like they were being ripped into a thousand pieces and scattered across space and time.

Then he realized something else. Chava's grip was loosening. He turned to look at his hand. The enigmatic Watcher was barely holding on now.

He met Decker's gaze, spoke a single word, although whatever he said was lost to the void. But Decker understood.

*Farewell.*

Then he let go and tumbled away into the emptiness. But it wasn't completely empty, because Tezcatlipoca was also there, appearing more solid than he had ever looked before. The smoke was gone, and now they could see his true nature. A grotesque creature with a head that reminded Decker of a jackal, with burning yellow eyes, and a mouthful of sharp, pointy teeth. A pair of curved horns protruded from the creature's skull. Dark crimson scales covered its body. The breath caught in Decker's throat, because it looked for all the world like the classic representation of the devil.

He wanted to look away, but couldn't, even as Chava tumbled across the void toward the dreadful creature. He reached out, opened his arms and wrapped them around the beast's torso, sending them both in the opposite direction, deeper into the void. Then, without warning, the emptiness contracted around them. There was another moment of intense discomfort, and then the world snapped back into place.

# SIXTY-FOUR

THE FIRST THING Decker saw when he regained his senses was an expanse of frothy blue ocean. He was standing at the edge of a bluff with waves crashing against the rocks beneath him. He took a step back, turned around to see Rory with his arm looped around Abby's shoulders, helping her to stand. A little further away, Cade and Saunders were staring up at a three-story steel and glass building that loomed over them, looking confused.

They were obviously on Earth, and exactly where Decker had wanted to take them.

Cade turned to him. "This isn't California."

"No, it isn't," Decker said. "It's Maine. Welcome to the headquarters of Classified Universal Special Projects."

"CUSP for short," Rory added. He looked around. "Where's Chava?"

An image of the Watcher falling through the void with his arms wrapped around Tezcatlipoca flashed through Decker's mind. "Gone. He let go of my hand. Sacrificed himself to stop the entity from reaching Earth."

Rory looked horrified. "He's still in the void?"

"It was his choice." Decker wondered if Chava had really

thought through his actions. If he had truly understood the choice he was making. But it was too late now, and he doubted anyone could have stopped him, anyway.

"What about the orb?" Cade asked. "If it's still in the possession of that creature—"

"It's not." Decker said, because a small spherical object lay in the grass several feet from them. He walked over and picked it up.

"The orb," Rory said.

"Yes." Decker thought he could still detect a faint vibration from somewhere within the orb, but it also could have been his imagination. "And we need to make sure that no one ever uses it again now that we know what's waiting if they do."

"I'll take care of that," Cade said, starting toward Decker with an outstretched hand.

"I don't think that will be necessary, Commander Cade," a voice said from behind them.

A voice that the Decker knew all too well.

He turned to see Mina striding toward them with several men at her rear that Decker recognized as members of the Ghost Team, CUSP's private paramilitary security and response force. The automatic rifles slung over their shoulders suggested Mina felt a show of force would be necessary. Or maybe she wasn't entirely sure that something hadn't come through the portal with them . . . such as an entity that looked a little too demonic for Decker's liking.

"The device belongs to us," Cade said, squaring his shoulders and folding his arms. "We are better equipped to keep it safe than you."

"Really?" Mina came to a halt, her arms at her sides. "Because none of this would have happened if you hadn't let the map and diary get stolen from right under your nose by a Russian sleeper cell."

"Those particular objects were not in our possession," Cade

protested. "They were at the California Museum Collections Center."

"Then maybe they should have been in your possession. The guard who got shot by the men who stole it would still be alive if you had possessed a little more foresight."

"It wasn't our call to make. We lacked jurisdiction. Besides, there was no way to know that someone would break into–"

Mina snorted and shook her head. "The people you work for have never had a problem with jurisdiction before. I can't imagine that a lowly museum administration would get in your way. We'll be taking the orb and keeping it safe."

"You just said it yourself," Cade shot back. "My employers have never had a problem with jurisdiction."

Mina looked unfazed. "That's because they've never directly crossed us before. You might have Area 51 and a bunch of other super-secret places tucked away around the world that I won't mention out in the open—call it a courtesy—but we have friends in high places just like you, and a lot more sway. I guarantee that."

Cade was silent for a moment, perhaps gauging whether he should press the issue. In the end, he just shook his head and said, "Time will tell."

"Yes, it will." Mina looked at Saunders. "My team will escort you and your man to the infirmary so he can receive medical attention, then we'll provide suitable accommodation until transportation can be arranged to take you back where you belong."

"By suitable I assume you mean secure," Cade said dryly.

"That's exactly what I mean. We can't have unauthorized civilians wandering around our facility, poking their noses where they're not welcome." Mina turned her attention to Decker, who was still holding the orb. "I think it's time we got that thing into the vault, where it will be safe."

"You won't hear any arguments from me." Decker started toward the building.

One of the Ghost Team members approached Rory and tried to help him with Abby, but she shrugged them both off. "I'm fine now. I can walk."

Rory observed her for a moment, then followed Decker. When he realized that Abby was with him, he glanced back over his shoulder. "Well?"

"I figure your boss will have me taken to that secure area. I am a civilian after all, and honestly, I've caused enough trouble."

Decker glanced toward Mina, expecting her to speak up, but instead, she shrugged.

Rory grinned and motioned to Abby. "Come on. Don't just stand there. You're one of us now."

# SIXTY-FIVE

**THREE WEEKS LATER**

DECKER RACED DOWN THE TUNNEL. Behind him, moving fast, he could hear the creature. It snorted and growled and sent stacks of ancient bones crashing to the floor as it gave chase through the catacombs, and he was overcome by a sudden sense of déjà vu.

"Decker." Daisy's voice sounded far away. It echoed through the tunnels and bounced back upon itself, making her location almost impossible to pinpoint.

Earlier that evening, in the hotel room that provided a not too shabby view of the Eiffel Tower, he had tried to memorize the plans of the catacombs Mina had given to them. But the system was vast, spanning a couple of hundred miles in its entirety, and even though he had only focused on the small portion that was relevant to his mission, it was an impossible proposition. He had done no better in remembering the twists and turns and dead ends than he had the previous month when they had last attempted to contain the deadly gargoyle that had been snatching people off the streets and murdering them in gruesome fashion.

He reached a point where four tunnels intersected, and for a moment he hesitated. In the heat of the moment, he couldn't remember if he was supposed to turn left or right. There was no time to think about it. If he stayed here for more than a second, the gargoyle would find him, and then it wouldn't matter.

He took a guess and turned left.

The tunnel stretched ahead of him into darkness, illuminated only by the beam of his flashlight. A couple of miles away, the tunnels would be brightly lit for the hordes of slack-jawed tourists who walked through them every day, gawking at the final resting place of long-dead Parisians who would never have imagined their earthly remains would become a tourist attraction. But only a mile of the tunnels had been opened to the public. Here, in the labyrinth beyond that small haven, it was cold and dark . . . and deadly.

He reached another intersection, turned and kept running. Hoping he was still going in the right direction.

A roar echoed down the tunnel behind him, sounding closer than ever. He wouldn't be able to outrun the creature for much longer, which was why he was so happy to see a glimmer of light ahead. He risked a glance over his shoulder, and there it was. The gargoyle. It was sprinting along on its hind legs, arms raking the piles of human skulls that lined both sides of the narrow passageway. Saliva dripped from its powerful jaws. The same jaws that had almost ripped his neck out on their last jaunt through these tunnels.

"I'm almost there," Decker shouted as he approached the end of the tunnel, where it widened into a large ossuary with even more bones.

"I'm ready," Daisy called back, sounding even closer now, which was a relief.

And then he saw her, standing on the far side of the bone room holding the gun—the same localized EMP weapon they had tried to immobilize the monster with before.

She waved frantically to him. "Out of the way."

Decker skidded to a halt, leaped sideways just as the gargoyle barreled into the room.

Decker turned and shielded his eyes as a pulse of bright blue light lit up the chamber.

He turned back, expecting to see the gargoyle immobilized on the ground, but just like the last time they tried to catch it, the beast was gone.

But not for long.

"Decker. Look out. Above you!" She was already aiming the gun again, but when she pulled the trigger, nothing happened.

He looked up, saw the gargoyle. It was on the ceiling; leathery wings curled around its body and razor-sharp claws dug into the soft rock of what had once been a vast mine system before it had been repurposed as a city of the dead.

It glared back at him, then swooped.

Another glaring blue light lit up the room.

Decker was momentarily blinded. He waited for the gargoyle to grab him, rip him limb from limb. But when his eyes adjusted, the creature was sprawled on the floor, turned back to stone and frozen with one arm reaching out, claws extended toward him.

"Well, that was fun." Colum O'Shea stood a few feet away, a second EMP weapon cradled in his hands. He looked at Decker. "How many times have I saved your hide now?"

Decker brushed himself off. "Not as many as I've saved yours."

"Okay, boys. You can save the chest-thumping for later," Daisy said, grinning. She looked down at the immobilized gargoyle. "Let's get the Ghost Team down here to secure this ugly chap before the EMP pulse wears off and we have to do it all over again."

---

Back at the hotel, Decker stepped into his room on the fifth floor and closed the door. It was almost two in the morning. He was weary and wanted nothing more than to hit the sack. But that wasn't going to happen, at least for a while, because there was something that he wanted to do more.

"I'm going to take a shower," he said to the woman who was standing at the window, gazing out over the city. "And then . . ."

"And then we can figure out why they call this the city of love," Nancy said, turning around and glancing toward the bed. Her eyes twinkled mischievously in the soft half-light. "Maybe we can figure it out twice if you're not too tired."

273
199

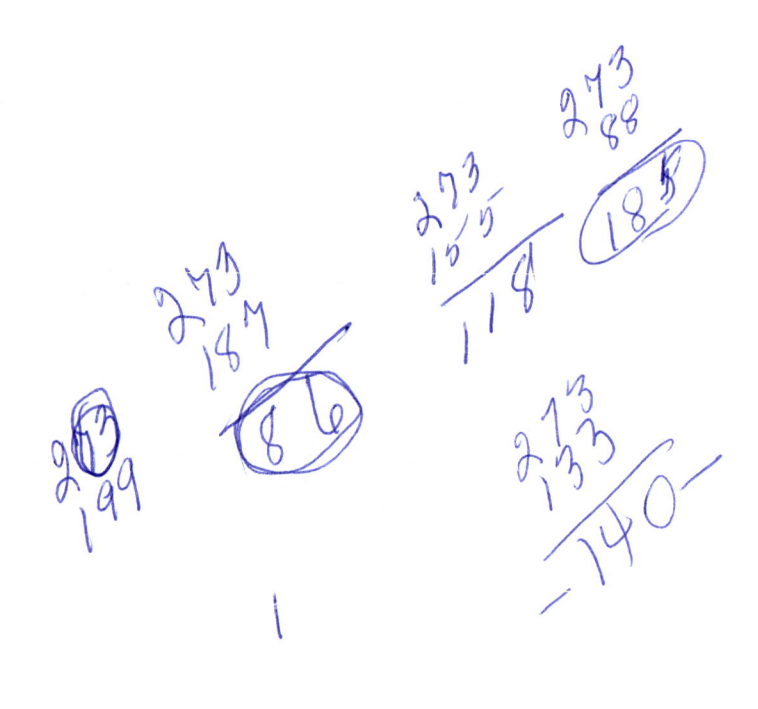

273
187

⑧ ⑥

273
155
―――
118

273
88
―――
185

273
133
―――
140

1

# ABOUT THE AUTHOR

Anthony M. Strong is a British-born writer living and working in the United States. He is the author of the popular John Decker series of supernatural adventure thrillers.

Anthony has worked as a graphic designer, newspaper writer, artist, and actor. When he was a young boy, he dreamed of becoming an Egyptologist and spent hours reading about pyramids and tombs. Until he discovered dinosaurs and decided to be a paleontologist instead. Neither career panned out, but he was left with a fascination for monsters and archaeology that serve him well in the John Decker books.

Anthony has traveled extensively across Europe and the United States, and weaves his love of travel into his novels, setting them both close to home and in far-off places.

Anthony currently resides most of the year on Florida's Space Coast where he can watch rockets launch from his balcony, and part of the year on an island in Maine, with his wife Sonya, and two furry bosses, Izzie and Hayden.

Connect with Anthony, find out about new releases, and get free books at www.anthonymstrong.com

Made in the USA
Coppell, TX
09 September 2025